Justin walked over to Paige's car

"Could I talk to you for a minute?" he asked, watching as she bent over the rear seat in search of the cups.

"This is not the time or the place to talk," she told him when she straightened.

"Maybe not, but I have something to say to you."

"Can't it wait?" She slammed the door shut.

"No, it can't."

She leaned back against the fender. "What is it?" she asked in a tone that was close to boredom. She didn't look at him, but out into the darkness.

"What is it?" he repeated in disbelief. "You're the one who's treating me like yesterday's garbage. What is wrong with you?"

She finally met his gaze. "How can you even ask me that after last night?"

Dear Reader,

When my husband asked our four-year-old grandson, Aedan, why he asks so many questions, he replied, "Because I'm curious." My husband looked at me and said, "Like his grandmother."

Curiosity is a good thing, especially in a writer. It's the reason I've written thirty-two books. I'm always looking for an answer to that age-old question "Why do people fall in love?"

For me every book begins with a question, a "what if" situation such as "What if two people who had been the best of friends suddenly found themselves in a romantic relationship?" Then I become like my grandson. I ask a lot of questions, most of them beginning with the word *why.*

I have to confess that sometimes it's easier to answer Aedan's questions regarding the universe than it is to figure out what motivates my characters. But I must find the answers. Because whether it's a four-year-old gazing at his grandmother as if she's the wisest woman on the planet or a reader telling an author her story touched her heart, the reward is priceless.

All the best,

Pamela Bauer

HAVING JUSTIN'S BABY
Pamela Bauer

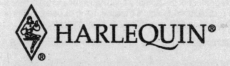

HARLEQUIN®

TORONTO • NEW YORK • LONDON
AMSTERDAM • PARIS • SYDNEY • HAMBURG
STOCKHOLM • ATHENS • TOKYO • MILAN • MADRID
PRAGUE • WARSAW • BUDAPEST • AUCKLAND

ISBN-13: 978-0-373-71481-0
ISBN-10:   0-373-71481-5

HAVING JUSTIN'S BABY

ABOUT THE AUTHOR

Best advice? Never forget there's no such thing as a perfect parent. **Mrs. Brady or Mrs. Cleaver?** Mrs. Cleaver. One husband, two kids. **Cloth or disposable?** Cloth at home, disposable on the go. **Favorite bedtime story?** *Goodnight Moon.* **Keeper quote from your mom?** "Don't throw out the baby with the bathwater." **I wish my baby could've stayed forever at age...?** Preschool. Kids that age are so sweet and innocent—and they still like to cuddle. **Most poignant moment?** That first smile made my heart sing. **What makes a mom?** When a tiny life becomes more important than your own. **Best story behind a baby name?** A friend who lives in California named her son Lake as a reminder of her family roots here in Minnesota, the land of 10,000 lakes.

Books by Pamela Bauer

In loving memory of a very dear, courageous
brother-in-law, Clarence (Bill) Greising.

PROLOGUE

THE SOUND OF THE PHONE ringing woke Justin Collier from a deep slumber. His right hand snaked its way under the sheet to reach for the cordless on the nightstand next to his bed.

"Justin here," he said in a sleepy voice against his pillow.

"It's me."

"Paige?" He sat upright. "What's happened? What's wrong?"

"Nothing's wrong," she assured him. "Everything's right. Really right."

"Then why are you calling in the middle of the night?"

"It's not the middle of the night," she said with a chuckle. "Where's Kyle?"

"I assume he's in his bed." He looked at the clock and grimaced. "Do you realize what time it is?"

"I didn't wake you, did I? I thought you'd be on summer hours."

Until a few months ago, Paige Stephens had shared a house in the Twin Cities with Justin and his friend Kyle Landon. The three had been inseparable since they were kids. Justin and Kyle were partners in a landscape business in St. Paul, but this summer Paige was working at the Cascading Waters Resort on Lake Superior. No way would she be calling at this hour unless it were an emergency.

"Yes, but that doesn't mean I get up at five. You should

know that—you used to live here or have you already forgotten us?"

"Of course I haven't forgotten you!"

"Good. So what's so urgent that you had to wake me before the sun is even up?"

"I'll tell you, but first I want you to get Kyle."

"You want me to wake him up?"

"Yes. I have something important to discuss with both of you."

"At five o'clock in the morning?" Justin groaned in resignation. "All right. I'll do it." Wearing only a pair of boxers covered with images of the characters on *Family Guy*, he made his way down the hallway.

"Lucky for you his door is open," he grumbled into the phone. It had been a long-standing rule that a closed door with a sock covering the knob served as a Do Not Disturb sign.

"Kyle," he called out repeatedly from the doorway until his friend and business partner stirred.

"What's up?" he asked as he sat up in bed. "Did I oversleep?"

"No, Paige is on the phone. She wants to talk to both of us so I'm going to put her on speaker." Justin pressed a button, then said, "Go ahead, Paige."

"Hey, Kyle. Sorry to wake you." Her voiced echoed as if she were speaking in a tunnel.

"Hey—no problem. You know you can call anytime." A sappy grin spread over Kyle's face. Justin should have expected it. It had been that way since the fourth grade. One word from Paige and Kyle turned into a marshmallow.

Paige and Kyle made small talk until Justin finally cut in. "So are you going to tell us what's so important that you interrupted our beauty sleep?"

"Yes. I figured out who I want to be maid of honor at my wedding," Paige replied. "You."

"You who?" Justin asked. "I only see two men here. I believe a maid of honor is a woman."

"Traditionally it is, yes, but there's no reason why it can't be a guy. It's supposed to be the bride's closest friend. That would be the two of you."

"You want us to wear dresses?" Kyle's voice rose a pitch.

"No, I don't want you to wear dresses," she said with a hint of impatience. "I want you to stand up for me—just like you have for the past twenty years. You'd wear tuxes, like the other men in the wedding party."

"But we'd be standing with the women," Kyle pointed out.

"There aren't going to be any women," Paige told them. "It's a small wedding. I'm only having a maid of honor, and Michael is only having a best man."

"So there'll be four men and you?" Justin asked.

"You guys sound like you don't want to do it." There was a plaintive note in Paige's voice.

"We didn't say that," Justin told her, although one glance at Kyle told him that not even his lifelong crush on their former housemate was going to persuade him to be a maid of honor at her wedding. He was gesturing "no way" with his hands and shaking his head.

"Then what are you saying?" she demanded to know.

Justin avoided answering the question. "Is your fiancé okay with this?"

"I haven't run it by him yet," she admitted.

"Don't you think you should?" Again it was Justin who spoke.

"I will, but first I wanted to ask you guys. I mean, you've been my best friends since the fourth grade. It wouldn't feel right to ask someone else."

Silence stretched between them, prompting her to ask, "You are going to do it, aren't you?"

Justin was about to say, "Let us think about it," when Kyle spoke. "Of course we'll do it."

Justin glared at him, but Kyle paid no attention. "Or at least one of us will."

Justin frowned. "What do you mean *one* of us?"

"I know the three of us have been friends for a long time and it's always been one for all and all for one," Kyle said, "but don't you think Paige should have only one of us as maid of honor. After all, Michael is having one best man."

"But I can't choose between the two of you," she protested.

"Then we'll choose for you," Kyle said. "We'll talk it over and let you know which one it'll be. Okay?"

Justin had a sinking feeling in his stomach.

"I'm okay with that if you guys are," Paige replied.

"Of course we are," Kyle said.

"Justin?"

Now was his time to protest. He should have said no, but he didn't. Because like Kyle, he didn't want to disappoint Paige. "I'm okay with it," he muttered.

As soon as she had hung up he turned to Kyle and said, "Why do I have the feeling that there is going to be no discussion as to which one of us gets to play the girl part at the wedding?"

"I would do it, but I can't," he said, climbing out of bed and pulling on a pair of jeans. "You know how I feel about Paige. It's going to be tough enough watching her marry Michael Cross. I can't do it standing right next to her and in front of everyone. You do understand what I'm saying, don't you?"

Justin exhaled a long sigh. "Yeah, I understand."

"Thanks, buddy." Kyle clapped him on the arm as he passed him on his way out of the room. "You'll make a great maid of honor," he called over his shoulder as he headed down the hallway.

No, he was going to make a terrible one. Paige should have chosen someone who would be happy for her, someone who would truly share in the joy of her wedding. That someone was not him. Because like Kyle, he was a marshmallow when it came to Paige. He'd been in love with her since the fourth grade. Only no one knew.

CHAPTER ONE

"YOU'RE NOT NERVOUS, are you?" Paige Stephens asked her fiancé.

"No. Why would you think that?"

"Because your knees are creating an air current under the table."

"Sorry." Michael Cross stopped wriggling and gave her a lazy half smile that caused a dimple to appear in his left cheek. "Maybe I do feel a little like Ben Stiller in *Meet the Parents*."

"There's no need to. The Colliers aren't my parents. They're just friends."

Paige took a sip of the ice water in her glass. Even though she didn't want to admit it to Michael, she felt a twinge of anxiety herself. That's why she'd chosen Betty's Pie Shop for lunch instead of the dining room at the Cascading Waters Resort. She didn't want to be under the scrutiny of her coworkers. The pie shop was always crowded with lots of noise and commotion. Fidgeting wouldn't be as noticeable among clanking silverware and clattering plates.

"They must be special friends if you want them to be host and hostess at the wedding."

"They are special. I've known them most of my life. I think I probably spent more time in their home than mine when I was a kid."

"Because of their son Justin?"

"No, because Nancy ran a day care and my father made me stay there even when I was old enough to stay home by myself. I can remember the exact moment my father sat me down and told me I'd be spending the hours after school at her day care. I cried and begged him to let me stay by myself. He didn't think that nine was old enough to be left alone and didn't believe me when I said I could take care of myself."

Michael smiled indulgently. "I bet you would have been just fine on your own."

"Of course I would have," she insisted. "I was a very responsible child."

"I believe you." He gave her the smile she found the most endearing of all of his grins—the one that made her feel warm and fuzzy. "You're such a capable woman. I can't imagine you were any different as a child."

"What a sweet thing to say. Thank you." She reached across the table to squeeze his hand. "No wonder I fell in love with you. You have a sensitivity that is rare in a man."

Actually he had quite a few qualities that she'd found to be rare in guys she had dated over the past twelve years. Michael was honest. Sincere. Trustworthy.

Until she met him she'd never believed in love at first sight, but all it had taken was one look from his deep-set eyes and a slow seductive smile on his lips and she'd been smitten. She had been a volunteer in the education building at the State Fair handing out buttons that promoted literacy. He kept returning to the booth until the entire front of his shirt was covered in "I like to read" buttons. She'd been charmed from the first moment he said hello—not an easy thing for any guy to do with her, especially one who made a living teaching golf. At first she thought it was the whole preppie look he had going—

the polo shirts, the casual pants, the carefully groomed black hair. But the more time they spent together, the more wonderful she found him to be.

"I aim to please," Michael said with a lift of his water glass. Then he looked again at his watch.

"Please relax," she urged him. "I don't think you were this nervous when you came to Thanksgiving dinner and had to meet my father."

"Probably because you talk about the Colliers a lot more than you talk about your dad. You're not very close to your dad, are you?"

She rubbed the moisture from the base of her water glass with her thumb. "We have issues."

"What kind of issues?"

She continued to run her fingers along the glass. "It goes back to when my mom died. It's nothing, really. We get along all right—you've seen us together. But we're never going to be as close as we were before my mom died."

She was grateful that he didn't ask why not. There were only two people who knew the root of her problem with her dad—Justin and Kyle—and they had promised her they would never say a word to anyone. Someday she would tell Michael the reason she couldn't trust her father, but not today.

"It's okay," her fiancé said in understanding. "I'm not that close to my parents, either."

"So you shouldn't be nervous about meeting the Colliers," she reasoned.

"I'm just wondering what their son told them about me."

"Justin wouldn't say anything negative," she told him, which produced a harrumph from her fiancé. "He wouldn't," she insisted, although she wasn't completely sure. Both Justin and Kyle were as overprotective as older brothers.

"He doesn't like me, Paige."

"Justin doesn't dislike you," she declared. "He just hasn't had time to get to know you. That's why I want you to come to the Bulldog Reunion with me."

"About that weekend…" he said, tugging on his right ear. Paige knew it was another sign that he was nervous. "Are you sure you want me there?"

"Of course I want you there! I want you to meet my friends from college." Her shoulders sagged. "Please don't tell me that you don't want to come?" She gave him her most appealing look.

He gazed into her eyes. "It goes without saying that I want to be with you. I'm just worried that the others won't appreciate having outsiders crash what's traditionally been a private event."

That's what Kyle and Justin had said when she'd suggested they bring guests to their annual retreat at the Cascading Waters Resort. The five friends who made up the Bulldog Reunion had met their senior year before college while working as kitchen and housekeeping staff at the year-round resort on the northern shore of Lake Superior. All five had attended the same college, and this would be their eighth reunion. To bring guests would change the tone and the purpose of their gathering, which was why Justin had warned her it might be the last time they had it.

Paige didn't believe him. Amber Carlson and Ben Hendricks, who completed their circle of five, were happy with her suggestion and planned to bring guests.

"This isn't like a regular college reunion, Michael. We're just five friends who get together to spend a weekend in what has to be the most beautiful part of Minnesota. One thing I should warn you about though. Do *not* drink Ben's dandelion wine. He brews it himself and it has quite a kick to it."

"You know that if you don't want me to drink, I won't drink," he said simply.

That was another thing she loved about him. Paige wasn't a teetotaler, but she didn't drink often, and it didn't bother Michael.

"A penny for your thoughts?" he said.

"I was just thinking how lucky I am." She glanced out the window at a view she never tired of seeing—the rocky shoreline of Lake Superior, the sparkling blue waters. "Moving up here for the summer was the best thing I could have done."

"Then you don't mind waiting tables at the Birchwood Room?"

Paige was an elementary-school teacher, but had taken a summer job as a waitress at the Cascading Waters Resort to be closer to Michael. "No, it's only for the summer. Once school's back in session I'll work as a sub until I can find a full-time teaching position in the area."

"I'm glad you like it here. I was worried you wouldn't want to call this home once we're married. I mean, you are a city girl."

"Yes, but do you know how many vacations I've spent on the North Shore?" It was a rhetorical question.

"That's not quite the same as living here year-round," he warned her. "I hope you're as enthusiastic about it come January." He grinned again and the dimple in his cheek appeared.

"If you're here, I'll be happy."

He squeezed her hand. "That's what I like to hear." He glanced past her shoulder and said, "I see a middle-aged couple who look like they're trying to find somebody. Do the Colliers wear University of Minnesota windbreakers?"

Paige turned and caught sight of her old neighbors, Justin's parents. She stood and waved, then sat back down, noticing that Michael's legs were moving even faster than before.

"They won't bite, I promise," she said softly.

As Paige expected, Nancy and Elliot Collier treated

Michael with a warmth and friendliness that put everyone at ease. That's why she wasn't surprised after lunch when Elliot accepted Michael's offer to show him the golf course at the Cascading Waters Resort.

It also gave Paige an opportunity to sit under the shade of an umbrella on the tiled patio of the resort clubhouse and have an iced tea with her former day-care provider. She wasted no time in asking Nancy, "So what do you think of Michael?"

"I think he's charming," she said with a smile. "And he's very attentive to you."

"He's sweet. I know he talks a lot about golf, but that's because he's passionate about it."

"It is his work," she pointed out. "So tell me about the wedding."

Paige took a sip of her iced tea. "It's going to be at the High Falls. That's always been my favorite spot on the North Shore."

"Ah, an outdoor wedding…it should be lovely."

"Did Justin tell you he's going to be my maid of honor—or maybe I should say man of honor," she corrected with a grin.

"He did say something to that effect," Nancy acknowledged.

Paige glanced out across the greens and saw Michael and Elliot riding on a cart. "I'm just grateful he said yes. He's not very excited about me marrying Michael. Neither is Kyle—but you probably already know that."

"Actually, neither one has said much about your engagement, but I'm not surprised that they're giving you a hard time. Ever since you three were kids they've put themselves in the role of being your protector."

"Well, we're not kids anymore and I don't need protecting. I know once I'm married my friendship with Kyle and Justin will change, but it doesn't have to end." It was a concern that had been on her mind ever since Michael had asked her to marry him.

"I don't think you have to worry about that happening. Over the years I've seen the way you three have handled the growing pains of friendship and I'd say yours has a pretty good foundation. It can probably weather just about anything. Now finish telling me your wedding plans."

Paige was more than happy to do as she requested. Sitting on the terrace with Nancy talking about flowers and formal wear reminded her of all those times she'd turned to her neighbor after her mother had died when Paige was nine. It was Nancy who had taken her shopping for school clothes and helped her with her homework. It didn't matter how many kids Nancy had in her day care, she always found time for Paige.

That's why she was disappointed when the older woman said, "It looks like our guys are back."

Paige could have sat and talked with her for hours.

"I'm so glad we had this time together," she said to Paige.

"I am, too. It's means a lot to me that you're going to be a part of our wedding celebration."

"I'm glad that day is going to happen, Paige. You've come a long way from the little girl who walked into my day care and announced she was going to hate boys the rest of her life."

"Doesn't every nine-year-old girl hate boys?" She tried to dismiss Nancy's comment with a chuckle, but they both knew what had precipitated the comment. Although Nancy had never pressed her to talk about her mother's death, Paige was fairly certain that the older woman was aware of the circumstances leading up to the automobile accident.

News of the crash had spread through the neighborhood quickly. Her father and mother had been arguing. Paige had heard them. So had many of the neighbors. What the neighbors hadn't heard was the reason why. Only Paige knew it was because of a woman her father had met during one of his business trips. That discovery had prompted her mother to pack her bags and drive off in her car. The last words Paige had heard her say to her father were, "I can't trust you."

"Paige?"

She realized that she'd been daydreaming and hadn't heard what Nancy had said. "I'm sorry. What did you say?"

"I said I'd like to credit Justin and Kyle as being good influences on you, but I honestly think it was the other way around."

"Does it matter?" Paige asked.

"No, not really. I'm just so proud of all of you. I think of all of my day-care kids, including you and Kyle, as my own, you know."

"I do, and I appreciate that."

"Good. Because I want you to know that no matter what happens between you, Kyle and Justin, I'm always here for you."

"Nothing's going to happen. We'll always be friends."

BY THE TIME Justin Collier arrived home the sun was low in the sky. Not even the approaching dusk could hide the condition of the seventy-five-year-old house he called home. When he and Kyle had bought the place shortly after graduating from college they had intended to fix it up and sell it within a couple of years. That was seven years ago. All the money that should have gone into home improvements had been sunk into the landscape company they'd started. Now their business was flourishing and the house still looked neglected. As Justin went to get the mail from the dented box nailed to the porch, he saw an exterior badly in need of attention.

He added paint to his mental list of things to buy next time he was at the hardware store. Summer was always the busiest season for J&K Landscapes and this year was no exception.

Even with the addition of several new employees, he and Kyle often worked twelve-hour days. He consoled himself with the knowledge that by late fall and early winter they would have the time to work on the house. He kicked the dirt off his work boots and went into the kitchen, which showed the same signs of wear as the exterior. Faded floor tiles, permanently stained countertops and dated appliances were fine for a couple of bachelors, but he knew why Paige had been after them to update the place.

Justin grabbed a beer from the refrigerator and sat down on a wooden chair at the table. He glanced at his mail and saw little of interest except for a neon-yellow envelope. He ripped it open and found a schedule for the Bulldog Reunion. In her usual efficient manner Paige had made all the arrangements for the weekend. Only this year there was something different. At the bottom of the invitation were the words *Friends are welcome.* Justin frowned.

As he folded the schedule he noticed a personal note.

Can't wait to see you. It's been too long. Love, P

Yes, it had been a while since he had seen her but that wasn't his fault. She was the one who had been in a hurry to pack up her things and move a hundred and fifty miles away as soon as she'd finished her teaching job. But it wasn't simply the distance separating them. The reason it had been so long since Justin and Paige had been together was she had fallen in love. Annoyance rippled through him at the thought of Michael Cross. Of all the men Paige could have fallen in love with, he didn't understand why she had chosen one so totally wrong for her.

He and Kyle had been suspicious of the golf pro the first

time Paige had brought him home. Not that it mattered to Paige. She was in love and didn't want to hear anything negative about her boyfriend. Ever since they were kids she'd been coming to them for advice, but before either one could tell her why he was wary of Michael, she'd looked at them and said, "If you can't say something nice, don't say anything."

He looked again at the Bulldog schedule. There was hiking, disc golf, sailing, volleyball, bonfires...all the things they had done in the past that had made everyone want to continue reuniting each summer. Only this year while doing the fun stuff, Paige would be looking at Michael with that lovesick-puppy gaze. Justin didn't want to spend one hour, let alone an entire weekend, with the lovebirds.

He'd always considered a weekend at the North Shore to be more like therapy. No customer complaints to deal with, no long hours out in the hot sun digging and planting. It was a chance to reconnect with nature and with friends. Spending any length of time watching Paige act all lovey-dovey with her fiancé would be more like punishment.

"I hope you didn't drink the last cold one."

Justin glanced toward the doorway to see Kyle had come home. He looked heat weary and physically exhausted as he walked into the kitchen.

"No, there are plenty more," Justin answered.

Kyle ambled over to the refrigerator and pulled out a bottle of beer then dropped onto a chair opposite him. He twisted off the cap and took a long drink before saying, "I think it's time we seriously consider accepting Harry Bonner's offer to buy into the business."

Justin sighed. "I thought we agreed that as beneficial as it would be financially to join forces with Bonner, it would also mean that we're no longer a small local company."

"No, we'd be a Midwest company. Bigger and better." Kyle took another drink. "We could hire the additional employees we need to bid on the larger commercial projects and you and I could devote more of our time to managing the company instead of doing the physical labor. We were business majors in college," he reminded Justin.

"I know, but I happen to like working with the trees," Justin reminded him.

"And that's fine. All I'm saying is that if we expand, we'll have the option to delegate more of the work. We'll also make more money. And *that* would be a good thing." He used his beer bottle as a pointer. "We could also afford to move to a nice place—something a little more modern than this place."

"Even if we sell the house we're going to have to fix it up a bit…put some fresh paint on the walls."

"Now you're starting to sound like Paige. She was always after me to put one of those designer colors on the walls…something called Mesa Sunrise."

Justin grinned. "It looked like pink to me."

"Yeah, well, I'm not living in a pink house. There's nothing wrong with white walls."

"Except these walls look more like dirty socks." Justin toyed with the label on the neck of his beer bottle. "The whole house needs work. Every year we say we're going to do it during our slow season and it doesn't get done."

"That's because there've been better things to do—like lie in the sun on a beach in Mexico," Kyle reminded him.

"Maybe this year we should think about staying home and taking care of the work that needs to be done around this place."

"I thought you wanted me to look up info on those nursery seminars that are being offered in Oregon—which reminds me." He sat forward, patting his pockets until he produced a folded piece of paper. "I have the name of a contact person. Another reason why it would be to our advantage to have Bonner come on board. You and I could take the seminar at the same time and still have someone running the company back here."

Justin pondered that a moment. "Good point. Maybe it is time we bring on another partner."

"What about the house? Should we have a real estate appraiser come out to take a look?"

"It wouldn't hurt, but I suppose we really ought to talk to Paige before we do anything. She has been our silent partner."

"Well, technically she isn't, but we've treated her like one since she invested her first paycheck as a teacher to help us get started."

"That makes her a part of us," Justin insisted.

"Then we'll tell her," Kyle agreed. "I'm sure she'll say that whatever we plan to do with the business is fine with her. We'll talk to her about it at the Bulldog Reunion."

"Speaking of the reunion...did you see this?" Justin slid the invitation across the wooden tabletop. "I thought we told her we didn't want to have outsiders."

"We did, but you know Paige. Once she sets her mind to something, she gets it done. And she wanted to bring her fiancé. She called me last week."

"I hope you told her we weren't bringing anyone."

"Of course I did."

"Good."

"But then I asked Tammy to come along."

Justin had been teetering on the back legs of his chair, but sat forward with a thump. "Are you telling me I'm going to be the only one flying solo? Why would you invite Tammy?" Kyle had only started going out with her recently.

"Hey—I had to," he insisted in a defensive tone. "Paige is going to be bringing that Tiger Woods wannabe and I didn't want to have to watch the two of them play kissy face all weekend. You know as well as I do that falling in love has changed Paige and not in a good way."

"I know it's affected her hearing." Justin grimaced. "She hasn't heard a word we've said about the guy."

"I think her common sense has been pushed to the back of her brain."

Justin didn't want to talk about Paige. "Look, I'm not going to feel much like going to the reunion if I'm the only one without a date," he said irritably.

Kyle raised his hands. "Just chill—you won't be alone," he said with a devilish grin. "I asked Tammy to bring her sister Tara for you."

Justin groaned. "Tell me you didn't."

Kyle was clearly perplexed. "What is wrong with you? You've seen Tara. She's not only beautiful, she's fun to be around. Why are you groaning? I did you a favor."

What was wrong was that he felt the same way as Kyle did about seeing Paige with Michael. But having Tara there wouldn't help. Only he couldn't tell him that, so he said, "You told Paige we weren't bringing anyone, which means she's made plans for eight people, not ten. You know how she hates a change in plans."

"I don't think she's going to care about two extra people."

"Yes, she will." The weekend was becoming less appealing by the minute. "Maybe we ought to just skip the reunion this year."

"And what about Tammy and her sister?"

He shrugged. "We could still go away—we just don't have to go to the North Shore."

"That would be fine with me, but what would we tell Paige?"

Justin didn't have to think about that one very long. "She'd never forgive us for skipping out on her, would she?"

"No, we're going to have to do this," Kyle stated with a shake of his head.

"And listen to her talk about her wedding plans."

This time it was Kyle who groaned. "Don't remind me. Ever since he gave her that diamond on Valentine's Day she's been like a broken record…the wedding this, the wedding that. Michael says…blah blah blah."

"It's only one weekend," Justin said for his benefit as much as Kyle's.

"So does this mean I can tell Tammy she can bring Tara?" Kyle stood, waiting for his answer.

"All right," he said, ignoring his instincts, which told him he was making a mistake. "I'll do it, but you're going to owe me big-time for this one."

"Hey—you'll be thanking me by the time the weekend's over," Kyle said with a cocky grin.

Justin hoped he was right, but his gut was telling him that this year's Bulldog Reunion was not going to be the carefree event it had been in the past. Still, he would go for Paige. He'd been looking out for her ever since that first day she showed up at his mother's day care. There were things that friends needed to do for friends. So instead of calling Paige and telling her he wouldn't be at the reunion, he went to look for his Bulldog sweatshirt.

CHAPTER TWO

DESPITE KYLE'S ASSERTION that it didn't matter whether there were eight or ten people at the Bulldog Reunion, Justin wanted to make sure that Paige knew he and Kyle had changed their minds and were now bringing guests. He wanted an excuse to talk to her—something he hadn't done for a while. So the day before they were supposed to head out of town for the reunion, he called her while he was on his morning break.

She answered her cell phone with, "You did it again, J.C." using the nickname she'd given him as a teen.

He smiled. "You were about to call me."

"I was. I guess we still have that special connection, don't we?" She sounded a bit amused by their uncanny ability to sense when the other was about to phone. "Do you realize how long it's been since this has happened?"

"We haven't talked much lately," he agreed.

"No, we haven't. But I am glad you called today because I was worried I wouldn't be able to reach you and I have to know what you think. You are never going to guess where I am."

"Dipping your toes in the Cascade River?" It was a favorite spot along the North Shore where they'd spent many a hot summer day. They'd hike along the upper region of the Cascade River where it tumbled and fell over rocks and boulders until they reached the Upper Falls. They'd bask in the sun on the flat rocks where the falls began, before following the winding trail as it twisted and turned its way back down the hilly terrain until they reached the area where the river was shallow enough for trout fishing. That's where they'd take off their hiking shoes and wade in the cool water, splashing around like kids.

"No." She sounded impatient. "I'm in a dressing room trying on a wedding dress."

Justin stifled his groan. "You're trying on wedding dresses the day before the Bulldog Reunion? Don't you have enough to do to get ready for the weekend?"

"Of course I do. That's why I'm standing here in a wedding dress."

She wasn't making any sense. More proof that love had made her crazy.

"I was on my way to pick up some munchies for the Bulldog Reunion when I passed this consignment shop and saw this wedding dress in the window," she continued. "How's that for serendipity?"

Paige excited over a dress was a novelty for Justin. Unlike most women he knew, she hated shopping, which was why he liked going to the mall with her. She used the "get what you need and get out fast" approach.

"I'm telling you, Justin, this dress could have been made for me. When you see it you'll know why I had to come in and try it on. And it's a perfect fit. What makes it unique is that it belonged to a woman who was married in 1942."

"You want to buy an old dress for your wedding?"

"It's not old, it's vintage," she corrected him. "This dress was worn by a woman whose fiancé was going off to World War II."

"Your fiancé isn't going off to war, is he?" he asked, trying not to sound hopeful.

"No, but you know *Pearl Harbor* is my favorite movie. Justin, this dress looks like something Kate Beckinsale would have worn if Ben Affleck hadn't gone missing and they had gotten married in the movie, which you know is what I wish had happened."

"And that's why you want the dress?"

"I want it because I like the way I feel in it—glamorous." She chuckled. "Me...glamorous," she said in a self-deprecating tone.

"I think you are," he told her, but she dismissed the compliment with a sarcastic "Yeah, right."

"Did I tell you the original owner was a schoolteacher?" She didn't wait for an answer but rushed on. "Oh, and here's something else. Guess where the wedding took place?"

"In a church?" He knew it was the wrong answer, but he hated playing Twenty Questions, which was what she seemed bent on doing, and all of them were on a subject that he found irritating—her marriage plans.

"You know I'm not getting married in a church," she chided him. "The bride who wore this dress in 1942 was married at the High Falls."

"So you're going to wear a dress that someone else has already worn to get married in the same place where you're planning your wedding?" The significance escaped him and he didn't pretend otherwise.

She sighed. "I should have known you wouldn't get it. I know you find my wedding details boring, but you are one of my best friends. At least you can pretend to be interested. I thought you'd be happy for me."

"I am happy," he lied.

"You don't sound like it."

Justin held the phone away from his ear momentarily. Who was this woman? Certainly not the Paige he knew. That Paige would never have gone shopping for a wedding dress the day before the Bulldog Reunion. But then that Paige had never been engaged before, either.

"Justin, you're there, aren't you?"

"Yeah, I'm here. I think you cut out for a second, but I hear you now."

"Good, because I need an honest opinion and you always give me that. You need to tell me if I should get this dress. The salesclerk took a picture of me with her camera phone and she said she can send it to you."

"Can't you just show the dress to me this weekend?"

"If I wait till then, someone else might buy it. The clerk told me she's already had several people asking about it. Besides, there's no room in the schedule this weekend for us to leave the reunion and go look at it. If I'm going to get this dress, I have to buy it today."

"But, Paige, you never make impulse purchases," he reminded her.

"That's why I need your help. Besides. You're my man of honor. It's your duty to help me select a dress."

He frowned. "Shouldn't your fiancé be the one helping you make that decision?"

"He can't. It's bad luck for the groom to see the bride's dress before the wedding."

Justin wondered briefly if getting rid of Michael Cross could be as easy as showing him a picture. That alone tempted him to tell Paige to send the photo so he could forward it to Michael.

Paige didn't wait for his consent. "The salesclerk is sending the picture now. Tell me when you get it."

Justin's phone beeped, indicating he had a message. With the touch of a button he found himself staring at a photo of Paige in a long white dress. It fell from her shoulders to the floor in a straight line that made her look taller than her five foot two inches. She looked graceful and feminine standing with her hands folded in front of her. Very different from the Paige he knew. She had always taken great pleasure in being a tomboy. Normally she wore her long brown hair in a ponytail, but today it fell across her shoulders in a way that reminded him of the film stars of the 1940s. No wonder she felt glamorous. The dress was stunning on her. The old-fashioned style suited her, reminding him that she'd never been one for fashion trends yet she always managed to look good.

"I didn't lose you, did I? Justin? Are you there?" she called out.

"Yeah, I'm here." He couldn't tell her that the reason for the dead air was that seeing her in the wedding dress had taken his breath away. The thought that she would be wearing it for another guy made him sick with envy.

"So what do you think?" she demanded.

There was only one answer he could give her. "I think you should buy it."

"Did you say buy it? You're cutting out on me. Are you in your car?"

"Yes, but it's not moving. I just went through the drive-thru of a fast-food restaurant and I'm eating French-toast sticks in the parking lot. Paige, I think you should buy the dress. It suits you."

"You really think so?"

"Yes."

"I am so glad you said that because I need a dress. You do realize the wedding is only seven weeks away, don't you? It's a good thing I had the summer off from teaching and moved up here, because I never would get everything done otherwise."

"You're happy then?"

"Of course I'm happy. Why wouldn't I be?"

"You're giving up a lot. Your job, your friends…"

"Marriage will be worth it," she said with confidence. "And I'm not giving up my two best friends. Oh shoot. I just got a low-battery warning on my phone. I've got to run. Thanks for calling me just when I needed you."

"Paige, wait! Before you hang up I need to talk to you about tomorrow."

"Oh, that reminds me. Could you come a little early? I want you to teach me to dance."

"You know how to dance," he reminded her.

"I'm not good at it and you know it," she chastised him. "Michael took me to this nightclub in Duluth and it was the worst date we've ever had. He loves to dance, but once he realized I have no rhythm, we hardly danced at all. You have to help me so I don't embarrass him."

Embarrass him? Anger nearly had Justin telling Paige exactly what he thought of Michael Cross and his *dancing* skills, but he knew it wouldn't do any good. She'd still think the guy was the prize of a lifetime. "Paige, you don't like to dance. Why not just tell him that?"

"I might like it if I were better at it," she said. "I thought about taking lessons but that freaks me out. There'd be other people watching me make a fool of myself. At least it doesn't matter if I look like a fool in front of you."

His thanks must have sounded sarcastic to her ears, because she added, "Hey, that's a compliment. So will you come early tomorrow?"

"I can't." He paused, thinking now was a good time to tell her that he and Kyle were bringing friends.

"Why not? I thought you and Kyle took the day off."

"We did, but there's something you need to know. We

decided to bring guests. I know you've reserved the Pinecone Cabin and it sleeps ten, so there shouldn't be any problem with two extra people, but just in case you planned any events that require partners or small groups, I wanted you to know there are going to be two more people. You're okay with that, right?"

She didn't answer and he worried that she was annoyed at the last-minute change.

"You did say we could bring guests," he reminded her.

Still there was no response.

Then he saw the tiny "call ended" message in the corner of his screen. "Paige, are you there? Paige?" he asked, even though he already knew the answer. He tried calling her again, but was immediately connected to her voice mail.

Frustrated, he flipped his phone shut. No doubt her battery had gone dead. He wondered just how much she'd heard. Guess he'd find out sooner or later. He hoped it was sooner.

PAIGE CAREFULLY MOVED the plastic garment bag containing the wedding dress from the backseat of her car into the small travel trailer she temporarily called home. When she'd decided to spend the summer at the North Shore, Michael had offered to share his apartment with her until the house they had leased would be ready for occupancy. She had opted to spend her remaining days as a single woman in a campground in what Michael called her bubblemobile. Although it was smaller than an efficiency apartment, it had all the amenities she needed, but its best feature was that she could be lulled to sleep each night by the gentle lapping of waves. She also liked that she could start each day with a hike to the pebbly shore of Lake Superior or a walk through the woods.

Today, however, she realized just how small her temporary home was. No matter how many times she rearranged the things in her closet there was no place for the dress. She finally gave up trying to find a spot for it and spread it across her bed. She would figure out what to do with it after she returned from her lunch shift at the Birchwood Room. She quickly changed into the black skirt and white shirt that were the uniform of the waitstaff at the restaurant and headed for work.

As she pulled into the employee parking lot at the resort, she looked for Michael's red Mustang, but it wasn't in the space reserved for the club's golf pro. He always gave lessons on Thursday mornings so why wasn't he at work? Thinking he must have been on an errand, she parked her car and went inside.

Because the lodge's restaurant was open to the public as well as to the guests of the resort, it was usually crowded over the noon hour, and Paige expected today would be no exception. Although the decor was rustic, with wagon-wheel chandeliers and fish and animal trophies lining the walls, crisp white linen tablecloths and fresh-flower centerpieces gave it a casual elegance that set it apart from the informal cafés along the Shore and made it a popular spot for tourists.

Although many of her coworkers were college and high-school students there for the summer, the resort relied on the local community for year-round employment. Paige had been pleased at how easy it was to renew acquaintances with staff members who had been working at the resort the summer she'd waited tables here before her senior year in college.

One of those workers, a woman named Kathy, greeted Paige when she punched in at the time clock.

"Paige! I didn't expect to see you today."

"Why not? I'm on the schedule," Paige reminded her.

"Yes, I know, but…" She paused before asking, "Is everything okay?"

"Yeah, it's great. In fact it's better than great." She went on to tell Kathy about finding her dress, but when the older woman looked a bit uneasy, Paige said, "I'm sorry. I must be boring you. I'm like one of those windup toys once I start talking wedding stuff."

"No, it's all right. Don't apologize. Your dress sounds beautiful."

They were joined by another of their coworkers, a redhead named Rosie. As she punched her time card, she said to Paige, "You look like you're in a good mood."

Paige grinned. "I am. It's a beautiful day."

"That's because she found her wedding dress," Kathy added.

"Well, no wonder you're so cheery," Rosie remarked. "Did you get it here in town?"

"No, in Grand Marais." Paige repeated the story she'd just told Kathy, explaining that she needed to find a place to store the gown as her trailer was too crowded. "I would ask Michael to take it but I'm not going to tempt fate."

"Oh, noooo," Kathy drawled. "You definitely can't leave it with him. That would be bad luck."

"That's right," Rosie agreed. Paige didn't miss the furtive glances the two women exchanged.

"It's too bad he's not feeling well," Rosie remarked.

"He's not feeling well?" Paige frowned. That would explain his vacant parking space.

"You didn't hear?" Kathy asked.

"Hear what?"

Again the two women exchanged glances.

"All I know is that he called in sick today and my David had to go in and cover for him." Kathy's husband was semi-retired and substituted for workers at the golf course when needed.

"It's funny that he didn't call me," Paige remarked. "Well,

I shouldn't say that because he may have tried but my cell phone battery died on me today."

"I'm sure he would have called you if it was anything serious," Kathy said. "He probably just has a virus."

"It's going around," Rosie added. "Chelsea in housekeeping called in sick today, too."

"She's not sick," Kathy said. "She's faking it. She went to Las Vegas."

A chill rattled through Paige. At one time Michael had dated Chelsea Kinseth, an outrageous flirt who thought no man was off-limits. She'd made no secret of the fact that she was still interested in Michael, and Paige suspected that it wouldn't take much encouragement for her to make a play for him.

Fortunately Michael had assured Paige that he was no longer interested in the woman, whose claim to fame was that for two years running she'd won the wet T-shirt contest at a local bar. Still, Paige had to fight the jealous twinge that made her want to drive over to his place and check on him during her break. She wouldn't, of course. Michael had given her no reason to suspect the two absences were connected. Besides, she trusted him and knew that it was simply a coincidence that they were both off sick.

The first half of her shift passed quickly as customers waited in line for the opportunity to eat the house special of red ribs and sweet-potato fries. During her break, Paige tried calling Michael's number, but all she heard was his voice mail. She left a message for him to call her and headed over to the reservations desk to see if she could get the key to the Pinecone Cabin. She planned to stock the refrigerator with beverages and fill the cupboards with snacks.

Behind the counter was a tall slender woman named Stacy Walker, who had been an intern at the resort the summer

Paige and the Bulldogs had worked as waitstaff. Now after seven years at the resort, Stacy had worked her way up to manager of customer relations. When she saw Paige, she greeted her with a smile and said, "You're just the person I'm looking for. I have something for you."

Expecting it to be the key to the cabin, Paige was surprised when she handed her an envelope with the resort logo on it. Scrawled across the front was her name in what appeared to be her fiancé's handwriting.

"Was Michael here today?"

"No, he left that last night and told me to give this to you when you came to pick up the key for the Pinecone," Stacy replied. "You are here for the key, aren't you?"

"Yes."

"I'll get it for you in just a minute, but I need to talk to these people first, okay?" She nodded toward the end of the counter where an elderly couple waited patiently for her attention.

Paige looked at the envelope and wondered why Michael hadn't simply called her and talked to her. Even if her phone battery wasn't working, he could have left a voice message for her. She stepped away from the counter and ripped open the sealed envelope. Inside was a single sheet of paper bearing a note in Michael's handwriting.

Dear Paige,
By the time you get this I will be on my way to Las Vegas.
I can't marry you. I don't want you to think that I don't love you because I do, but I need some time to think over some things. I didn't want to hurt you, but right now I feel that if we were to marry, it wouldn't be fair to you.
I'm really sorry. Love, Michael.
P.S. You can keep the ring.

For a moment Paige was too stunned to even breathe. Then she gasped and leaned up against the wall of the lobby. Michael had jilted her? Why? The question banged around in her head like a bad headache. She reread the letter and saw nothing that she hadn't seen the first time she'd read his note. He needed time to think...he was confused...so why did he have to go to Las Vegas?

"She went to Las Vegas." Kathy's words echoed in her head. *"She's not sick. She's faking it."*

Paige had a flash of memory. She was sitting in the resort's lounge a couple of weeks ago, having a soda with some of the other waitstaff. Chelsea Kinseth entered and announced to anyone who would listen that someday she was going to go to Las Vegas to take the biggest gamble of her life. Paige had thought she wanted to get a job as a showgirl, but now she wondered if that gamble was running off with Michael.

She shook her head. No, she wasn't going to jump to conclusions. She gazed at the diamond on her finger. Surely Michael wouldn't have given her such an expensive ring if he hadn't planned to marry her. She quickly reread the note, but the message was the same.

"Paige, is everything all right?" Stacy asked.

With unsteady hands Paige folded the note from Michael and shoved it into her apron pocket next to her order pad. Tears misted in her eyes but she wasn't about to let anyone see them. "You'll have to excuse me," she said and rushed out the front door of the lodge and into the parking lot, where she took long, deep breaths of fresh air, willing her body not to give in to the urge to cry.

This couldn't be happening to her. Michael wouldn't do this to her. She walked over to the employee section of the parking lot, hoping to see his red Mustang. It wasn't there.

She followed the paved walkway leading to the golf course, her stride brisk as she made her way to the clubhouse. If there was one person who would know what was going on, it was Gus Reynolds. He was the golf-course groundskeeper and Michael's closest friend at the resort. She found him tending the garden outside the clubhouse, his portly figure bent over a bed of impatiens.

"Well, look who's here," he said, getting to his feet to greet her. "I thought you'd be in Vegas by now."

Any hope Paige had that the letter was some cruel joke was gone. "Michael told you he was going to Vegas?"

"He didn't exactly tell me. I saw his e-ticket. We both use the same computer." He winked. "I figured something was going on. Every time I came in here he'd be on the Internet looking at Las Vegas sites. When I saw the list of wedding chapels I figured you two were running off to get married or something."

"No."

His voice softened. "I'm sorry. I just assumed."

"Stacy said he called in sick."

"Well, I guess that's one way of getting time off without using vacation days, isn't it?"

Paige didn't respond. What could she say? There could only be one reason why Michael had been using Google to search for Las Vegas wedding chapels. He was going to marry Chelsea.

Pain shot through her, making her want to crumble right there in front of Gus. But she didn't. She simply turned around and headed back up the paved walkway leading to the lodge.

Ever since she'd read Michael's letter she'd been fighting the tears, but on her way back to the lodge she gave up the battle. She dropped onto a small concrete bench and wept.

She hated crying. It was for wusses and she was no wuss.

She especially hated crying over a guy, but this was not just any guy. This was Michael. Her fiancé. She looked again at the ring on her finger. This morning she'd dangled it in front of the consignment-store clerk's eyes as if it was her most prized possession. Now it hurt to look at it. She yanked it from her finger and almost threw it across the carefully manicured grass into one of the golf course's water hazards. Almost. Paige could be just as emotional as any other woman, but she had an advantage. Her brain rarely allowed her emotions to govern her decisions.

She didn't know what would become of the diamond, but she didn't want its fate to be the same as that of a golf ball whose owner had botched a swing. Hoping that out of sight would mean out of mind, she slipped the ring into her pocket, wishing it was as easy to hide the ugly stuff that had happened to her today.

Only there was no way she was going to be able to keep what had happened a secret. She wondered how many of the resort's employees already knew that Michael had dumped her. Suddenly the furtive glances exchanged between Kathy and Rosie made sense. Kathy's husband worked at the golf course. The rumor mill had put two and two together.

It was such a humiliating thought Paige didn't know how she was going to face anyone. Maybe she wouldn't face them. Maybe she would just go get her purse, punch her time card, walk out and never return. Ever.

The thought was a tempting one. There were only a couple of weeks left of the summer season anyway. It would be so nice not to have to face a single person at the resort. She could just imagine the looks of pity.

But as badly as she wanted to run away from it all, she couldn't. She had responsibilities—a job, a lease on a trailer, a lease on a house. And the Bulldogs would be coming for their reunion weekend.

Her hurt turned to anger. She was supposed to be introducing her fiancé to Ben and Amber this weekend, not making excuses as to why he wasn't there. Only, she wouldn't make excuses. She would get through the next three days one way or another.

She pulled out her cell phone, took several deep breaths and punched the number one on her speed dial—the house phone she had at one time shared with Justin and Kyle. It rang once then rolled over to voice mail.

After the beep she said, "Hey, it's me. I need to talk to you. Bad." Her voice was wobbly and she was worried that they'd be able to tell she'd been crying. She took another deep breath and said, "I'm having, like, the worst day of my life. Michael's on his way to Vegas with his old girlfriend and I'm here at the Cascading Waters feeling like…well, you can imagine how I feel…and I really need to talk to you." Losing the battle of fighting tears, she ended with, "I have to get back to work. Call me when you get this."

Again she thought about getting in her car and never coming back. But she knew that sooner or later she would have to face everyone at the lodge, so she went back to work.

When she walked into the Birchwood Room, the first person she saw was Kathy. "You've been crying?" She flung an arm around her shoulder. "Is there anything I can do to help?"

"You know, don't you?" Paige asked, even though she was almost certain of the answer.

The older woman nodded slowly. "I was hoping it was just a rumor. I'm sorry, Paige. It was a really low thing for the two of them to do. Why don't you ask if you can take the rest of the afternoon off?"

Paige knew it would mean extra work for the remaining waitstaff. "No, it's all right. It's better if I keep busy. I'll go wash up and be right out."

"Sure. Go ahead. Take as much time as you need. Rosie and I can cover for you."

"Thanks." Paige visited the ladies' restroom and washed her hands and face, determined that none of the other employees would see just how deeply hurt she was by Michael's rejection. To her relief the lunch crowd was heavy and she didn't have time to dwell on what they may or may not have heard. When her shift finally ended, Paige left with the knowledge that as difficult as it had been to stay at work, at least she'd had the satisfaction of knowing she'd fulfilled her obligation.

When she got back to the trailer she saw the box of decorations staring at her from the tiny tabletop, reminding her that she had another job to finish before she could do what she really wanted to do—go to bed and forget the day even happened. She needed to take the food and beverages over to the Pinecone Cabin and hang the decorations. And she would, but first she needed some time alone to let her jangled nerves rest.

At only five foot two she could easily curl up onto the small sofa that pulled out into a bed. She sighed and closed her eyes, trying not to think about Michael and Chelsea cuddling up to one another at a wedding chapel in Vegas.

"This should not be happening to me—it's just not fair," she said to herself as images of the two of them together tormented her until she fell asleep.

AS JUSTIN HEADED FOR HOME he knew exactly what he wanted. A cold beer and a shower and in that order. Then he was going to meet several of his friends at the Saints game, where he'd get a couple of hot dogs and have another cold beer. It was the perfect way to spend a hot summer evening and there was nothing like baseball to take his mind off a woman he shouldn't be thinking about. Ever since she'd sent him the phone photo of her in her wedding dress, Paige had been on his mind.

It hadn't been one of his better days. It had started with a flat tire on his pickup that had put him behind on his appointments for the rest of the day. As part of his job selling the nursery stock, he also had to respond to complaint calls. He usually had one or two follow-up calls a week to check on the condition of the plants and trees he'd sold clients. Today alone he'd had three callbacks, but it was the last one that had been the most difficult. It was to a golf course.

After listening to Paige carry on about her wedding dress this morning, it was the last place he wanted to be. He hated golf, and the fact that Michael Cross had Paige playing the game was like a burr in his sock. Paige was no more interested in golf than Justin was, yet she now spent more energy worrying about getting a tee time than she did getting tickets to a ball game.

And if it wasn't enough that the trees he'd sold the golf course had died, while he was doing the inspection, one of the landscape employees had tripped getting out of the way of a golf cart and broken an ankle. Justin was the one who took him to the hospital emergency room where they had ended up spending most of the afternoon. He'd had to cancel the remainder of his appointments for the day, which was not the way he wanted to start his three-day weekend.

He took an unusually long shower, allowing the water to wash away the frustrations of the day. By the time he had toweled himself dry, he felt relaxed and ready to spend the night with the guys drinking beer and talking baseball.

As he was getting dressed, his cell phone beeped. It was Kyle sending him a text message telling him that he was having a DND night at Tammy's. They had been roommates long enough for Justin to know that DND was code for Do Not Disturb. Justin messaged him back, telling him he was going to the Saints game and would see him in the morning.

Then he finished dressing, grabbed his Saints cap and was about to head out the back door when he noticed the blinking message light on the house phone. His finger automatically hit the play button.

As he suspected, the first two messages were from telemarketers trying to convince him he needed his carpets cleaned and new windows installed. He glanced impatiently at his watch, thinking that if he had to run through a string of such calls he'd miss the start of the game. He was about to press the stop button when he heard Paige's voice.

"Hey, it's me. I need to talk to you. Bad. I'm having, like, the worst day of my life. Michael's on his way to Vegas with his old girlfriend and I'm here at the Cascading Waters feeling like…well, you can imagine how I feel…and I really need to talk to you."

It was followed by a double beep indicating it was the last message recorded.

"That son of a bitch," Justin muttered as he took the steps two at a time. When he reached his room he grabbed the duffel bag with his Bulldog sweatshirt already in it and began stuffing it with clothes. On his way back down the stairs he called his buddies and told them he wouldn't be at the Saints game. As he was about to walk out the door he started to dial Kyle's cell then stopped. Kyle was DND.

So instead of phoning Kyle he went to a drawer in the kitchen, pulled out a piece of paper and began to write.

Kyle, Call me when you read this. Paige needed help so I left a day early. J.C.

As he stuck the note to the refrigerator with a loon magnet, he thought it was probably a good thing that Kyle was with Tammy tonight. Because he was a little in love with Paige, Kyle might not be able to console her without letting those emotions get in the way.

Justin, on the other hand, was much better at hiding his feelings for Paige and wouldn't forget that she wanted him to be her friend, not her boyfriend. As he climbed into the pickup he said to himself, "Just hang in there, Paige. Your best friend is coming to the rescue."

CHAPTER THREE

PAIGE AWOKE with a start, hearing a pounding near her head. After only a couple of seconds, she realized that someone was banging on the metal door of her trailer. She sat up and a sharp pain shot through her neck. She'd been curled up like a pretzel on the narrow sofa and was now paying the price. She peeked through the louvered window and saw Stacy in the gold blazer that identified her as one of the managers at the lodge.

"Paige, are you in there?" she heard the woman call out.

Paige stumbled toward the door and unlocked it. "I'm here," she said, rubbing her sore neck. "I'm sorry. I fell asleep after work." She moved to one side and gestured for her to come in. "Why are you here?"

Stacy stepped into the small trailer. "You never came back for the key to the cabin." She dangled a large diamond-shaped plastic key ring in midair.

"Oh. Thanks." Paige took the key from her and stuck it in her jeans pocket. "Do you want something to drink? Some water or a soda?"

She shook her head. "No, I'm fine. What about you? How are you doing?"

Paige suspected from the look of sympathy on the blonde's face that she'd heard the news about Michael and Chelsea. "I suppose you know what happened."

"I've heard nasty rumors, but all I know for certain is that Michael quit his job."

"He quit? I thought he'd called in sick."

"Apparently he left a resignation letter in his desk drawer."

Paige sank back down onto the small sofa. "I guess he and Chelsea plan to stay out there for good." She was surprised that she could even say the words without crying. But it was as if she was talking about someone else's life, not her own, and they came out on a note of indifference.

"I'm really sorry, Paige. For what it's worth, that girl has no shame when it comes to men. It didn't matter to her if he was engaged or not."

"You don't need to make excuses for him," Paige told her. "Any way you look at it, it's still the same outcome." She swallowed back the lump in her throat. It would have been so easy to break down and cry, but she was determined not to do that. Especially not in front of Stacy, who always looked so composed. "I'd rather not talk about any of it if you don't mind."

"I don't mind at all," Stacy assured her. "I didn't come here to talk about Michael Cross. I just wanted to bring you the key and to let you know that if there's anything I can do to make your Bulldog weekend easier, I'm here." She spread her arms in a welcoming gesture. "You are still having your reunion, aren't you?"

"I don't see any way out of it now." Paige tried to keep her voice even, but it wasn't easy.

"Do you want a way out? At this time of year I'd have no trouble renting the cabin at the last minute. You'd lose your deposit, I'm afraid but…"

"No…no…I can't cancel." She scrubbed her hands across her face as if the motion would clear her head. "Everything's such a mess."

"Maybe I can help clean it up."

"I'm not sure there is a way to clean up this one."

Paige was grateful Stacy didn't give her any of the words of encouragement women usually got after being dumped by their boyfriends. Stacy looked around, her gaze landing on the snacks and beverages lining the table and counter. "Is that stuff for your reunion?"

· "I have a small box of decorations, too." Paige nodded at a box on the counter beside the food supplies. "Michael was going to help me get the cabin ready tonight."

Stacy placed a hand on the box. "I'll take his place. I may not be as tall as he is, but I'm not afraid to climb a ladder."

"Michael's not afraid of heights," Paige stated.

"Ever seen him on the chair lift at Lutsen?"

"No, but he doesn't like to downhill ski. He does cross-country."

"Has he hiked the Baptism River Trail with you?"

Of all the trails in the Superior National Forest, it had some of the steepest drops. She'd climbed it often with Justin and Kyle, but never with Michael. She tried to remember hiking to any of the breathtaking lookouts in the various parks along the shoreline, but most of their dates had been spent golfing. The one time they'd stopped at the Split Rock Lighthouse, he'd told her the reason he wasn't going to climb the circular stairs to the top was he'd twisted his knee and wasn't supposed to do stairs.

Stacy hoisted the box of decorations into her arms and said, "If you get the door for me, I'll take this for you." When Paige hesitated she added, "Look, there are some things you can control and others you can't. You'll feel better about the ones you can't control if you take care of the ones you can."

"I suppose everyone at the resort knows what's happened by now."

"Paige, you can't worry about what people think. You did nothing wrong. Michael is the one who should be feeling ashamed, not you. Now, is there anything else you want to take over to the cabin besides what's here?"

"The rest of the stuff is already in my trunk."

"Why don't we put everything in my Escape and you can ride with me," she suggested. "There's no reason for both of us to drive."

A few minutes later Paige was in the front of Stacy's SUV heading for the Cascading Waters Resort. The Pinecone was the largest of nine cabins that formed a horseshoe behind the main lodge at the resort. She took comfort in knowing that each cabin had a private parking area, which meant it was unlikely they'd run into any of the other employees.

Tires crunched on gravel as Stacy parked next to a towering white pine. Because of the wooded setting, the evening sun was but a flicker through the foliage.

Paige appreciated the fact that Stacy made no mention of Michael or the broken engagement as they hung the few decorations from previous years and stocked the refrigerator and cupboards with beverages and food. While they worked they talked mostly about the changes Stacy had seen throughout her lifetime as a resident on the North Shore. As they were hanging the last of the posters, Paige's stomach growled.

"I bet you haven't had any dinner, have you?" Stacy asked.

Paige shook her head. She hadn't eaten lunch or dinner but she hadn't exactly been hungry, either.

"We'll go over to the Birchwood when we're finished here," Stacy offered. "My treat."

"That's really thoughtful of you, but it would probably just be a waste of money," she said, shoving her tape dispenser and scissors back in her tote bag. "I don't feel much like eating. You know what I mean?"

"Oh yes, I do," she acknowledged with a nod. "I've had my heart broken. I know where you're at tonight and it's not a good place to be."

"No, it isn't, which is why I think I'll just go home and go to bed." Paige turned off the lights on their way out of the cabin.

"No, no, no." Stacy wagged her finger. "You most certainly will not go home and have a pity party for one. I have a better idea."

Stacy's better idea was to stop and pick up a couple of sandwiches at a local deli on the way back to Paige's trailer. When she pulled up to a liquor store, Paige said, "Unless you want something, you don't have to stop for me. I get headaches from alcohol."

"I'll just be a minute," was all Stacy said before disappearing inside. She returned carrying a couple of brown bags. As she set them on the bench seat between them, the contents rattled.

Seeing Paige's wary glance, she said, "It's mostly fruit juices. I'm going to make us some punch."

"You don't need to spend your night off babysitting me," Paige said.

"Who said anything about babysitting? I know we haven't had a lot of time to get to know one another, but you're still a girlfriend and girlfriends don't let other girlfriends have pity parties for one. So consider tonight an opportunity for me to show someone in the sisterhood how to look at the positive side of breaking up. And there is a positive side. You just can't see it yet, but believe me, it's there."

Paige tried to smile, but she didn't think that anything Stacy could say or do would dull the pain of losing Michael. All of her life she'd been a "glass is half-full" person, weathering breakups with guys better than most women she knew. But never had she expected that getting jilted could hurt so badly.

When they arrived back at the campground, Stacy insisted it was too nice out to eat indoors. She instructed Paige to build a campfire in the fire pit next to the trailer while she mixed the punch.

A short while later Paige found herself on an Adirondack chair in front of a crackling fire with a sandwich in one hand and a concoction Stacy called her "men are pigs" punch in the other. Paige wasn't sure just what it was she was drinking. While she had been gathering wood, Stacy had been inside the trailer pouring a variety of liquids into her blender. The result had been a surprisingly delicious fruit drink that had Paige wondering if it contained much alcohol.

"You make a pretty good fire, Paige," Stacy told her as a birch log popped and sizzled in the dancing flames. "One thing I've learned over the years is that there is nothing that a man can do for you that you can't do for yourself."

Paige really didn't want to talk about the value of men and changed the subject. "Thank you for stopping and getting these sandwiches. I guess I was hungry after all."

"They're are not as good as Tony's, but they're not bad," Stacy said.

Tony was the chef at the Birchwood and a good friend of Stacy's. Paige felt a bit guilty that she'd refused Stacy's offer to eat at the resort restaurant. "You understand why I didn't want to go to the Birchwood, don't you? I don't think I could have taken one more person glancing at me with that pitiful look that says, 'Oh, you've been dumped, you poor thing.'"

"If they're looking at you with pity they're making the assumption that you've lost something of value," Stacy said in between bites of her sandwich. "You haven't."

"You're right. He's worthless. So is Chelsea." Paige lifted her glass toward the starry sky. "To the worthless Michael Cross and his worthless bride, Chelsea."

"Uh-uh, the toast should be to Michael and Chelsea for saving you from making the biggest mistake of your life." Stacy raised her glass to Paige's.

Paige took another sip and suddenly realized that there indeed was plenty of liquor in the fruit drink. She felt a warmth spread through her, tickling her insides.

"A friend of mine tried to warn me that Michael would be trouble," she said, gazing up at the stars.

"All men are," Stacy stated with authority.

"Tell me the truth. Was I the only one who didn't know he was still seeing Chelsea?"

"I don't think anyone knew for sure, but it was hard not to notice how she was always hanging around him. And they did have a history." Stacy got up and reached for Paige's empty glass. "You need a refill."

"Better only make it a half." She giggled. "I think I'm getting a little tipsy."

"Nothing wrong with that," Stacy said, and disappeared into the trailer, only to return with another full glass.

"I know one thing," Paige said after taking another sip. "I will not get involved with someone who works at the same place as I do. Today had to be the most humiliating day of my life. I used to think the people who worked at the resort were nice, but now…"

"Hey—they are nice, but like everyone else they talk," Stacy said in defense of her coworkers. "If you're going to be mad at someone, it should be Michael. He's the one who gave them something to talk about."

"Ever since I got his letter I've been trying to figure out

what I could have done differently in our relationship, but he acted as if he was really happy."

"Paige, this is *not* your fault."

"Then why do I feel like it is?"

"Because you're a woman and men want us to feel that way…like we're to blame for everything that goes wrong in a relationship."

"Well, it doesn't help that some women buy into that crap. Maybe our problem was about sex. But if sex was so important to our relationship, he shouldn't have told me he understood my reasons for wanting to wait until we were married to sleep together."

"You never had sex with Michael!" It was a statement, not a question.

Paige gasped. "I can't believe I told you that."

"It's okay. I'll treat it as a confidence. You have my word." Stacy made a cross over her heart with her right index finger.

"I've always believed that I would only have sex with one man—the one I married. It was a gift I wanted to give my husband on our wedding night. That's why Michael and I were waiting until we were married…or at least I was waiting. He was obviously doing it with Chelsea." Paige took another sip of her punch then asked, "Do you think if I had been sleeping with Michael, he would have still run off with her?"

"Now you're starting to sound like one of those women who believe the crap men are peddling. You and Michael had an agreement. He broke it. It's that simple. Case closed."

"You're right. Even if we did have sex, he might have still run off with Chelsea."

"Exactly." Stacy lifted her glass in acknowledgment. "There's no excuse for his behavior."

"I can't believe he dumped me like that. He could have at

least told me face-to-face. He's chickenshit. And pig shit, too." She giggled.

"He's afraid of heights," Stacy reminded her.

"And bees. He runs like a girl when he sees one. He told me it's because he's allergic to them, but I think he's just afraid."

"He's vain. Have you noticed how he can't pass a mirror without admiring himself?"

With each sip of the fruit drink Paige found it easier to find fault with her ex-fiancé. By the time she was on her third glass of Stacy's special concoction, she was convinced she'd been unhappy with him.

"Now aren't you glad you're not going to marry the man?" Stacy asked.

"Yeeeesss! I'm happy he's gone and I hope I never have to see him again!" she proclaimed in a loud voice as she stretched her arms toward the sky.

"Didn't I tell you I'd get you to see the positive side of him leaving?"

"Yes, and thank you, thank you, thank you," she said, bowing theatrically. "Oooh—look, our fire is going out."

"Got anything you want to burn? Maybe some pictures?" Stacy asked, arching an eyebrow.

Paige snapped her fingers. "That's it. I'm going to burn his pictures. Watch my drink for me." She disappeared inside the trailer and returned with a handful of snapshots in one hand and a cardboard box in the other. She tossed the photos onto the fire and watched them burn. "Good riddance."

"What's in the box?" Stacy asked.

Paige removed the lid and a pile of papers floated onto the flames. "Scorecards from our golf games. He wanted me to save them. Nobody cares about your stupid golf scores, Michael!" she shouted into the fire.

"Feel better?" Stacy asked.

"I feel great!" She ran back into the trailer and came out waving a piece of paper.

"What's that?"

"It's my Top Ten list…you know, my list of the ten most important traits a guy needs to have to be a good boyfriend. I thought Michael had all ten, but it turns out he was missing the most important one."

"Which is?"

"A guy should be trustworthy." She tossed the paper into the fire and made several more trips into the trailer, each time coming out with more things to burn. But it was the last article that brought Stacy to her feet. Folded over Paige's arm was her wedding gown.

"I have one last thing to get rid of. I just bought this today. Can you believe that? Today of all days. I buy my wedding dress and my fiancé runs off with another woman."

Alarmed, Stacy rose to her feet. "You're not thinking of putting that in the fire, are you?"

"Sure. Why not? I'm never going to wear it."

JUSTIN'S ROAD TRIP went about as well as his day had gone. After being stuck in rush-hour traffic leaving St. Paul, he'd hit road construction that caused another delay and made him wish he'd ordered more than a super-size soda when he stopped at a fast-food drive-thru. Other than three Salted Nut Roll candy bars he'd found in the glove compartment of his pickup, he'd had nothing to eat since lunch, which was why as soon as he reached Paige's he planned to take her out somewhere decent for dinner. She could pour her heart out to him just as easily over a thick, juicy prime cut of beef as she could over a burger. But if she wanted fast food, he would sacrifice the steak.

Thinking of being with her had him pushing the pedal a little closer to the metal. As the sun went down and the air cooled, he turned off his air-conditioning and rolled down the windows, loving the feel of the breeze rushing through the cab of his pickup. He turned up the volume on his CD player so the sounds of the Dave Matthews Band blared in stereo all around him. The music was so loud he didn't hear the siren. It wasn't until he glanced into his rearview mirror and saw the flashing red light that he knew he'd been a little too eager to get to see Paige. He cursed under his breath and pulled off onto the shoulder of the highway.

"Is there a problem, Officer?" he asked in his good-citizen voice.

"Know how fast you were driving?" the policeman asked.

"Sixty-five?" Justin ventured to guess.

"Eighty-two. Could I see your driver's license, please?"

Justin didn't miss the way the officer's eyes scanned the cab of the pickup. Surely there was nothing suspicious about a guy's having three empty candy wrappers and a super-size beverage cup from a fast-food restaurant on his front seat. So why was the man's face wrinkling as if there was?

"Are those your shoes?" he asked, pointing to the pair of athletic shoes on the passenger-side mat.

"Yes."

"You're not driving barefoot, are you?"

"No. I have on sandals."

"Step out of the vehicle, please."

Justin climbed out, smoothing down the wrinkles of his khaki shorts as he unfolded his long legs. The officer looked at his feet, then back up at his shirt. Justin was grateful he wasn't wearing a T-shirt with some irreverent saying on the front. It was only because experience had taught him it would be wise not to challenge the authority of anyone wearing a badge and carrying a gun that he managed to stay calm and wait for the officer to issue the ticket. As he pondered his situation, he thought it was a good thing that Michael Cross had left town or else Justin might have kicked his skinny little ass when he got to the resort.

But he didn't want to waste time thinking about the weasel. Paige was the one he worried about. He hoped she was all right. Knowing her, he expected to find her at home cleaning her tiny trailer. That's what she usually did when she was stressed—organized her cupboards and drawers. She loved to put things in order, especially when her mind was in turmoil.

Paige wasn't like most women he knew. She got angry and got over it. She didn't dwell on the bad stuff. She couldn't. It just wasn't in her nature. And she rarely resorted to tears. That's why today when he'd heard her voice crack with emotion he knew that this breakup was different from others. And that was the reason he had immediately jumped in his pickup and hit the road. She needed him.

Yes, it was only as a friend, but that was the way it had always been and he'd accepted it could be no other way a long time ago. Even if Paige had given him any indication that she wanted to take their friendship to the next level—and she hadn't—he wouldn't have been able to follow through on it. The reason they'd been able to stay close for so long was because early on in their friendship they'd agreed that no matter how tempting it might be to test the waters of romance, they were first and foremost friends. It was why Kyle hadn't acted upon his adolescent crush on Paige. And why neither of them would ever know of *his* love for her.

Justin couldn't risk losing her. If she were to ever find out that he had feelings for her, she might withdraw emotionally. It was the kind of revelation that once it was out there, you could never take it back. He'd been friends too long with Kyle and Paige to take such a chance.

So Justin's was the shoulder Paige cried on when she needed one—which was seldom. More often she simply used him as a sounding board. Although he knew she had a soft center, she'd spent most of her life showing the world how tough she could be. She'd get angry, talk about the problem, then get over it and move on. It was one of the things he loved about her. Her resiliency. That and the fact that she wasn't the kind for emotional outbursts. He could use some of that self-control himself as the officer handed him a speeding ticket.

By the time he reached the campground where she was staying it was dark. He'd only been to her place once—when he and Kyle had helped her move. He followed the dirt road that wound through the campground, looking closely at the numbers that identified the different sites.

But he didn't need a number to point out where Paige lived. She was standing on a lawn chair swinging a wedding dress around as if she was getting ready to toss it into the campfire. "What the…" he mumbled to himself as he scurried out of the truck.

"That better not be the dress that nearly cost me a client this morning," Justin said as he approached the campfire.

Both women turned at the sound of his voice. "Justin! You're just in time. Get it? Just-in?" She giggled and he raced over to swoop her off the chair.

"Hey—what are you doing?" she protested.

"Bringing you down to my level so you can give me a

proper welcome and thank me for coming to you in your hour of need, although it looks as if you've been doing all right without me."

With the wedding dress still in her arms she pulled him to her and gave him a hug so that he nearly got a mouthful of satin.

"You came all the way up here to make sure that I was okay?"

"Yup, once again Justin to the rescue." He looked over his shoulder at her companion. "I have a habit of doing this."

"What a good friend you are," Paige gushed as she released him. "I am so glad you're here. You're just in time to see me burn the last reminder of the chickenshit."

When she moved to toss the dress into the fire, he stopped her. "You're not burning that thing. It has a history."

"Oh, you mean the schoolteacher and the soldier." She sighed. "They were so in love."

"That's why you shouldn't burn the dress." He took the gown from her hands.

"That's what I've been trying to tell her," the blond woman said, and suddenly Paige found her manners.

"Justin, you remember Stacy, don't you? She's in charge of customer relations. Stacy, this is Justin, my best friend and maid of honor."

"Maid of honor?" Stacy lifted her eyebrows inquisitively.

"It's a long story," Justin said. They made small talk, and Justin told her that he was one of the Bulldogs and would be staying for the weekend.

Stacy finally said, "I really should get going." She turned to Paige. "You don't mind, do you?"

"You don't have to go because Justin came," Paige told her.

"No, but it's late and I do have to work tomorrow."

Paige covered her mouth. "Oh, I forgot. Thanks for all your help tonight," she said, giving the other woman a hug.

As Stacy prepared to leave, Paige said, "What about the stuff you bought for the men are pigs punch?"

Stacy dismissed her concern with a flap of her hand. "Keep it."

"Men are pigs punch?" Justin repeated.

"It's really good," Paige told him. "You have to try it—even though you're not a pig."

Justin looked at Paige. "Are you sure about that?"

"Yes, I am. You're my best friend." Then she turned to Stacy and gave her a hug. "Thank you so much for teaching me how to see the positive side of getting dumped."

Justin was at a loss for words. He'd expected to find Paige angry and hurt, but he hadn't expected to find her drinking. He asked Stacy if she needed a ride home, but she assured him she'd had only one glass of the punch a few hours earlier, so she was fine. As she drove away, he knew the first thing he had to do was put the wedding dress out of sight.

"What are you going to do with that?" Paige asked as he started walking with the dress toward his truck.

"Put it away so you can return it and get your money back."

"I don't care about the money. I want to burn it. Bring it back here," she ordered him.

He ignored her and kept walking. He was fairly certain that come tomorrow she'd be glad the satin gown wasn't among the ashes of the fire pit. "You may feel differently tomorrow."

She followed him. "No, I won't. I don't ever want to see that stupid dress again. I don't want any memories of Mr. Michael 'I'm a chickenshit' Cross."

"Then I'll return it for you."

"Why would you want to do that?"

"Because you said there's a story behind it," he said, draping it across the seat of his pickup.

"Yeah, and it's a nightmare. You can take it back to the consignment shop but no one's going to want to buy it now. Everyone in town knows what happened."

He could see it would do no good to argue with her as to the worth of the dress so he simply said, "Then we won't return it. Why don't you go inside and get me a beer."

"I don't have any beer but Stacy left the punch and it's really good. You can drink it even though you're a guy."

"Maybe we should have some coffee."

"Coffee? You don't drink coffee." She gave him a puzzled look before saying, "Ah, I get it. You think I'm drunk." She giggled. "I've only had two glasses, Just-in." She stressed each syllable of his name. "Enough to make me realize I'm better off without Mr. Chickenshit."

"You just made my point. You're swearing, which means you've definitely hit your limit of alcohol."

"You're sounding like a big brother again, Just-in. I don't need a big brother tonight. I need a friend. And if you are my best friend you will help me celebrate the end of my engagement." She held up her left hand and wiggled it in the air. "See. No ring."

His eyes widened. "You didn't throw that in the fire?"

"Nope. I flushed it down the toilet." Seeing the expression on his face, she laughed. "I'm kidding. It's inside. Now, are you going to join me in a glass of punch or not? Stacy made it extra weak because she knows it doesn't take much to give me a headache."

"Why don't you just bring me a soda."

She shoved her fists to her waist. "Did you or did you not drive all the way up here a day early to help me make it through the nastiest day of my life?"

"I did," he assured her.

"Good, because that's what friends do—they're there for each other when you need them, and right now I need you to be my best friend, not my big brother. Nothing bad is going to happen to you or me just because we have a couple of glasses of men are pigs punch."

He thought about it briefly and decided if sitting around the campfire drinking made her forget about her broken heart, who was he to say she should stop? "Okay, go inside and get us some punch."

As she climbed the steps to the trailer she called out over her shoulder, "If you're not going to burn the dress, we're going to need more wood for the fire. There's a pile of it on the other side of my car."

While she was inside he gathered several birch logs and added them to the fire. It was quiet on her campsite. A small awning extended from the trailer under which she had a bistro-size table and chairs. Although the campsites were fairly close together, trees afforded a privacy that made it feel as if they were in the middle of the wilderness.

Justin leaned back in the chair and closed his eyes, listening to the sounds of nature all around him. The steady chirping of the crickets, the buzz of insects. He smiled to himself. Paige loved the outdoors and didn't mind the bugs. It was one of the many things he found attractive about her. She wasn't given to princesslike behavior. If a spider crawled up her leg she wouldn't run screaming in circles.

"You're not sleeping, are you?"

He opened his eyes and saw her standing over him, a glass in each hand. "Too bad I already took all the food over to the Pinecone, otherwise we could have made s'mores. You got a great fire going."

He sat forward and poked at it with a bare tree branch,

causing the burning wood to crackle. Then he tried the punch. "Man, this is sweet. No wonder you like it."

"I told you. It's like a fruit smoothie."

"It certainly goes down smoothly, but I'm warning you, this might have the same effects as Ben's dandelion wine."

She waved her finger at him. "No skinny-dipping or you might wake up with mosquito bites in places you've never had them before." Again she giggled.

"I'm more worried about you waking up with a whopper of a hangover."

"Who cares? After what I've been through today, a hangover is nothing."

He sat in the chair Stacy had vacated and reached across to take Paige's hand. "I'm sorry you got hurt, Paige. You were too good for the guy, and if he were here right now I'd beat the crap out of him."

"I should have listened to you. You were right about him. He's a loser."

"You said he ran off to Vegas with another woman?"

"Chelsea, the biggest bee-otch in town. But I don't want to talk about it." She squeezed his hand. "I'm so glad you're here."

"Me, too. Tell me what the plans are for tomorrow."

He hoped to get her talking about the Bulldog weekend, but despite her assertion that she didn't want to talk about her broken engagement, she said, "He must have been with her all those times when I couldn't reach him and he told me he was working."

Justin tried to distract her. "Ben and Amber are coming tomorrow, right?"

"They used to date."

"Ben and Amber? That's news to me." Her next words made him realize that she wasn't talking about their college friends.

"Chelsea did everything she could to get him back. She's not a nice person, Justin."

"I thought you didn't want to talk about her?"

She ignored his comment. "She's a schemer and she has no morals. She didn't care that he was engaged to me. And what makes this whole mess even worse is that everybody at the Cascading Waters knew what was going on. Well, everyone but me."

Again he reached over to touch her. "He was the wrong man for you, Paige."

"But it felt so right."

That made him cringe inside.

She took another sip of her punch and said, "Well, that's it for me. I'm through with men. They can't be faithful. It's not in their genes."

"Hey—what about me? Haven't I been a faithful friend?"

"Yes, but you don't count." He would have liked to tell her that he could count if she'd give him a chance, but she was back on the subject of Michael Cross.

"Michael and I got along so well," she said in a wistful tone. "Do you know we never had one single argument?"

"That tells me he was wrong for you," he said with a tilt of his glass.

"What are you talking about?"

"If two people never argue it's because one person is always getting her way."

"You mean me," she said in indignation.

"You can be rather bossy," he said with good-humored affection.

"I didn't boss Michael around!" she denied emphatically.

"Okay, you didn't. Let's not talk about him. How about if I take you to get something to eat."

"I'm not hungry. I think the reason they ran off to Las Vegas is that Chelsea wanted to get him away from me so I couldn't talk him out of it. She's probably the one who told him to dump me in a letter rather than face-to-face."

"He left you a letter?"

"Uh-huh. I'd show it to you but I burned it." She proceeded to tell him the rest of the details of her broken engagement, which only made Justin more disgusted with Michael Cross.

"You're better off without him, Paige."

"Don't I know it! Now I don't have to play that dumb old game of golf."

"That's right."

"And I don't have to make a fool of myself on the dance floor."

"You don't."

"And I don't have to listen to talk radio in the car."

"Nope."

"I can listen to music." She jumped up. "Hey—you know what we need? Tunes. I'll get my boom box." She disappeared into the trailer and came out with the CD player.

"You still have that thing?" he commented when she set the old boom box on the small table between the two chairs.

"And all of our favorite music," she said as she punched a button that filled the air with the sounds of Faith Hill.

"You mean all of *your* favorite music," he corrected her.

She leaned her head back against the wooden chair and stared up at the starry sky. "Remember when we saw Faith Hill in concert at the convention center? That was such a great night."

"For you, maybe."

"You and Kyle had fun. Admit it."

"Kyle may have, but I only went because you promised to

clean our apartment for a month. You know I'm no fan of country music."

"It's better than that heavy-metal stuff you listen to. And at least no one threw up on me at Faith Hill's concert. I will never ever go to another heavy-metal concert again. Eeewwww. That was so gross."

"It was. Kyle and I shouldn't have taken you with us."

"You mean you shouldn't have dragged me with you," she corrected him.

"We didn't drag you there," he denied. "And don't forget that we left in the middle of the concert to take you home."

"You two are the best friends a girl could have."

"Careful, Paige," he warned. "You're dangerously close to getting slobbering sentimental."

"I don't care."

"If that's the case, then you've definitely had too much of Stacy's punch. You work very hard at keeping those feelings bottled up."

"Ouch." She slapped at her hand saying, "A mosquito bit me."

"Time to move this party inside?" He stood up and began kicking sand over the remains of their fire.

"But I like it out here," she protested.

"You'll like it inside, too. Come." He offered her a hand. "Besides, it's getting cold and I don't want to drag out my sweatshirt."

She put her hands in his and allowed him to pull her to her feet. He liked how warm her hands felt in his and wished he could pull her close and feel her soft body next to his. When she lost her balance momentarily, he steadied her and turned her around, pointing her in the direction of the trailer.

"Don't forget my boom box," she told him as he gave her a gentle nudge.

He grabbed the CD player and followed her to the trailer. When they were inside he asked, "Is there somewhere for me to sleep?"

She placed her hands at her waist. "Don't tell me you want to go to bed? We're supposed to be having a party."

"We'll have a party, but if I'm going to have to drive to look for a motel room I'd better not drink any more of Stacy's punch." The punch may have been mostly fruit juice, but because he hadn't had any dinner, it didn't take much to give him a buzz.

"You're not going to a motel. You can stay here." She pointed to the bench seat behind the table. "That pulls out into a bed. I don't think you want to sleep on the sofa. It's skinny."

"You sure you don't mind?"

"Mind? Justin, you're my best friend." She threw her arms around his neck and clung to him. "I'd sleep on the floor before I made you go to a motel."

When she finally released him he pointed to the travel-size refrigerator and asked, "Do you have any food in that thing? I haven't had dinner."

"Not much. I ate most of my meals either at the lodge or at Michael's. He's a great cook." Justin wondered if that was why she thought she was in love with him—was being a good cook number one on her Top Ten list? He would have asked but he didn't want to encourage her to talk about Michael.

"A sandwich would be fine," he said.

"I know. I'll make you a PB&J—just like I used to do in college," she offered.

"Okay. I'll wash up."

He left her rummaging through the cupboards in the minuscule kitchen. When he returned she was sitting on the bench seat, her shoulders drooping. Next to her on the tiny table was a loaf of bread, a jar of peanut butter and a container of jelly.

When she saw him she said, "Look." In her hands was a red plastic spoon with a handle that had a heart shape at the top of it.

"You're holding a spoon. So what?"

She held it up for his inspection. "It's not just any spoon. It's from my very first date with Michael. We were at this charity golf tournament and they were selling fat-free ice-cream sundaes with these heart-shaped spoons because they were raising money for heart health. I had hot fudge and he had caramel."

She had a look on her face he knew well. He'd seen it often when they were kids. It was her "I want to cry but I'm not going to because I'm not like the rest of the girls" look. Only he was fairly certain that she'd had just enough of Stacy's punch that she wasn't going to be able to keep up the tough-girl act.

"You know what?" Justin said, taking the spoon out of her hand and tossing it into the sink. "I don't need anything to eat after all."

"He said he loved me, Justin," she told him in a tiny, troubled voice.

"I know. He probably said a lot of things he shouldn't have."

He looked at her and it was as if a dam broke. Tears flowed down her cheeks. He pulled her into his arms and let her cry into his shirt. "It's okay. Everything's going to be all right."

But she didn't want to be comforted. She pushed him away. "N-n-no, it isn't," she stammered between sobs.

He tried again to take her in his arms. "Please stop, Paige."

Again she pushed him away. Her expression reminded him of the way she'd looked when she was eleven and her dog, Boots, had been hit by a car.

"Paige, you're letting the alcohol mess with your mind," he said gently but firmly.

She stood up a little straighter. "He might not marry Chelsea if I call him and tell him how I feel." She spotted her cell phone on the counter and reached for it. "I'm going to call him. I should have called him before now. I don't know what I was thinking."

Justin wasn't sure what he should do, but he knew he couldn't let her make a fool of herself because she'd been drinking. He put his hand over hers. "Stop, Paige. You don't want to do that."

"Yes, I do." She tried to wrestle the phone from him, but he wasn't about to let her have it.

"What if he's already married?" Justin asked.

"He can get unmarried."

"Paige, you're not making any sense."

"I need to talk to him, Justin," she pleaded. "Please! I have to!"

He could see that nothing he said was going to stop her from making the call. He released his grip on the phone and she pressed one number. Justin held his breath as she waited for the connection to be made. It wasn't long before she pulled the phone away from her ear and tossed it onto the counter in disgust.

"He didn't answer," she said quietly, then slumped down onto the bench seat, holding her head in her hands. He could see she was trying not to cry, but she couldn't stop her body from trembling with emotion. "I didn't think he would be like my father."

He wanted to say, "He's not. Your father is a good guy," but that wasn't what she wanted to hear. Instead, he stooped down in front of her and pulled her hands away from her face so she had to look at him. "What can I do to help?"

"Nothing. There's nothing anyone can do."

She looked like a limp rag doll sitting on the bench seat.

He took her hands in his and pulled her to her feet. "There's only one thing that's going to help. Sleep."

"But I haven't made you a sandwich."

"I'll make my own." He looked around the tiny trailer. "Where do you sleep in this place?"

She pointed to a curtain at the opposite end of the trailer. "In there."

He walked over and shoved the curtain aside to see a full-size bed with pink linens. Across one end was a pair of light green pajamas and on the floor were matching flip-flops.

"There's not a lot of room," she said as she followed him across the narrow space.

"I'll tell you what. I'll go out to my truck and get my bag and you can do whatever it is you need to do to get ready for bed." Justin stepped outside the trailer and headed for his truck. He gave her enough time to use the restroom and get into bed before he went back inside.

But when he returned she was still fully clothed. She was curled up in a fetal position on the bed and crying again. It broke his heart to see her in such pain.

"You didn't put your pajamas on," he scolded her gently, leaning over her.

She sat up and thrust herself into his arms. He sank onto the bed, cradling her as if she were a child.

As she sobbed against his chest, he said, "Hey, where's that girl who said she was too smart to cry over any guy?"

"I'm not feeling very smart tonight. I feel stupid."

He pushed her away for a moment so that he could stare into her face. "Michael Cross is the stupid one for walking away from you. Any guy who lets someone like you get away is an idiot."

Once again she buried her head against his chest. "You're just saying that because you're my best friend."

"I'm also a guy and I know what makes a girl hot and what doesn't, and you definitely have what it takes."

She lifted her head. "You really think so?"

The look on her face did something funny to his insides. He swiped at the stray tear on her cheek with his thumb and brushed back a lock of hair that had fallen across her forehead. "Yes, I really think so."

"Then prove it." Her words held a bold challenge.

"And how would I do that?" he asked, taking the bait on the hook she dangled.

"Do I really need to tell you the answer to that?" she said in a teasing voice. She pushed him back against the pillow so that she was sitting on top of him, her legs straddling his midsection.

They were playing a provocative game and he liked it. Suddenly he was very much aware of things that normally didn't draw his attention, like the fact that he could see the outline of her nipples through her T-shirt. And the kind of perfume she wore made him want to nuzzle her neck. And the way her hands clung to his shoulders made him wonder how they would feel on his bare skin.

"Are you thinking what I'm thinking?" she asked.

"That Stacy's punch was some crazy love potion?"

"Don't you like that warm feeling it gives you?"

"Yeah, but it's messing with my thinking."

"Why? What do you want to do?"

"You don't want to know."

"You know what I want to do?" she teased provocatively.

"What?" he couldn't resist asking.

"This." She lowered her head and placed her lips on his. It wasn't the first time she'd kissed him, but this was nothing like the gesture of affection they usually exchanged.

The way his body responded made him think that Stacy

had concocted a love potion. Paige may have initiated the kissing, but he was the one who took it to another level, exploring not only her mouth but her body as they rolled around on the bed. He forgot the reason he was in her trailer, forgot just about everything except that she was making him crazy with desire.

"Don't stop," she begged when he pulled back for a moment.

"I have to stop now or pretty soon there'll be no stopping."

"I don't want to stop. It feels too good." Her fingers toyed with the buttons on his shirt.

She was right. It did feel good. Way too good. As he gazed into her eyes he saw the same desire that was coursing through his veins. He knew he should ask her if she was sure this was what she wanted, but she was kissing him again and her hands were going to those places that made him stop thinking.

"You're making me crazy," he said, his body trembling at her touch.

"Tonight crazy is good," she whispered against his lips.

He hoped she was right.

CHAPTER FOUR

THE MINUTE PAIGE AWOKE she knew something was wrong. For one thing she was naked. She always wore pajamas to bed, so why hadn't she put them on? And she could hear water running. Who was in her shower? Her questions were answered when she reached for the sheet and saw a pair of men's shorts.

She gasped in horror as she remembered how they came to be at the foot of her bed. "Oh, no, it can't be," she mumbled to herself, scrambling to wrap the sheet around her. "I didn't…I wouldn't…I couldn't…"

As she glanced around she saw a pair of dark blue boxer briefs on the floor and a little voice in her head said, "Oh yes you did."

"No, no, no," she repeated silently, her eyes squeezed shut. "Please let this all be a bad dream." But closing her eyes couldn't keep the images away. They flashed like a slide show in her memory, sending a rush of heat through her body. If she could have pressed a delete key and erased every single one of them she would have, because they were photos of an event that should never have happened.

She'd slept with Justin. The evidence was all around her. The tousled sheets, the sound of the shower, his underwear on the floor.

She tried to sit up but the throbbing in her head and the nausea in her stomach had her falling back against the pillows with a moan. She shouldn't have had anything to drink. She draped an arm over her forehead trying to block out the light of day.

Justin had shared her bed. Justin, not Michael, the man she wanted to marry. Only Michael didn't want to marry her anymore. The realization just compounded her misery. Until this morning she thought it would be impossible to feel worse than she had felt yesterday. She was wrong. Being dumped by Michael may have dealt a blow to her heart, but getting drunk and sleeping with Justin was a blow to her conscience.

Sex was supposed to be an expression of love. She'd lived by that code all twenty-eight years of her life, making a promise to herself that when she did commit to the man who would be her partner for life, she would be his and his alone. The first time she had sex was going to be special and on the most important day of her life. Only now that dream was gone and its loss brought a tear to her eye.

She shuddered and pulled the covers even closer to her body. If only she could pretend last night hadn't happened.

But it had happened, and the sound of the water being turned off in the shower reminded Paige that Justin hadn't gone anywhere. He was here in her trailer and she was going to have to face him soon. It was such an intimidating thought that had she not been naked she would have grabbed her keys and run out the door.

But there was no running away from the mess she'd created. She was in no condition to do much of anything except wait for Justin to appear, which he did in only a matter of minutes. He stepped out of the tiny bathroom, naked except for the towel wrapped around his waist. His brown hair was askew, as if he'd toweled it dry and hadn't combed it. Yesterday she might have thought it looked funny. Today it looked sexy.

Uncomfortable with the direction of her thoughts, she rolled onto her side so that her back was to him, trying to minimize the awkwardness she felt. It didn't help. Her memory produced another slide show of her making love to him.

"How are you feeling?" he asked.

"Sick."

"I warned you that Stacy's punch was going to give you a hangover."

"That's not why I feel awful. We're friends, Justin. Friends. And we did something we never should have done." She avoided looking at him as she spoke. "Now, I would appreciate it if you would just get dressed and leave."

"Don't you think we should talk about this?"

"I don't want to talk. I just want to forget it happened. If someone had told me yesterday that things could be worse today than they were yesterday, I wouldn't have believed it. But they are."

"Paige, it was just sex."

She reached for a pillow and threw it at him. "Just sex? There is no such thing as just sex!" She groaned in frustration. "You know how important it was for me to be a virgin when I got married."

"Are you saying last night was your first time?"

"You know it was."

He had the decency not to argue with her. He stared at her briefly, then shook his head and went back into the tiny bathroom, slamming the door. He was only gone a couple of minutes when he reappeared, looking exactly as he had when he left—the white towel around his waist and his hair spiking in dozens of directions. "You didn't act like it was your first time."

She wasn't sure whether she should take it as a compliment

or an insult. "I told you I was only going to have sex with one man in my life. My husband."

"Paige, you said that when you were sixteen. We're not teenagers anymore."

Again she turned away from him, staring at the wall of her trailer. She felt him sit down beside her and put a hand on her shoulder, but she flinched at his touch. "Paige, I'm sorry. I shouldn't have said that it was *just* sex. I do know how important it is to you not to sleep around. That's why I was so surprised last night when—"

Again she interrupted him. "Will you please stop talking about it?"

He was quiet for a moment before saying, "What can I do to help?"

"Nothing."

"Come on. There has to be something."

"No, there isn't." She should have known he wouldn't leave it at that. He could never let anything go without discussing it.

"I'm sorry we got carried away last night and ended up having fun in a way neither of us expected," he told her. "If I could go back and change what happened I would, but I can't."

Fun? She didn't want to go there. She wouldn't go there and she wouldn't think about a single moment of the pleasure she'd had last night. In her world friends didn't sleep together for fun.

"No, you can't change anything," she told him tersely. "The time to do something was last night and you didn't."

"No, and neither did you," he reminded her. "If it makes you feel better to blame me, then go right ahead, but you were the one who—"

This time she threw the other pillow at him. At close range it hit him in the face, causing him to get up from the bed.

"Don't say another word. You know I wasn't myself last night. I was crying. You know I never cry unless I'm on-the-floor miserable."

He stood leaning against the closet door, acting as if he didn't have a care in the world. "So you're saying you wanted to have sex for comfort?"

"I did not *want* it," she denied hotly. "I was distraught and it didn't help that I'd had some of Stacy's punch. You know I rarely drink and even the slightest bit of alcohol makes me do things I normally don't do."

"That's what I don't get," he said, folding his arms across his chest. "You clean when you're upset. You organize and sort and straighten. You don't drink."

"She was trying to help me feel better. Believe me. If I had known this was going to happen I would have cleaned out every drawer and closet five times instead of drinking that punch." It bothered her that he was close enough that she could smell the soap he'd used in the shower. She was conscious of his naked chest in a way she'd never been before and she didn't like it. "You need to get dressed and get out of here."

"And where is it that you want me to go?"

"I don't know." She averted her gaze so she wouldn't notice how great his abs looked. Funny how she'd never noticed them before today. Maybe he'd been working out. "You can't stay here."

"That's not what you were saying last night."

"You're my best friend. You're supposed to be making things better, not worse."

Again he apologized. "I'm sorry, but I don't think I can make them better, Paige. Only you can do that."

"Me? What am I supposed to do?"

"Look. I don't want to argue with you. Why don't we get dressed and we'll go get something to eat."

"How can you think about food right now?"

"Because I'm starving. I didn't get dinner last night and it's almost noon now."

She gasped. "Ohmigosh! I have to get dressed. What if someone comes early for the Bulldog Reunion? What if Kyle comes here and sees this?" She looked around frantically.

"Paige, until a couple of months ago you were our roommate. Why would he think anything except that I stayed at your place?"

"He can't ever find out about this," she warned.

"He won't. Believe me, I'm not going to say anything to him. He is my business partner besides my best friend."

"It's going to be awkward enough just having to be around the Bulldogs this weekend." She hung her head in her hands. "I don't know how I'm going to face them. I wish we could cancel the weekend."

"Maybe we should cancel," he suggested.

"We can't. Everyone's already made plans. The cabin's been rented. I can't just say, 'I'm having a bad day. Don't come.'"

"It wouldn't matter to me if you did. I didn't want to be here in the first place. I was only doing it for you."

That realization gave her a moment's pleasure but it was short-lived. "Don't say that."

"Why not? It's true."

There was an awkward silence broken by a musical ring tone. "That's mine," he said, and scooped up his shorts from the floor to pull his phone from one of the pockets. "It's Kyle."

She grimaced and shook her head, mouthing, "Don't tell him you're here."

He turned his back to her and answered the phone. "Where

are you at? Oh—you're already on your way up here? Yes, I'm here with her right now."

Paige's stomach tightened. Justin moved into the small kitchen area of her trailer, but that didn't prevent her from hearing his end of the conversation.

She listened as he gave short answers to Kyle's obvious questions, saying nothing that would give him reason to think Justin had been anything but a shoulder to cry on. The conversation was brief, and when Justin was finished, he came back to her bedroom area and said, "Satisfied?"

"Yes, thank you."

"If you're not going to eat breakfast with me, I might as well go." He paused, as if waiting for her to ask him to stay, but she couldn't.

She simply said, "I think that would be best."

He disappeared into the bathroom without saying another word to Paige. When he emerged a few minutes later he was dressed in jeans and a blue shirt that matched the color of his eyes. As usual his Saints baseball cap sat cocked to one side on his head, giving him a boyish look that was so familiar, yet today he looked different to her. That's because he *was* different. He'd changed from friend to lover and she couldn't pretend that it hadn't happened.

"What time do you want me at the Cascading Waters?" he asked. "I left home in such a hurry I didn't bring my schedule."

He'd always teased her about her need to have things down in black and white, but today there was a biting edge of sarcasm in his tone and she didn't like it. "Dinner reservations aren't until eight, but almost everyone is checking in between three and five."

"Okay. I'll see you there," he told her, and left without saying another word.

As soon as he was gone she wished she hadn't sent him away. He was the one person she'd always been able to talk to about her problems. Kyle wasn't exactly the sensitive type. Only today Justin was the problem. And that made her feel empty inside. She quickly showered and dressed, then did what she always did when she was upset. She organized her cupboards and drawers until it was time to head over to the Pinecone.

"LET'S SEE," the waitress said as she flipped through the order slips. "You had the two eggs over easy, a side of bacon and the wild-rice pancakes." She found Justin's bill and set it down on the counter. "Anything else I can do for you?" she asked, looking over the rim of her reading glasses.

"No, that'll do it, unless you know how to turn back the hands of time," he said with the lift of an eyebrow.

"Uh-oh, had one of those nights, did you?" she asked as she refilled his coffee cup for a third time. "If your girlfriend's mad at you, there's a florist shop five miles down the road."

If it was only that easy, thought Justin. "Thanks for the tip, but I don't think that's going to work."

"I haven't met a woman yet who didn't love a big beautiful bouquet of flowers." She gave him a knowing smile before moving on to another customer.

She hadn't met Paige. Justin had seen her reaction to receiving flowers on more than one occasion. Each time she'd grumbled about what a waste it was to buy something that was going to be dead in a few days when the money could have been used for something more useful—like an oil change in her car.

For as long as he could remember she'd been like one of the guys, which was why what happened last night had been so unexpected. Over the years they had slept in the same tent on camping trips, shared a hotel room on spring break and even lived together in the same house, yet they had never come close to sharing anything more than a platonic kiss and hug. That was because he had respected the boundaries of friendship the three of them had established.

No, Paige was definitely not like other women. He doubted there were many twenty-eight-year-old virgins. That announcement had certainly caught him off guard. When they were teenagers they had talked about sex—as teens often do. But as their friendship had matured, they had gradually stopped talking, respecting each other's privacy.

He wished he could get the picture of her wrapped in that sheet this morning out of his head. They were just friends, which was why he needed to forget how great last night had been. Maybe they shouldn't have slept together, but there was no denying that the sex had been good. At least for him. Last night he'd fallen asleep believing that it had been good for her, too, but this morning she hadn't acted as if it had. Suddenly, instead of being best friends who confided in one another, they were two people who'd had a one-night stand and couldn't wait to put it behind them.

Paige had made it perfectly clear this morning that having sex was definitely a mistake that would not be repeated. Not exactly what a man in love wanted to hear, but he shouldn't have expected anything else. She'd never given him any reason to believe he would ever be more than a friend.

If things had been different between them, he would have suggested they spend the day together. Instead, he was sitting on a bar stool at a counter lined with strangers and she was cleaning her trailer. He had no doubt that she was scrubbing and straightening and sorting and doing whatever she could to work through the stress and anxiety of the past twenty-four hours.

He had expected that she would be upset by Michael

Cross's betrayal, but the extent of her emotional outburst had caught him off guard. Paige had never been one for histrionics. He could only hope that after spending a few hours alone she would be her old self again and able to put things in perspective. Her life was not ruined and she was not going to be cursed with an unhappy marriage because they'd had sex last night. Nor would anyone else have to know. He was good at keeping secrets. After all, he'd kept his love for her to himself all these years. Not even Kyle knew. Especially not Kyle.

Thinking of his friend and business partner gave him an uneasy feeling. There were no secrets between them. Until today there had never been any reason not to be open with each other. Now there was. He'd slept with Paige.

He left a tip on the counter for Millie the waitress and headed for his truck. It was too late for regrets. He needed to stop thinking about last night and act as if nothing had happened. For the sake of his friendship with Kyle and his friendship with Paige.

So he got in his pickup and drove to Tettegouche State Park. He changed into his hiking boots and followed the High Falls Trail until he reached the suspension bridge. He leaned against the rail to take in the view of the Baptism River before continuing to the steep cliff that offered the most panoramic view of the falls. It was the spot where most hikers turned around and went back, but Justin was up for a challenge today and he decided to take the rugged hike to the base of the falls. The guidebook said it was one hundred and eighty-four steps, but he and Paige had counted only one hundred and eighty-two.

He didn't count them on this trip, but as he ascended, then descended to the base of the falls, his mind was filled with thoughts of Paige. She had planned to be married at the High Falls, at a lookout in the park that was easily accessible for guests. But when Justin arrived at the end of the trail and found himself on the grassy knoll at the base of the falls, he knew that this was where he would choose to be married, where he could smell and practically taste the water as it roared over the rocky cliffs.

Again he thought of Paige and how she had felt in his arms last night. His musings were interrupted by the vibration of his cell phone in his pocket. Flipping it open he saw that he had a voice-mail message from Kyle. He must have tried phoning while Justin was out of cell-tower range.

As soon as he was back at the trailhead, he punched in Kyle's number.

His friend answered the phone with "We're at the Pinecone. Where are you and Paige?"

"I just finished hiking to the High Falls," Justin answered. "I'm not sure where Paige is."

"You didn't leave her alone, did you?"

"She didn't want to come with me," Justin answered.

"How is she?"

"As I told you this morning, she's okay." It wasn't exactly the truth, but he didn't want to talk about Paige.

"I know you didn't want to say too much because she was there with you this morning when I called, but has she been crying at all?"

"A little," he said evasively.

"I wish you had told me that creep had dumped her last night. I would have come right up."

"You were at Tammy's," Justin reminded him. "Besides, there's not much you could have done."

"Yeah, you're probably right. It's a good thing Michael Cross left town or I just might kick his ass."

"Ah, the guy's not worth the trouble," Justin said.

"You and I know that, but she's crazy about him. The wedding is all she's talked about lately."

"She's not going to want to talk about it this weekend."

"She won't have to. It's probably a good thing we're having the reunion. You know as well as I do the way she copes with disappointment is to keep busy. She needs the distraction of the reunion. Being in charge is the best remedy for her broken heart."

Justin wasn't as convinced but said, "I hope you're right."

"We'll keep her so busy she won't have time to think about that jackass," Kyle stated with confidence. "It's going to be a good weekend."

"Maybe."

"What do you mean maybe? Of course it will be. So when are you coming over to the Pinecone? Tara's been asking about you."

Tara. He'd conveniently put his blind date out of his mind. He grimaced. How was he ever going to get any time alone with Paige with Tammy's sister expecting him to entertain her?

"Give me about an hour," he told Kyle. "I want to hike the Baptism River loop before I head over to Cascading Waters."

Justin was about to hang up, when Kyle said, "Hey, before you go I want to say thanks. I owe you big-time."

"No, you don't."

"Yeah, I do. For letting me have my night with Tammy. I know you gave up your Saints game so you could come up here and be with Paige."

Guilt washed over him. "There's no need to thank me for that. We're all friends."

As Justin snapped the cell phone shut he could only hope that Kyle never had any reason to feel differently toward them. One thing he did know for sure. He was going to feel as if he was walking a tightrope this weekend.

FOR THE FIRST TIME in the history of the Bulldog Reunion, Paige was not going to be the one greeting everyone as they arrived. According to the schedule she had drafted, "check-in" at the Pinecone began at three o'clock, yet she had deliberately waited until it was almost four before getting in her car and driving the short distance to the resort. She wanted to make sure that other people would be there when she arrived so she wouldn't have to be alone with Justin.

As she drove to the resort, uncertainty fluttered in her stomach like a butterfly unable to find the right flower. It was bad enough that everyone would know why she was attending the reunion without Michael. Now there was the added discomfort of having to be around Justin and pretend that nothing had happened.

As she pulled up to the log cabin she saw three vehicles—Kyle's car, Justin's pickup and an SUV that she assumed belonged to either Amber or Ben. Anxiety tightened her chest as she parked at the end of the row. Taking a deep breath, she grabbed her duffel bag and got out of the car.

As she climbed the steps to the cabin she heard women's voices. None of them sounded like Amber. She frowned. Ben was the only one bringing his girlfriend, so why did she hear more than one unfamiliar female voice?

She found her answer when she stepped inside. The screen door creaked as it slammed shut and all eyes turned toward her. Gathered around the eating counter that separated the kitchen from the living room were three men and three women. Paige felt like an intruder on a party for six.

Kyle eased his tall, lanky frame off the bar stool and came toward her, his arms outspread. The automatic smile that usually beamed from behind his brown goatee was missing, his green eyes full of compassion as he hugged her, saying softly in her ear, "How are you doing?" He pushed her back to arm's length and looked her over as if he expected to find she was covered with break-up spots.

She pulled her hands away from his. "I'm okay."

"It's gotta hurt."

She nodded, swallowing back the lump in her throat.

"I'm really sorry, Paige. I know how excited you were about getting married, but that guy was all wrong for you." He deliberately kept his voice low so the others wouldn't hear their conversation, but that didn't ease Paige's discomfort. "I hate that he hurt you the way he did. Are you sure you're going to be okay?"

"Yeah, I'm fine."

He slung an arm around her shoulder and gave her a squeeze. "I know it's tough right now, but you'll get through this. You're strong, Paige."

"You're right, I am," she said with more confidence than she was feeling at the moment.

"And if you need someone to lean on, Justin and I are here for you. And you have the Bulldogs. We'll help you get through this bad time. We want you to just sit back and relax."

"Kyle, I don't know these people" She looked sideways at the women gathered around the counter. "Who are they?"

"One is Ben's fiancée, the other two are with me and Justin."

"You brought guests?" she squeaked in a voice barely above a whisper.

"You said we could."

"But you told me you weren't going to!"

"Yeah, I know, but we changed our minds. It's not a problem, is it? This place sleeps ten."

"But I only brought enough food for eight!"

"So we go buy more food if we need it. There's a grocer right down the road."

"But everything is set up for eight people." Of course with Michael gone, there would have been just seven of them.

"Yes, and we have one more—nine. It can't make that big of a difference."

"Yes, it can." For the umpteenth time in the past twenty-four hours she felt like crying, but she refused to give in to her emotions. "I can't believe you did this to me. I've just been dumped by my fiancé and now this."

"I'm sorry," he said, wrapping his arm around her affectionately. "I wouldn't have brought the girls had I known what was going on with you and Michael."

"Justin didn't tell you?"

"Not until I was halfway up here."

"Just great," she drawled sarcastically.

"It's not his fault, so don't be mad at him."

How could she not be angry with Justin? Not once in the past few weeks had he mentioned he was even seeing anyone, yet here he was with a guest for the weekend. That meant he'd slept with Paige last night knowing that this weekend he would be hooking up with someone else. The nausea that had been with her earlier in the day returned with a vengeance.

"I don't want to be here," she whispered.

"Don't say that, Paige. You're the reason we have the Bulldog Reunion."

From across the room she heard, "Hey, are you going to let that Bulldog join the party or what?"

"In a minute," Kyle called back to him. "I've never known you to hide away and lick your wounds." The words were a challenge, one he knew she wouldn't refuse.

She allowed him to steer her toward the kitchen, where Ben stood with arms wide. "Hey, give me a Bulldog bear hug."

It had become a tradition—greeting each other with an exuberant embrace. She allowed him to spin her around as they clung together.

"Gosh, it's good to see you," he said as he released her. "You haven't changed a bit this past year."

"Neither have you," she said honestly. He still had the same boyish good looks that had earned him the nickname Doogie Howser in college, only now he had a soul patch on his chin.

"Oh yes I have. I'm a much nicer person thanks to this lady." He reached for the sole redhead at the counter and introduced her to Paige. "This is Jolene."

Paige smiled and shook the hand she offered. "Welcome to the Bulldog Reunion."

"I'm really looking forward to it. Ben's told me how much fun you have. I just hope you don't mind outsiders crashing the party."

"No, not at all," Paige said. "We decided it was time we brought guests."

Kyle spoke then. "That's why Justin and I brought these two lovely ladies." He stepped between the two blondes. "Tammy, Tara, this is my best friend Paige."

The two blondes smiled and acted as if they didn't have a clue what had been going on in Paige's world, but the look in their eyes told her they knew she had just been jilted by her fiancé.

"Paige, Tammy and Tara Martin," Kyle said, making the introduction. "They're sisters, but you probably already figured that out." He grinned sheepishly.

Except for the fact that they were both skinny, wore lots of bling and had dark roots on their blond heads, Paige didn't think they looked at all alike. Not that it mattered. She was still trying to get over the shock that they were at the reunion. The sisters made the appropriate small talk and Paige muttered something equally inconsequential, all the while aware of Justin staring at her.

She refused to look at him. She couldn't look at him. She was too angry.

She heard Ben say, "She needs something to drink. Tell Justin what you want, Paige. He's tending the bar."

There was no way she was going to even look at Justin, let alone ask him for a drink. "No, I'm fine for now. I'll have something later."

"I hope you don't mind that we dug out the food," Ben said as he reached for a handful of trail mix.

"No, not at all," Paige told him. "That's why it's here."

"Try the Buffalo wings," Kyle said passing her a plate. "Tammy made them and they're fabulous."

"I'll wait a bit. Thanks."

They stood around the bar talking for what seemed an eternity to Paige but was actually only about fifteen minutes. No one asked where her fiancé was, so she could only assume that Justin had filled everyone in on what had happened. That was probably the reason they were being so attentive to her. She wished they would stop. The last thing she wanted was pity and she didn't want to be the center of attention the entire weekend.

But since Kyle and Justin had brought guests, she knew that was exactly what was going to happen. When Amber arrived there would be four couples and one single. She was the single. The extra woman. A fifth wheel. The odd one out. Had she walked into a room full of total strangers she would have felt more at ease than she did with this group.

The claustrophobia she thought she'd licked as a child returned, making her fidget uneasily. She needed space, which was why she suggested, "Why doesn't everyone move into the other room. It's much more comfortable."

"You're going to join us, aren't you?" Tammy asked as they carried the trays of food into the living room, where the guys collapsed into oversize leather chairs.

"Sure. I just need to take care of a few things first."

"That translates into cleaning up the mess we made," Kyle said with an affectionate grin in her direction.

"Let me help," Jolene offered, staying behind while the others made themselves comfortable in the gathering room of the cabin.

"No, you go sit," Paige told her.

"You sure?"

Paige nodded. "They've probably already told you I'm the organizer. They weren't kidding. I am and I like doing it."

She was relieved when Jolene finally joined the others and she had the kitchen to herself. Her solitude was short-lived, however. She had just started on the dishes when Justin turned up at her side.

"Paige, I need to talk to you," he told her quietly.

"Please go away," she whispered, glancing nervously over her shoulder to see if anyone noticed them together.

"Are you going to be like this all weekend?"

"Like what?"

"Refusing to even look at me?"

She stared down at the sinkful of soapy water. "Please, just go back to your girlfriend."

"She is not my girlfriend," he said in a barely controlled whisper.

"Do you always go away for the weekend with women you aren't attracted to?" Before he could answer, the sound of a horn honking announced the arrival of the last Bulldog.

"Amber's here," Kyle called out, and all eyes turned toward the door.

In her typical fashion, Amber Carlson, the fifth and final Bulldog, made a grand entrance. She burst into the log cabin saying, "All right, I'm here and I have just one question. Would somebody please tell me why there is a wedding dress on the front seat of Justin's pickup?"

CHAPTER FIVE

THE OCCUPANTS of the cabin froze. All conversation ceased and Justin thought Paige, who had started toward the door to greet Amber, looked shell-shocked.

No one moved or spoke until Ben turned to Justin and said, "You have a wedding dress in your pickup? What's up with that?" Jolene immediately shushed him with a gentle elbow to his side. "Wrong thing to say. Sorry."

For the first time since she'd arrived, Paige looked at Justin as if she wanted his help. In her face he saw anxiety and wished he could pull her aside and let her know that other than telling Kyle that her engagement was broken, he'd given no one any details of their evening last night. He also wanted to explain how he'd been roped into bringing Tara to the reunion. He could tell by the way Paige had reacted that she had jumped to the wrong conclusion about Tara. There were a lot of things Justin wanted to say to Paige but he couldn't say any of them as long as they had an audience.

Amber misread the awkwardness in the room and with a sly smile asked, "Hmm. Is the Bulldog Reunion going to be the setting for a surprise wedding this weekend? Maybe two people can't wait until September to tie the knot?"

"No!" Justin corrected that misconception. "No one's getting married this weekend."

The uncomfortable silence that followed told Amber just how wrong she was. "Sorry." Her smile was apologetic. She squeezed her eyes shut and said, "I think I'll go out and come back in and we can start over."

"Don't be silly." It was Paige who spoke first.

Amber opened her eyes and looked around carefully. "So how is everyone?" she asked quietly, almost as if she was afraid of the answer she might get.

"We're great. Aren't we?" Kyle's arms encompassed everyone in the cabin. The others made appropriate sounds of agreement.

Paige, however, contradicted all of them. "No, you're not. You're all worried you're going to say the wrong thing and upset me." She crossed the pine floor until she stood next to Amber. "That's because it's my wedding dress in Justin's pickup and everyone knows why it's there."

"No, they really don't," Justin assured her. "I haven't told anybody."

"Then I will," Paige said, "and maybe we won't have to talk about it for the rest of the weekend and everyone can stop looking at me as if they're worried they're going to say the wrong thing."

"Paige, you don't owe anyone any explanations," Kyle said as he sat down in one of the comfortable leather chairs near the fireplace.

She ignored him and spoke directly to Amber. "The reason Justin has my dress is he was worried I was going to burn it. I got a little carried away getting rid of the clutter in my life last night. Since I'm no longer engaged, I figured I didn't need the dress and I was going to throw it in the campfire, but Justin arrived in time to save me from making an expensive mistake."

Amber gasped. "You broke up with Michael? Oh, Paige, I

am so sorry. I didn't know or I wouldn't have said anything about the dress." She gave Paige a hug full of sympathy and understanding.

"It's okay," Paige repeated several times to a penitent Amber, who kept apologizing. Finally Paige turned to the group gathered in the living room. "It really is okay. You don't need to tiptoe around the fact that I'm no longer engaged. I don't want nor do I need any special treatment this weekend. I'm fine."

Justin could see by the tightness in her jaw that she wasn't. As usual Paige was very good at hiding her emotions, but he knew her well enough to see beneath her calm exterior. She was suffering.

Amber must have seen it, too, because she put one arm around Justin and the other around Paige and announced to the others, "Excuse us just for a few minutes. We're going outside to get my stuff from the car." She ushered both of them out the door and onto the front porch, where she again apologized to Paige.

"Gosh, I am so sorry for those remarks about the dress."

"Will you please stop?" Paige said. "I told you I'm fine."

"Come with me to the car and you can tell me all about it." Taking Paige by the hand, she led her down the wooden steps. As the three of them walked around to the small parking area at the side of the cottage, Amber asked Justin, "What do you think? Is she really okay?"

"It doesn't matter what he thinks," Paige retorted, and Amber's mouth dropped open in surprise. "I told you I'm fine and I am."

"No, you're not! You wouldn't snap at Justin that way if you were okay."

Justin grimaced. "It's all right, Amber. She's just tired."

"I'm sure she is. We both know she always puts the needs of everyone else before her own. It wouldn't matter what was going on in her personal life. She would still do the Bulldog Reunion because that's the kind of person she is."

"You don't need to talk about me in the third person," Paige pointed out irritably. "I'm right here."

Amber threw an arm around her and gave her a quick squeeze. "Yes, and I'm glad you are. You need your friends at a time like this."

"That's what I've been trying to tell her," Justin added.

Paige sighed. "Look. It's been a really stressful twenty-four hours. Until yesterday I thought my fiancé was going to be here with me this weekend. And yeah, it hurts that he's not, but you know me, Amber. I'm strong. I'll get through this."

"Of course you will," Amber said with confidence. "And if there's anything I can do to help, you'll let me know, right?"

"Yes, now can we please stop talking about this?" Paige begged.

"Of course we can," Amber assured her with a pat on the arm. "It looks like we're going to have a full cabin this weekend. I counted three unfamiliar faces. I take it the guys all brought girlfriends."

"Kyle and Ben did," Justin clarified. "Tara's not my girl-friend."

That had Paige clicking her tongue, a sound that didn't go unnoticed by Amber, who glanced skeptically at Justin, then back at Paige. "Okay. She's not your girlfriend."

"So where's your guy?" Paige asked Amber when they reached her car.

"Oh, wouldn't you know he couldn't make it." She popped open the hatchback and reached for a suitcase.

Justin said, "I'll get it," and hoisted the bag out.

"The military canceled his leave at the last minute," Amber told them, grabbing a small cooler before slamming the hatch shut. "At first I was so bummed, all I wanted to do was stay home and bawl my eyes out all weekend, but I forced myself to come."

"I'm glad you did," Paige told her as they started back toward the cabin. "It wouldn't be the same without you."

"It's probably not going to be the same anyway. Boy, talk about things getting turned around. You and I were supposed to have our guys here and they're not, and Justin and Kyle weren't supposed to bring guests but they did." Amber rolled her eyes. "Not the greatest start to our first attempt at bringing guests to the Bulldog Reunion, is it?"

Again Justin found himself wanting to explain why Kyle had brought Tara and Tammy, but at that moment the screen door opened and Kyle leaned out to say, "Hey, Paige. I thought you said you brought paper cups? I can't find any."

"I must have left them in my car. I'll get them." Instead of following the others up the hand-hewn log steps, she headed back to the parking area.

Justin wasn't about to let this opportunity escape. He handed Amber's suitcase to Kyle. "I'll let you make the introductions. I need to talk to Paige."

He was relieved that Kyle didn't protest and disappeared with Amber into the cabin. Justin walked over to Paige's car and found her bent over the rear seat in search of the cups.

"Paige, could I talk to you for a minute?" he asked.

"This is not the time or the place to talk," she told him when she straightened.

"Maybe not, but I have something to say to you."

"Can't it wait?" She slammed her rear door shut and faced him.

"No, it can't."

She leaned back against her fender and sighed. "What is it?" She didn't look at him, but out into the blackness of the night, staring at nothing in particular.

"What is it?" he repeated in disbelief. "You're the one who's treating me like yesterday's garbage. What is wrong with you?"

She finally met his gaze. "How can you even ask me that after last night?"

"I thought we were putting last night behind us. Paige, if you keep freezing me out someone is going to suspect something is going on between us and you don't want that, do you?"

"No," she agreed quietly.

"I'm not looking forward to this weekend any more than you are, but we're stuck here. You're unhappy because the person you wanted to share the weekend with isn't here. Well, let me tell you. The person I didn't want to share the weekend with is here and that doesn't exactly make my day."

"Then you should have done something about it before she got here," she chastised him.

"I couldn't and you know why. Kyle left St. Paul before we were even out of bed this morning."

"You two told me you weren't bringing any guests," she countered. "Just when were you and Kyle planning to let me know there would be two extra people?"

"I was going to tell you yesterday morning but your phone went dead before I had a chance."

"The day before the event is not when you announce you're bringing extra people." She groaned. "I don't know why I didn't see this coming. I should have known that neither one of you would be able to stand being a single guy this weekend if the rest of us were paired up."

"You're all wrong about that. I didn't bring anyone. Kyle was the one who set this up."

"Oh, please. Let's not revert to the 'Kyle made me do it' 'No, Justin made *me* do it' routine. I had hoped that was gone with our college days."

"He didn't make me do anything because I haven't done anything. Tara is Tammy's sister. She's nothing to me."

"You know what? I really don't want to know about your relationship with Tara."

"That's just it—I don't have a relationship with her," he insisted. "The only reason she's here is because Kyle was worried Tammy would feel out of place not knowing anyone."

"Oh, so it's all about being a couple of sensitive guys?" she said with a generous dose of sarcasm. "I'm touched,"

"Kyle wanted to bring Tammy, which is why I agreed to Tara's coming along. I didn't do it because I wanted to. I did it as a favor for a friend."

"I'm sure Kyle appreciates your gesture of friendship. I mean, it is the ultimate sacrifice, isn't it? Having to spend an entire weekend with a single girl who's practically drooling over you."

"Whether you want to believe it or not, I was just trying to help a friend."

"Like you helped me last night?"

Her words were like a slap in the face. "That's not fair. I don't know what you want me to say about last night. It happened. Maybe it shouldn't have, but it did."

"There's no maybe about it. You know darn well it shouldn't have happened. You knew that girl was coming up here this weekend, yet last night you…" She trailed off, turning away.

Was she jealous? His heartbeat quickened. "And if I hadn't known she was coming up here…would that have made any difference as to how you feel about last night?"

"No!"

"I didn't think so," he said quietly.

She remained silent, biting down on her lower lip.

"You know what, Paige?" He held up his hands in surrender. "I'm done saying I'm sorry and I'm done being your punching bag. If you want to blame someone for what happened, go stand in front of a mirror. You'll find the person you're looking for. Now, I'm going back inside and I'm going to try to have a good time this weekend. Are you coming with me?"

She was silent for so long he thought she was going to tell him she'd rather go in alone, but then she said quietly, "I'll come with you."

PAIGE VIEWED the weekend as a series of hurdles to cross. The first had been getting her broken engagement out in the open. Now that she'd successfully made it past that obstacle, she could move on to the next one. The sleeping arrangements.

The Cascading Waters Resort consisted of a lodge and nine guest cabins. The Pinecone was the largest of the log cabins nestled in the woods of the Superior National Forest. Although each cabin was within walking distance of the main lodge and restaurant, the density of the pines gave one the impression of being in the wilderness. Paige had chosen the Pinecone for its size and because it reminded her of a small ski chalet.

In previous years the bedrooms had been assigned on a first come, first served basis. The Bulldogs would park their duffel bags and suitcases wherever they wanted to sleep and no one complained. Normally Paige was the first one at the cabin, but because the three couples had arrived before her, she wasn't sure just whose gear was in which bedroom.

Shortly before dinner Ben's girlfriend, Jolene, brought the

issue to light. "You're going to have to excuse me," she announced to the small group gathered around the stone fireplace. "I need to get ready for dinner."

"I want to change my clothes, too," Amber said. "Which room are we in, Paige?"

"I'm not sure. My stuff is still by the door." She watched to see where the other three women went. Jolene disappeared into the bedroom that was closest to the living room, and Tara went into the bedroom at the far end of the cabin. That left the middle bedroom, which she expected Tammy to use, but instead she went into the bathroom.

Paige's uncertainty must have shown on her face because Kyle said, "Amber, you can either have the middle bedroom downstairs or you can take the one in the loft."

Paige frowned. That meant only two bedrooms were occupied. Were Kyle, Justin and their dates sharing one? A shiver of disgust traveled through her at the possibility.

"We'll take the loft, Paige," Amber stated, then in an aside whispered "We'll leave the couples to the first floor. It'll be less embarrassing for us, don't you think?"

Paige nodded. It would be a relief to be upstairs in the loft where she could have her own space far away from them. She was about to retrieve her duffel bag, when Justin grabbed it.

"I'll get it for you." His arm bumped hers as they both went for the bag at the same time. She flinched at the touch, hoping that no one noticed.

"Yay! Chivalry isn't dead!" Amber declared as he reached for her suitcase as well. She followed him up the stairway to the loft. When Paige would have gone up after them, Kyle stopped her.

"Hey. You sure you're doing all right?"

"I'd be much better if you would stop asking me that," Paige replied.

"Okay." He looked around the living room. "I've been debating whether I should bunk in with Justin or sleep out here."

"You're not—" She stopped herself. It was really none of her business where Kyle or Justin slept.

"No, I'm not sharing a room with Tammy. What do you think I am? An insensitive toad? Your engagement just ended and Amber's boyfriend is stuck on some military base."

She folded her arms across her chest. "In other words, Tammy wanted to share a room with her sister."

"You got it." He gave her a sheepish grin.

She gave him a playful slap on the arm. "You like her, don't you?" she said on a more serious note.

"It's that obvious?"

"To me it is. You forget. I've been around when you've dated girls you haven't liked so much."

"So what do you think of her? Honest answer."

"Kyle, I just met her."

"I know, but what's your first impression?"

She shrugged. "She seems nice."

"She is. So is her sister. That's why I wanted them to come this weekend. You have to admit they're both very friendly and easy to talk to."

Paige didn't have to admit anything, but she didn't want to argue with her friend so she simply said, "Yes, they are."

"And they're smart."

"Then why are they here with you and Justin?" she managed to ask with a straight face.

"Okay, go ahead and make a joke of it." He shook his head. "Can I ask you something?"

She shrugged. "Why not?"

"Is everything okay between you and Justin?"

She hoped her face didn't look as red as it felt. "Why wouldn't it be?"

His eyes narrowed. "You think I can't see there's tension between the two of you?"

"There is?" She feigned innocence. "There's no reason for there to be," she lied.

"I thought maybe you were mad at him because he kept your wedding dress when you wanted to get rid of it."

She chuckled. "Hardly."

"Good, because he was just looking out for you last night. I mean, you do realize what could have happened if that dress had caught fire while you were dangling it over the flames? You could have gone up in smoke along with it."

"I hadn't thought about that," she admitted.

"No, but lucky for you Justin was there."

"Yeah, lucky for me," she echoed, thinking, "If only you knew."

They were interrupted by Amber calling down from the loft. "Hey, Paige. There aren't any pillows on the beds up here."

"Looks like your services are needed," Kyle said with a nod toward the upstairs.

"I better check to see if anything else is missing before I call housekeeping," Paige said, relieved to be able to end their conversation. "I'll see you at dinner."

She wished they didn't have to eat in the dining room at the lodge. Yet if she didn't go to dinner, she risked giving the impression that she was sitting home wallowing in self-pity. Wimping out would also mean that Amber would be the only unattached woman. So Paige washed her face, changed her clothes and walked over to the lodge with the rest of them.

She expected to have a horrible time, but she actually found herself enjoying dinner. She was seated at the end of the table next to Jolene, who had the kind of personality that could put anyone at ease. Like Paige, she was an elementary-school teacher and loved to talk about education issues.

The only awkward moment in the evening came when Stacy Walker stopped by their table to ask if they were satisfied with their accommodations. Paige was certain her face must have been the color of a bad sunburn. She could only hope that the low lighting in the dining room kept people from noticing. Fortunately Stacy was visiting their table as a representative of the resort and discreetly said nothing about their night at the campfire.

"Thanks for helping me out yesterday," Paige said to her as she came around to her side of the table. For the benefit of the others she added, "Stacy's been instrumental in helping me set up our weekend in the Pinecone."

"My pleasure," Stacy said with a sincere smile. "We love having the Bulldog Reunion every summer."

"Just why is it called the Bulldog Reunion?" Tammy wanted to know.

It was Kyle who answered. "That was the mascot at the university we attended. We really are a bunch of Bulldogs."

"We will be later tonight when I drag out the dandelion wine," Ben said.

"No! Not the dandelion wine," Kyle protested. "Don't you remember what happened last year when we drank your home brew?"

"That's the problem," Justin said with a grin. "Some of us can't remember."

"Uh-uh, none for me this year," Amber said, holding up both hands. "I only had one glass of that stuff and I had such a bad hangover I nearly missed the sunrise picnic."

"At least you didn't end up in the creek skinny-dipping," Paige told her with a grin.

"Oh—you heard about that?" Kyle asked. He turned to Tammy. "A few Bulldogs—who shall remain nameless—had a little too much dandelion wine and ended up taking a late-night swim in the Cascade River."

Talk turned to memories of previous Bulldog Reunions. By the time everyone had finished dinner, a consensus had been reached that the next event on the Bulldog schedule should be to build a bonfire in the fire pit next to the cabin.

Paige tried to excuse herself, but a chorus of voices saying, "Aw, come on. Don't go in. It's way too early to go to bed," pleaded for her to change her mind and join them.

That was the way the entire weekend went. Every time she said she was going to skip an event she was coerced into participating. The Bulldogs went sailing on Saturday morning and hiking in the forest Saturday afternoon.

Paige told herself she went along so that Amber wouldn't feel out of place with the three couples, but the truth was she didn't want the others to think she was sitting back at the cabin in a blue funk. She was not one to feel sorry for herself and she was determined that no one would think she was crying over a man.

She was grateful when the clouds rolled in on Saturday evening. If she was lucky it would rain and she wouldn't have to watch Tara use the cool evening temperatures as an excuse to huddle close to Justin around the fire. If there was nothing going on between them, as Justin insisted, it wasn't for a lack of effort on Tara's part.

Amber noticed it too and commented to Paige while they were preparing dinner.

"Maybe I'm being overly sensitive because my guy

couldn't make it here this weekend, but am I the only one who thinks Tara's PDA is a little overboard?"

"She knows what she wants and she's going after it," Paige answered as she pulled a cast-iron frying pan from the rack overhead.

"You don't think she's already got it?"

Paige didn't want to even consider the possibility, so she simply shrugged and said, "Don't know and don't care."

"Well, you should care. Justin's your best friend. You want him hooking up with someone like that?"

She didn't but she wasn't about to admit it. Her relationship with Justin wasn't what it used to be. Every time she looked at him she felt an ache deep inside her, reminding her of what had happened the night before.

"He's never asked for my approval of his girlfriends up to this point so I doubt it's going to start now." She tried to sound as nonchalant as possible.

"Have you noticed how she keeps trying to get him to do things without the rest of us?" Amber stood at the sink washing vegetables. "She wanted to go back to the lodge after lunch and spend the afternoon in the spa instead of hiking."

"She doesn't know him very well if she thinks he's going to give up hiking for a hot tub."

"I wonder—" Amber began, only to stop abruptly. Paige looked up from the chicken she'd been chopping to see why she'd gone silent and realized Tammy was coming toward them.

"Can I help?" the blonde asked.

Before Paige could decline her offer, Amber said, "Sure. Grab a knife and you can help me cut up these veggies. We're making fajitas. I'll do the onions and you can do the peppers."

Tammy looked around, as if unsure where to begin. "You

can grab one of those knives in the carving block on the counter," Paige told her.

"Oh…thanks," Tammy said with a smile.

To Paige's dismay, before Tammy had even started slicing, Amber got a long-distance phone call from her boyfriend and left the room to talk to him.

"It's been a great weekend so far," Tammy said. "Kyle says you're the reason everything has gone so smoothly."

"I've had a lot of practice. This is our seventh reunion." Paige watched Tammy carefully cut off the end of a green pepper so she wouldn't wreck her acrylic nails. "You know you don't have to help in the kitchen. You're a guest."

"Oh, but I want to help. It's the least I can do to thank you for your hospitality. I know you weren't expecting me and Tara, yet you've been very gracious about us being here."

"I'm glad you could come." Paige gave the obligatory response. "Kyle says you like to cook."

"I do, but I'm not very good at it," she admitted with an almost shy grin.

"Judging by the appetizers you brought, I'd say you're a very good cook."

"I bought them at Byerly's," she confessed. "But please don't tell Kyle."

"I don't think he's dating you for your culinary skills."

"No, but you're, like, the perfect hostess. You're so together. So organized and everything."

It was then that Paige realized how young Tammy was. There was a youthful innocence hidden behind the bling. She found herself warming to the younger woman.

"I was wondering," she continued. "Maybe you could tell me what Kyle's favorite foods are. If I'm going to learn how to cook, I might as well start with stuff he likes."

"Then you can pretty much make him anything," Paige told her. "But if I were you, I would make him cook for you. Don't do what I did. I spoiled those two by cooking for them when we were in college."

"You three are really close, aren't you?"

"Yeah. We have been ever since we were kids. We were neighbors, plus Justin's mom did day care. That's how I met those two. I was a tomboy so I hung out with the guys more than the girls."

"What about when you were teenagers…didn't you ever want to date either one of them?"

"No!" she was quick to answer. "That's never been an issue—not even when we went away to college together. They are so not like the kind of guys I date."

"So you're like family?"

She shrugged. "More or less. We've just been really good friends for a long time."

"That's what I told Tara. She's worried that there's something going on between you and Justin."

Suddenly Paige understood the offer to help with dinner. Tammy had been sent to get information. Until last night the words would have rolled off her tongue automatically, but Paige found it difficult to say, "That's ridiculous."

"That's what Kyle said, but Tara seems to think there's some kind of chemistry between the two of you."

"It's not chemistry," Paige said, annoyed at the images the word brought to her mind. She squeezed her eyes shut, hoping to block out a naked Justin. "I told you. We're just good friends."

"I'm glad to hear that because Tara really likes him a lot and I wouldn't want to think that she's poaching."

"Poaching?" Amber walked back into the kitchen. "Is someone going hunting that's not supposed to?"

"I was just telling Paige that Tara really likes Justin, although I don't know why. He hasn't been very nice to her. I mean, Kyle said Justin wanted her to come up here for the weekend, but he hasn't been acting like it."

Amber came to Justin's defense. "He took her sailing, didn't he?"

"Well, yes, but…" Tammy paused.

"What do you think, Paige? Has Justin been ignoring Tara?"

"I haven't noticed," Paige said in place of what she wanted to say—that Tara was hunting a two-legged deer that didn't want to get shot. "Would you get the salsa out of the cupboard for me?" she asked her college friend.

She was relieved when Tammy asked Amber if everything was okay with her boyfriend and conversation turned to Amber's plan to fly out and see him at the military base in September.

When thunder and lightning put an end to any hopes they had of having another campfire after dinner, Kyle suggested they sample a couple of the North Shore's finest clubs. For the first time all weekend, excitement glowed in the faces of the Martin sisters.

Everyone agreed it was a good idea—everyone but Paige. Justin noticed her lack of enthusiasm and asked, "You're going to come along, aren't you?"

"I don't think so."

Kyle groaned. "Come on, Paige. You have to join us."

"Why? So you can have a designated driver?"

"No, because it won't be the same without you," Kyle answered.

She could feel all eyes on her. "Some of those clubs are open until two."

"So?" Kyle shrugged.

"So we're having the sunrise picnic tomorrow." As it had been every summer for the past seven years, the final activity for the weekend was a trek to their favorite outcrop of rocks on the shore of Lake Superior, where they would watch the sun rise over the water. When Tara heard of the plan she made a face and said, "You get up at what time?"

"Around fiveish." It was Amber who answered.

"What time is sunrise?" Tara wanted to know.

"At 6:02," Ben answered. "I checked it out already, which means we should be at the shore by about five-thirty. We don't want to miss a single minute of it."

"If you haven't seen the sun rise over the lake, you don't want to sleep through this," Kyle assured her.

"Can't you just take a picture with your camera phone and show it to the rest of us?" Tara asked.

"A picture can't do nature justice," Ben said.

"I'm sure it's an awe-inspiring experience, but I may have to pass if we're going to be out partying tonight," Tara told everyone.

"We could just stay up all night," Kyle suggested, which drew a chorus of groans. "Hey, that's why we had our very first sunrise picnic if you recall." For the guests' benefit he added, "We happened onto our first sunrise the summer we were college students working here at the resort. We had partied all night and ended up seeing the most glorious sunrise."

"I don't know about anyone else, but my days of staying up all night are gone," Amber said.

"Mine, too," Paige agreed.

"I hope that doesn't mean you're going to wuss out on the sunrise picnic?" Kyle said.

"No, I'm going to wuss out on the clubbing tonight," Paige answered.

"Okay, then we'll change plans," Ben suggested. "We'll hang out here and play board games."

That produced several audible sighs, prompting Paige to say, "You don't have to stay home because of me."

"Yes, we do," Amber assured her. "We've always done everything as a group. It's the Bulldog way."

Which meant that Paige was going to spoil everyone else's party if she didn't go. After several moments of deliberating she said, "All right. Let's do it."

CHAPTER SIX

AS SHE DID EVERY YEAR, Paige announced that those who wanted a wake-up call for the sunrise picnic should put their shoes outside their door. Justin didn't need a wake-up call. After a restless night, he was out of bed well before Paige's alarm was set to ring. He pulled on a pair of jeans and a hooded sweatshirt, then slipped into his sandals and headed down to the shore. He noted an absence of shoes outside the bedroom doors, which had him wondering if he and Paige would be the only ones watching the sunrise.

He hoped that would be the case. There had been too much tension and misunderstanding between them this weekend and he wanted to put it to rest. Watching the sun rise over Lake Superior had always been one of their favorite things to do together. Some of their best conversations had taken place on the giant slab of rock at the water's edge. Being alone with her would give him the opportunity to say the things he should have said Friday morning.

Like sometimes something exciting happened between two people that was totally unexpected. Neither one planned for it to happen, which was one of the reasons they didn't know how to act around each other after it did. Spending the night together didn't have to be a negative in their friendship. It could be a positive.

He paced back and forth. Who was he trying to fool? Besides breaking an unwritten rule of friendship—he'd totally ignored his own code of conduct. Never go to bed with a woman unless you both understand what's at stake. Be smart when it came to sex.

There had been nothing smart about the way he and Paige had approached that night. At first he had tried to assuage his guilt by saying that he'd always been a little in love with her, so he wasn't being irresponsible sleeping with her. The reality was that Paige wasn't in love with him. She had only turned to him because she'd been rejected by the man she loved. She and Justin had had Band-Aid sex. She had wanted to feel better, and judging by the way her body had responded to his, she'd achieved her goal. Unfortunately, with morning came the removal of the Band-Aid, and ripping it off exposed a raw wound that left her feeling vulnerable and ashamed and frustrated.

It was the shame part that bothered Justin. He very seldom had regrets, but in this instance he did have one. That the first time he'd had sex with Paige hadn't been under better conditions. For so many years he'd fantasized about what it would be like for her to beg him to make love to her that when she actually did, he didn't care that she was on the rebound.

She wanted to blame their behavior on Stacy's punch. He knew better. Had he not had anything to drink he would have had sex with Paige. Only he wasn't about to tell her that because he knew it would only make things more complicated. She might find out what his true feelings were for her and that was something he couldn't let happen.

He shook his head, wishing he could forget the pleasure he'd found with her on Thursday night, because now, instead of thinking of her as Paige the tomboy who'd climbed trees with him and Kyle, she was Paige the seductress who'd captivated him in bed. For the sake of his friendship with her and Kyle, he needed to think of her as that girl in the neighborhood who played hockey with him and Kyle in his backyard, not as the woman who'd invited him to share her bed.

"What? Did you forget to bring a blanket?" It was Kyle.

Justin felt a wave of disappointment at the sight of his friend walking toward him. It meant any chance of being alone with Paige was gone.

"Lucky for you our party planner sent one with me." He spread a plaid woolen blanket across the flat rock.

"It's chilly this morning," Justin answered.

"No kidding. Are we nuts to be out here or what?" Kyle glanced at the mist hanging over the lake. "Might be too much moisture in the air to get a decent sunrise. Those are clouds on the horizon."

"I didn't expect to see you," Justin answered honestly. "Where's Tammy?"

"Asleep. I had a hunch that after last night we were going to be a small group this morning."

"That's all right with me."

"Yeah, me, too. Paige was in the kitchen making coffee when I left. She told me to bring these." He set a box of pastries down in the center of the blanket. "I hope she's in a better mood than she's been in all weekend. She's been trying to act as if nothing is wrong but you can see she's hurting bigtime. God, it makes me sick to see her pining over that zero Michael Cross."

"She's done a pretty good job of keeping it together," Justin noted.

"Yeah, but you and I know that's only because she doesn't want everyone to think she's falling apart. Has she said anything to you about moving back to the Cities?"

He shook his head. "No, but I don't know why she would want to stay up here."

"Me neither," Kyle agreed. "I think we should tell her she can move back in with us."

Justin picked up a pebble from the shore and tossed it, hoping to skip it across the water. It sank immediately. "That's all right by me, but she might not want that."

"Why wouldn't she?"

Guilt clung to Justin like the morning mist hung over the lake. "I thought we were going to put the place up for sale?"

"Yes, but it takes time to sell a house. Paige needs to be with friends." He glanced back toward the cabin. "I think I see her coming now."

Justin saw her slender figure walking unevenly across the rocks. Like him she wore a hooded sweatshirt and jeans. He thought that she looked as if she wanted to turn around and go back when she realized it was just the three of them, but after a brief pause she continued walking toward them. When she reached the blanket she sat down next to Kyle. Justin continued to try to skip pebbles on the surface of the lake.

"Coffee or hot chocolate?" she asked Kyle as she opened a picnic basket that contained two insulated carafes.

"Coffee for me," Kyle answered.

Without a word she filled three cups, two with coffee, one with hot chocolate, and set them on the opened lid of the basket. Justin saw it as a positive sign. She knew he didn't drink coffee and had made the hot chocolate for him.

Kyle took a sip of the coffee and sighed. "Boy, did I need that. Especially after last night. Thanks, Shortstuff." He used the nickname he and Justin had given her when they'd been kids playing basketball in Kyle's driveway. She'd always been at a disadvantage because of her height, which was why she usually wanted to play the game of horse. What she lacked in height she made up for in accuracy.

"You're welcome." She pulled out a small stack of napkins from the basket and set them beside the box of pastries.

"You didn't hear anyone else stirring, did you?" Kyle asked, reaching for an iced cinnamon roll.

She shook her head. "Amber told me not to wake her when we went to bed. No one else left shoes outside their doors. I thought I was going to be the only one out here." She took a sip of coffee then gazed over the top of her cup at the horizon. "I don't think they realize what they're missing."

For several minutes they sat sipping their warm beverages in silence, watching the sky's color change from dark blues to deep pinks. As the sky lightened Paige said, "The way the clouds are scattered makes the sky look like pink cotton candy."

Her hair was pulled back in a ponytail as she gazed out across the expanse of water that seemed as endless as the ocean. Justin looked at her hands. She had long, delicate fingers that should have belonged to a musician or an artist. He remembered how those fingers had caressed his naked skin, and a wave of longing washed over him just as the water lapped at the boulders along the shore. He forced himself to look away for fear of revealing what he was trying so hard to conceal.

As the ball of fiery yellow rose up over the horizon she broke the silence. "Another new day. Another fresh start."

Kyle nodded. "That's the beauty of dawn. We get another chance to make it a good day. Here's to new beginnings."

He held up his cup, and Justin and Paige each clinked theirs against his in a toast.

"You have another chance, too, Paige," he continued. "You can start over and put all the bad stuff of the past few days behind you."

"I know," she said quietly, staring out at the rising sun.

"Justin and I are here for you, aren't we, buddy?"

"Definitely."

She shifted uneasily but Kyle didn't seem to notice.

"I'm glad it's just the three of us this morning," Kyle said, leaning back on one elbow. "It feels like old times, doesn't it?"

"Yes," Justin agreed, but Paige remained silent.

"I know it hasn't been easy for you this weekend, having so many people around, especially people you hardly know." Kyle's words were addressed to Paige.

She shrugged. "I survived."

"Yes, you did, but then I knew you would. You always manage to keep it together. That's why we let you hang out with us when we were kids. You weren't a crybaby."

"And I'm not now. Crying doesn't change anything," she said with a lack of emotion.

"No, but some people find it cathartic," Justin offered.

"Some, but not Paige," Kyle said with admiration in his voice. "Lucky for us cleaning is her therapy. Man, the cabin has been spotless this weekend."

"Are you complaining?" she asked.

"No. I know it helps you work through stuff in your head, but I wish you would have played more and worked less."

"I did play."

"Yes. You were a good sport." Kyle gave her shoulder an affectionate squeeze. "But I'm glad we have this time this morning, just the three of us. And I want you to know that if you find cleaning isn't doing the trick and you need to talk, we'll listen."

"I don't need to talk about it," she insisted, again turning her gaze to the wide expanse of water.

"Okay, but if you ever do…" he trailed off.

"I know. You're here for me. Look. There's a ship coming into the harbor."

Justin followed the direction of her finger and saw a freighter slowly moving across the water. It was so far off that it looked as if it could have been one of the toy battle-ships he and Kyle had played with as kids. That was the way Paige was making him feel right now—small and insignificant in her life.

Kyle, thinking he was being helpful, said, "I also want to tell you that when you're ready to get back into the singles scene, Tammy says she has a friend she'd like you to meet."

"I'm through with men," she stated firmly.

"You say that now because you're hurting," Kyle said gently. "But don't worry. Once you're back in the Cities with us we'll make sure you have some fun. Speaking of that...you are going to move back in with us, aren't you?"

"I don't know. I haven't thought about what I'm going to do."

Justin decided to join the conversation. "When is the lease up on your trailer?"

"Not until the end of September. I was going to move into Michael's place after the wedding." There was a flatness to her tone that had Justin wondering if she was hiding her emotions or if she had accepted that her engagement was off.

"I was thinking that as long as Justin and I are here, we should move your stuff today. We can probably fit everything in the back of his pickup. It would save another trip up here and you're probably anxious to get home."

"I can't just leave," Paige answered. "I was hired to work ten weeks this summer and I still have two left."

"I'm sure your boss would understand if you said you wanted to cut out early," Kyle said.

"He probably would, but I can't ask him for that favor."

"You don't have to," Justin told her. "I already spoke to him and he told me it's not a problem if you want to go home."

That brought Paige to her feet. "You spoke to Lou about me?"

"I did work here at one time, Paige," Justin reminded her. "He's a good guy and he understands the situation."

"But you had no right to ask him anything for me!" she protested. "I can't believe you did that!"

"I thought I was doing you a favor," he retorted, getting to his feet.

"A favor? Going behind my back and talking to my boss?"

"Paige, why are you mad at him?" Kyle had risen to his feet, too. "He was only looking out for you."

"I don't need him looking out for me," she shot back. "I can make my own decisions, talk to my own boss and live my life without any help from him." She emphasized her words by pointing her finger at Justin.

Kyle glanced first at Paige, then at Justin, shoving his hands to his waist. "Okay. What's really going on here? You two have hardly spoken to one another all weekend. Now when you finally have a chance to talk, you're spitting fire at each other."

"Nothing's going on," Justin denied.

Kyle looked at her. "Paige?"

"I agree. It's nothing. Absolutely nothing." She looked at Justin as if to remind him of just how unimportant their night together had been.

Their body language alone was enough for Kyle to have his doubts. "We've been friends too long for me not to know when something's not right. So what is it?"

Now was the time for the two of them to come clean, yet how could they with the fate of their friendship—not to mention Kyle and Justin's business—hanging in the balance?

When Paige looked at Justin he saw the plea in her eyes. She didn't want Kyle to know the truth. Neither did Justin. That left only one choice. Avoid telling the truth.

"Paige thinks I'm happy that Michael cut out on her," Justin told him. "I haven't been able to convince her that she's wrong."

"You never liked him," she added, as if giving her approval of his attempt to cover up what had really happened.

"No, I didn't, but that doesn't mean I wanted you to be hurt," he retorted.

"I don't need to hear 'I told you so,'" she replied.

"Hey, I came when you called," Justin reminded her. "I even got a speeding ticket trying to get here as quickly as I could."

"You did?" Kyle and Paige said in unison.

"Yes, and all I heard was how your life was over because some loser who wasn't good enough for you cut out on you." Justin didn't need to fake his anger.

"All right, just calm down," Kyle said, making hand gestures of conciliation. "Going back over this isn't doing anyone any good. Let's get back to the issue here." Kyle looked at Paige and asked, "Do you really want to spend two more weeks here?"

"No," she said, wrapping her arms around her middle.

"Then let us move you out of the trailer and back into the J&K boardinghouse," he said. "We already know that Lou will understand if you tell him you're leaving, and why subject yourself to the unpleasantness of seeing the newlyweds?"

Paige frowned. "Someone's going to get stuck working my hours. I don't want to do that to anyone."

"I know how you feel about leaving something unfinished, but there might be someone who would be happy to have the extra hours," Kyle pointed out. "Why don't you find out before you make your decision?"

Justin thought she looked as if she wanted to refuse, but finally she sighed and said, "All right. I'll ask, but I don't want to take any crap if it turns out I don't go today."

She packed their cups into the picnic basket and grabbed the box of pastries. "I'm going back to the cabin. Don't forget the blanket when you come."

As she disappeared up the trail, Kyle looked at Justin. "She's definitely hurting but I think once she's home it won't be long until it's like old times again."

Justin nodded in agreement, but it was a meaningless gesture. There was no way things would ever be the same again.

"YOU WANT THIS HERE in the kitchen?" Kyle asked. "It says *Dishes* on it."

Paige pointed to one of the few spaces left on the counter that wasn't already cluttered with moving boxes. "You can put it there." She couldn't believe how fast her life had changed. Instead of planning a wedding and looking forward to her future as a married woman, she was returning to the life she thought she'd left behind. The thought of unpacking all the things she'd so hastily packed up that morning had her slouching against the counter in dismay.

"If you can't look happy to be home, can you at least not look as if you've been sentenced to twenty years in the women's correctional facility at Shakopee?" Kyle asked as he set the box down. A smile softened his words.

Paige thought the kitchen at the correctional facility probably had newer appliances if not better company. It wasn't that she didn't appreciate her best friends' offer for her to move back in with them, but she'd reached a point in her life when she didn't want to be rooming with two men. She'd never been fond of big anything, and this house was way too big for her taste. And even though it had four bedrooms and three baths, she would occasionally bump into a guy going from one to the other.

In the past there had never been any awkwardness between them when it came to privacy issues. But that was before she and Justin had crossed a line they shouldn't have crossed. Now she felt uneasy around both men. Mostly she was angry at Justin. Maybe it wasn't his fault that they were in this predicament, but she couldn't help feeling that he had let her down. She hated secrets, and now she was forced to keep one from Kyle. And she would keep it, because to reveal what had happened between her and Justin would change the friendship of the three of them forever.

That's why she made a special effort to smile at Kyle and say, "I'm sorry. I really appreciate you and Justin letting me stay with you for a while. I'm going to try really hard not to walk around with my lip on the floor."

"The guy's not worth it," he repeated for what had to be the hundredth time.

"I know," she replied as she had every other time.

"And you can stay as long as you want," he said with a reassuring smile. "But I do need to tell you about a couple of changes we made while you were gone."

As if on cue a woman came skipping down the stairs and into the kitchen. She wore a bright orange tank top and a pair of jean shorts and looked as comfortable in the house as if it was her right to be there. Suspicion had the hair on the back of Paige's neck rising.

"Hi. You must be Paige. I'm Angie." She extended her hand, which Paige shook. "I can see the guys haven't told you about me, have they?"

Since she acted as if she belonged in the house, Paige's first thought was that she was someone's girlfriend or a new roommate. Since both Justin and Kyle had brought women to the Bulldog Reunion, she assumed it had to be the latter—a rather unsettling possibility she hadn't considered.

"Angie's one of the changes I was talking about," Kyle told her. "She cleans once a week."

A cleaning woman? Paige thought the pigtailed redhead looked as if she should serving beer instead of cleaning toilets. "Well, that explains why there aren't any dirty dishes in the sink."

"Angie usually comes on Wednesdays, but when I found out you were coming home today I called her, and she was good enough to come over and get the place looking presentable for you." Kyle turned to the redhead and said, "I can't thank you enough. We really appreciate it."

"No problem," Angie said with a cheerful grin. "Is Justin around? I need to talk to him."

"He's out in the garage but he should be in shortly," Kyle answered.

"I'll go find him," she said, and Paige felt a rare sensation—jealousy. Which was ridiculous, because she had no reason to be envious of the woman who cleaned Justin's room.

Angie flounced out of the kitchen as breezily as she had come in. "A cleaning lady?" Paige asked with a lift of her brow.

"Hey—you should be happy. At least you didn't come home to a mess."

Paige wondered if that was the only reason Angie had been employed. *Meooww*. She chastised herself. The guys had done a nice thing. She should be grateful, not catty.

At that moment Justin came in carrying Paige's wedding dress, Angie bouncing along behind him. "What do you want me to do with this?" he asked Paige.

"I wish you hadn't brought it home," Paige answered.

Justin remained silent, waiting for an answer.

"Oh my gosh! It's gorgeous." Angie admired the gown. "Is it yours?"

"No," Paige answered curtly

"It's a long story," Justin told Angie, then looked at Paige. "We need to find someplace to store it. Either that or get rid of it."

"I told you, I don't care what you do with it." Paige turned her attention to the contents of the box Kyle had carried in.

"You don't want it?" Angie looked aghast. She fingered the beaded bodice gingerly. "This reminds me of the dress my grandmother wore on her wedding day. How old is it?"

"Dates from the 1940s. Isn't that what you said?" Justin refused to allow Paige to ignore them.

"Then you shouldn't just throw it out," Angie said. "If you don't want it, why not donate it to the Goldstein Museum at the U. They're always looking for vintage clothing for their collection."

As much as Paige hated to admit it, donating the dress to a museum at the university did make sense.

"We could check into it." Justin looked at her. "What do you think, Paige?"

She shrugged. "Fine."

"On the other hand, the dress could net cash," he said, glancing at her speculatively.

"I'm sure you wouldn't have any trouble finding someone to buy it," Angie gushed. "It's beautiful."

When Paige remained silent, Justin said, "We don't need to make a decision today. Do you think you can find room for it in my closet?" He looked at Angie.

"Oh, I think we can fit it in. I moved all of those books and magazines you had piled on the closet floor into that spare closet in the den. You'd be surprised the space that freed up."

"You're organizing their closets?" Again Paige had an ir-rational sense of jealousy, as if the other woman had usurped her role in the house.

"We didn't know you'd be back," Kyle told her.

Of course they didn't. She hadn't known herself. So why did it bother her that Angie moved about the house so freely after just a few months?

As she unpacked the small box of groceries she'd brought back from her trailer, she discovered that the cupboards had been rearranged, too.

"Where's the cereal?" she asked no one in particular.

"Oh, it's in the cupboard to your left," Angie told her. "It's more convenient if it's next to the refrigerator, don't you think?" She looked adoringly at Justin and asked, "Is there anything else I can do for you?"

"I can't think of anything." He looked at Kyle. "What about you?"

"No, the place looks great." He reached into his wallet and unrolled several bills, which he handed to Angie. Good grief. They'd never offered to pay her for cleaning up after them.

Angie sidled up to Justin and batted her eyelashes at him. "Would you be so kind as to give me a ride home? My roommate dropped me off because my car's been acting funny."

"I can take you," Kyle offered, which brought a slight wrinkle of disappointment to Angie's face, although she hid it well. "I'm going to the ATM to get some cash. I'll swing by your place on the way."

As soon as they left, Justin said, "I'm glad Kyle took her home, because we need to talk."

Paige knew this moment was coming. As much as she

wished they didn't need to discuss what had happened between them, if they were going to be living under the same roof, they had to clear the air.

"Then let's talk." She sat down at the kitchen table and motioned for him to sit across from her.

"This weekend was tough and neither one of us was prepared for what happened," he began. "But we've had time now to think about things. I hope we can discuss this calmly."

It annoyed her that he thought she was going to get upset. She took a deep breath and said, "Maybe the best way to put this behind us is to say nothing."

"Is that what you want to do?"

"Look, you don't have to worry. I'm over it." It wasn't exactly true, but she hoped that if she told herself often enough, that it would be one of those self-filling prophecies.

"You're over it?" he repeated suspiciously.

She moved her clasped hands from the table to her lap so he wouldn't see how tightly she was clenching them. "We made a mistake, we've both acknowledged it was a mistake, and we've agreed it won't happen again. Is there really any point in rehashing everything?"

He had that look in his eyes that meant he wasn't quite convinced. "I just want to make sure that what happened isn't going to threaten our friendship. I've heard stories of how casual sex can be the finish line for friends."

Casual sex. Of course that's what it was. Intellectually she'd had this conversation in her head a dozen times. Yet emotionally she was having trouble accepting that's what it had been. Justin, on the other hand, appeared to have no problem relegating their night together to casual-sex status. But then she suspected it wasn't the first one-nighter he'd had.

Just as he had on so many other occasions, he seemed to

know what she was thinking. "I'm okay with not talking about it anymore, but there's just one thing I want to clear up. Contrary to what you might think, I'm not in the habit of having one-nighters."

She got up from the table and turned her back to him. "It really doesn't matter."

He got up and followed her over to the counter. "Yes, it does. I don't want you to think you were just some girl I picked up and—"

"Please." She stopped him with her hand. "You don't need to say anything else. I'm over it."

"Turn around and look me in the eye and say that," he ordered her.

She took a deep breath and slowly turned around. When she gazed into his blue eyes she saw anguish. She should have known that he would be agonizing over what had happened. He was a man of principle, a guy who would never take advantage of a woman. Yet that was the very thing she had accused him of.

"You didn't take anything from me, Justin. I gave it to you willingly. Whether that was wise or not doesn't matter. We can't undo what happened so we might as well forget it and move forward. Do you think we can do that?"

"Yes, but let me say one more thing,"

"You already said one more thing," she reminded him with a half grin, trying to lighten the tone of their conversation.

"This is going to be my last one more thing," he promised.

"Okay."

"I behaved irresponsibly and I'm sorry. More than ever you needed me to be your friend that night and I let you down. I want you to know that it was a mistake that will never be repeated."

Mistake. Casual sex. Unimportant. He was saying everything she had already said to herself a gazillion times, so why was she disappointed rather than relieved?

"You believe me, don't you?" he asked, staring at her with an intensity that made her feel as if he could see right into her soul.

"Yes." It was what she wanted to hear, so why didn't she find his words comforting?

"Good. Because now that you're living here, I want things to be the way they were before you left." He moved away from her to open the refrigerator and pull out a soda.

"They will be," she said, watching him pop the tab and take a swallow. "It's going to be hard to be around Kyle, though."

He nodded. "Yeah, it is. I have to tell you, I don't feel very good about what was said this morning at the sunrise picnic when the three of us were talking about being honest with each other."

"I know. It bothered me, too," she admitted. "The reason our friendship has survived the test of time is because we haven't kept secrets. It's never been two against one. It's always the three of us or nothing."

"But this is in a class separate from all the other stuff we've shared as friends," Justin rationalized.

"I know."

She exhaled a long sigh. "If he knew that we…" She pointed her finger at him, then at herself, and shook her head.

"He'd feel betrayed. He's my business partner as well as my friend. I can't hurt him that way."

"Me neither," she said quietly. "We're just going to have to keep what happened that night to ourselves and live with the guilt."

"Agreed. So are you okay with everything?"

"Yeah, I am," she answered honestly.

"Good, because we're going to be seeing a lot of each other.

My dad's birthday's coming up and I know my parents expect the three of us to be there like we've always been in the past."

For as far back as she could remember the Colliers had hosted a party the first weekend in September to celebrate Elliot Collier's birthday and to kick off the start of the football season. Paige had received the invitation only last week and had responded that she would be bringing a guest—her fiancé. Now she would have to face everyone as a jilted bride to be.

"You are planning to go, aren't you?" Justin asked.

She didn't hesitate to say, "Yes. You know I would never miss your dad's birthday."

"I hoped you would say that."

"Then I'll get some flowers for your mom."

He reached for her hands and clasped them within his. "So are we friends again?" he asked with a smile that sent goose bumps up and down her spine.

She nodded. "We're friends."

"And we agree—not another word about that night?"

"We agree," she echoed.

He let go of her hand and wrapped his arms around her in a hug. It was the kind of embrace that prior to Friday night she would have thought of as a comforting, reassuring gesture of friendship. But the minute she felt his arms around her, a wave of longing rushed through her, reminding her that no matter how much they wanted to pretend that things were back to the way they used to be, it wasn't true. When he touched her she felt an emotion she didn't want to feel for him— desire. It was something she couldn't let him see.

As she pushed him away he asked, "Then we're okay?"

"Yes. We're okay."

"Good, because I need my friend Paige."

He smiled again, the familiar grin she knew so well, the

one that always made her feel that no matter what happened, she had someone to lean on. It gave her hope that maybe they could go back to being the best of friends. Then he turned and walked away, and as he left the room she wasn't thinking about what a great friend he'd always been to her. She was remembering what it had been like to make love with him and regretting that it would never happen again.

Send For
2 FREE BOOKS
Today!

I accept your offer!

Please send me two free *Harlequin Superromance*® novels and two mystery gifts (gifts worth about $10). I understand that these books are completely free— even the shipping and handling will be paid—and I am under no obligation to purchase anything, ever, as explained on the back of this card.

336 HDL ERRV   **135 HDL ERVL**

Please Print

FIRST NAME

LAST NAME

ADDRESS

APT.#   CITY

STATE/PROV.   ZIP/POSTAL CODE

Offer limited to one per household and not valid to current subscribers of *Harlequin Superromance*® books.

Your Privacy — Harlequin Books is committed to protecting your privacy. Our Privacy Policy is available online at www.eHarlequin.com or upon request from the Harlequin Reader Service. From time to time we make our list of customers available to reputable third parties who may have a product or service of interest to you. If you would prefer for us not to share your name and address, please check here ☐ .

▲ Detach card and mail today. No stamp needed. ▲ **GF-HSR-03/08**

CHAPTER SEVEN

PAIGE SPENT most of her first week at home looking for a job. Because teaching contracts had already been awarded for the upcoming school year, she didn't expect to find a full-time position as an elementary-school teacher and was prepared to hire on as an on-call substitute in the district where she had worked the previous year. By Friday, however, she had an offer for a full-time position at a private school in suburban St. Paul that was losing their third-grade teacher because of a family emergency.

When Justin and Kyle heard she was employed, they insisted on celebrating by taking her out to dinner. Paige had known them long enough to realize that if they were celebrating anything, there would be a group of people involved. It would have been much easier to decline their offer and stay home with a frozen dinner, but she wanted to show them and all of their friends that even though Michael may have broken up with her, he hadn't broken her spirit.

The place they chose for dinner was a local sports bar and grill that had been a favorite hangout of theirs ever since they'd been teenagers. Besides great food, including Paige's favorite, barbecued baby back ribs, it had TV screens on nearly every wall so that no sporting event went unnoticed. As Paige expected, they were joined by several friends. What she didn't expect was to see Tammy and her sister Tara.

"Hey, Paige. It's good to see you," Tammy said, giving her a hug. "Congratulations on landing the job."

"Thank you. It's a relief to be employed again," she said honestly, noticing that Tara didn't make any attempt to hug her but simply said hello. She didn't think she'd have to worry about Tammy's sister wanting to make conversation with her. She had eyes for only one person—Justin.

"I hope you don't mind but I invited a guy I work with to join us," Tammy said. "He's really nice."

Paige groaned silently. She was being set up—either an act of pity or a way to balance the numbers. She should have stayed home.

"I'm sitting between you and Kyle," she told Justin, grabbing ahold of his shirtsleeve as they waited in the entry for the hostess to seat them.

"I don't have a problem with that," he replied.

"You'll just have to put Tara on the other side of you." She deliberately kept her voice low so as not to be overhead.

"Why do you think I even want her anywhere near me? I'd much rather sit next to you."

It wasn't said in a flirtatious way, yet Paige felt a tiny shot of adrenaline upon hearing his words. Standing in the crowded lobby she noticed how tall Justin was compared to other men in their circle of friends. And he was much better looking. He was really cute. No wonder Tara was after him.

Feeling uneasy at the direction of her thoughts, she nudged Justin and said, "Tara's got it bad for you. She can't take her eyes off you."

"She knows I'm not looking for a serious relationship," he whispered.

"I don't know why you say that to women. Don't you know that those words only encourage them? They must like a challenge or something."

"I tell them that because it's the truth." He gazed at her intently.

Yes, it was, which was why she shouldn't be noticing things like the way his eyes darkened to an exquisite shade of blue when he focused on one thing—or person. Or how broad his shoulders looked when he wore a knit shirt.

"Hey—I may not have many of those Top Ten traits you want in your ideal guy, but at least I'm honest."

"I don't have an ideal guy," she told him.

He chuckled. "What about your *list?*"

"I burned it," she admitted. "At the campfire. I figured it wasn't reliable. I mean, Michael met all the criteria on my list and look what happened."

"Are you going to make a new one?"

"Why? I don't need one."

"You're just going to go with your instincts when it comes to men?"

"No, I'm just not going to go out with men, period." Out of the corner of her eye she saw Tammy pushing her way through the crowd toward them, dragging a man with a curly blond head. "Oh no. I think the setup is here." Justin was about to turn his head but she stopped him with a hand on his arm. "Tammy brought a friend. She thinks she's doing me a favor."

"So that's why you're hanging on to me as if I were a life vest," he said, glancing down at her hand.

She released him immediately. "Usually a blind intro is about as pleasant as a trip to the dentist," she said, studying the guy coming toward her. "Remember. I'm sitting between you and Kyle."

"Paige, this is my friend Ryan," Tammy introduced the man at her side. "He sells insurance. He can probably figure out a way to save you money on your car insurance. I know he saved me a bunch."

Ryan, it turned out, was a decent guy, but a major bore. When Paige made it clear that she was perfectly happy with the coverage on her car, he proceeded to tell her the details of how he'd worked his way up from messenger to salesman at the insurance company. As the hostess led their group to a table near the back of the restaurant, Paige tried to discreetly separate herself from him, but he wasn't about to be given the slip.

In the meantime Tara had insinuated herself between Paige and Justin, brushing up against him as they walked through the crowded restaurant. Paige found herself wishing she could change places with her, not just because she wanted to evade Ryan, but because she wanted to be the one leaning up against Justin, feeling his strength. That sudden awareness of him in a physical sense made her uneasy. Just because she had slept with him didn't mean that she should start having funny sensations every time she looked at him.

True to his word, Justin came to her side as everyone sat down at the table. "Paige, why don't you sit between me and Kyle."

She could see that neither Tara nor Ryan was happy with the seating arrangement, but she didn't care. She was grateful that Justin had sensed her uneasiness. Later, as they rode home together, she thanked him for rescuing her from the pride and joy of the insurance industry.

"You didn't have a good time tonight, did you?" he said, giving her a sideways glance.

"I know you and Kyle meant well, but you know me—I

could have stayed home, had food delivered and been just as happy," she answered honestly. "I'm not much for crowds."

"Eight people do not make a crowd."

"Not to you, no."

They rode the rest of the way in silence, but it was a comfortable silence, giving Paige hope that everything really was going to be okay between them. When they arrived back at the house, she said, "I'm going to bed. I'm tired."

"Okay. See you tomorrow." He bent over to kiss her on the cheek as he'd done a thousand times in the past. His lips were warm against her skin and she had to fight the temptation to grab his chin and kiss him properly on the lips. For a moment their eyes locked and she wondered if he was thinking the same thing. Then he pulled back and said, "Good night."

"Good night," she echoed and started up the stairs.

She was halfway up when he said, "Paige?"

She turned around, hoping he was going to tell her to come back down and give him a real kiss. But all he said was, "I'm glad things are back the way they used to be."

"Me, too." She'd been thinking the same thing on the way home, so why was she disappointed?

"Because you wish he wanted you as much as you want him," a tiny voice in her head answered. She chastised herself for even thinking such a thing and went to bed.

WHEN PAIGE AWOKE on the morning of Elliot Collier's birthday party, the first thing she did was reach for the bottle of antacid tablets on her nightstand. Thanks to all the stress in her life, indigestion had become a regular companion. Each morning she vowed she would eat healthier meals, but as usual when she was stressed, she lost her appetite.

As she put the bottle back she noticed her cell phone was

blinking, indicating she had a voice-mail message. She punched a button and saw that she had indeed missed a call. When the number popped up on the screen, she gasped. It was Michael.

How long she stared at the phone debating whether or not to listen to the message, she didn't know, but finally curiosity won the war with her common sense. She punched in the numbers for her voice mail and listened.

"Paige, it's me. I just called to say I'm sorry…really sorry about leaving the way I did. Please call me. I need to talk to you."

It had been over four weeks since he'd left and she'd canceled the wedding arrangements. Why would he be calling her now? What did he want? To get back together with her? For one brief moment her heart raced at the possibility, but then she snapped out of the fantasy. She erased his message from the voice mail, then tossed the phone carelessly onto her bed.

She showered and dressed, then turned her attention to the lesson plans she needed to prepare for the upcoming week at school, but she couldn't discard Michael's memory as easily as she did his message. Hearing his voice had resurrected feelings she thought she had buried for good.

She pulled open the small drawer in her nightstand. Still sitting there was the velvet box containing her engagement ring. She lifted it in her hand and stared at it. Inside was a symbol of love and fidelity. Michael had professed both, but had proven neither. She didn't open it, but put the box back in the drawer.

Unable to concentrate on her lessons, she finally went downstairs to find Justin alone in the living room. "Where's Kyle?" she asked.

"He went to get Tammy. I told him we'd meet him at my parents'. If you're ready, I'll get my keys and we'll go."

"I'm going to drive myself." She didn't say she might want

to call Michael on the way because she wasn't going to call Michael...or was she? "I have a lot of preparation to do for school tomorrow so I won't be staying very late."

"I can always bring you home."

"Wouldn't it make more sense for me to just drive myself?"

"I don't mind bringing you home."

Not wanting to make an issue of it, she accepted his offer and went into the kitchen to get the bouquet of fresh flowers she'd purchased for his mom. As they made their way to the neighborhood where they had both been raised, apprehension tickled her nerves, especially as she thought about seeing Justin's mother.

Paige knew it was irrational, but she worried that Nancy Collier would be able to tell just by looking at her that she and Justin had slept together. It was probably because Nancy was the one woman who knew Paige better than anyone else.

The woman had done her best to fill Paige's mother's shoes, making sure Paige had a woman's influence in her life. Paige hadn't made it easy for her. She didn't want a substitute mom. She wanted her own mother, and if she couldn't have her, she was determined to get by without anyone's help.

And she had, but even a stubborn Paige realized that there were times when it was nice to have a woman around, like when she needed a haircut or new school clothes. By the time Paige was a teenager, the rough edges in their relationship had been smoothed.

As Paige expected, Nancy was the one who greeted her and Justin at the door, giving each of them a hug and a kiss on the cheek. She gushed over the flowers then she turned to Paige and asked, "Are you okay? You look a little pale." She gave her the kind of scrutiny a mom gives a child who's just fallen off her bike.

"I feel good but I'm a little tired," Paige answered. "I haven't been getting enough sleep. There's always so much to do at the start of a new school year."

Nancy continued to look her over and Paige was certain that she was wearing her guilt like a fake tan and at any minute Justin's mother would scold the two of them for doing something they weren't supposed to do—just as she'd done on many occasions when they were children.

But she simply smiled and said, "Then it'll do you good to relax with us today."

"Why don't you come watch the game with me," Justin suggested to Paige.

"I will, but first I want to help your mom with dinner."

Nancy patted her hand. "That's not necessary, but you're always welcome. You know that."

Paige followed her into the room where she'd spent many hours as a child. Nancy no longer had the day care in her home, but there were still signs of its existence in the warm kitchen decorated in bright yellows and greens. Like the small chalkboard on the wall where she used to write the day's menus. Today it simply said, Happy Birthday, Elliot!

"What can I do?" Paige asked looking around the kitchen.

"You can tell me how you really are," Nancy replied, giving her even closer scrutiny than before. "I'm sorry about Michael."

Paige was tempted to tell her he had contacted her, but she didn't want anyone asking her questions she didn't have the answers to herself. She simply said, "I don't understand why he let me make all those wedding plans...why he didn't tell me he was having doubts."

"Maybe he didn't want to admit them even to himself," Nancy suggested.

She shrugged. "Whatever. It doesn't matter." She didn't want to talk about Michael, especially not today, when her feelings for him were so ambiguous. "If you don't mind, Nancy, I'd rather not talk about him."

"Then we won't. I just want you to know that I'm here for you if you do need to talk." She patted Paige's hand.

"Thank you. I appreciate that. Now how about you let me help you get the food on the table?" Paige rolled up the sleeves on her blouse.

"That would be lovely. You can whip the cream for the fruit salad. There's an apron in that drawer in front of you."

Paige opened the drawer and pulled out a white chef's apron, which she slipped over her head and tied around her waist. She was about to start the electric mixer, when she saw a woman wearing a long skirt and frilly blouse enter Nancy's kitchen.

"Hi, Mary," Paige called out to the middle-aged woman who always had a smile on her face and could tell you everything that was happening in the neighborhood.

"Well, Paige. I heard you were going to be here today. I'm so glad to see you." She gave Paige a bear hug that made her acutely aware of the fragrance she wore.

Although Mary Adelmann and her husband never had any children, they had hosted the annual summer block party and had always treated the neighbor children like extended family. Eight years ago when Mary's husband died suddenly, most people thought she would move back to her hometown in South Dakota, but she stayed in St. Paul and continued working as a cook at the local elementary school. Paige was glad because Mary and her father had become very good friends, and although Paige knew her father would never want to remarry, he needed a companion.

"I've come for ice," Mary said, holding an ice bucket in one hand, its lid in the other. "But first I have to say hello to this young lady." She pulled out one of the stools at the eating counter and sat down. "How are you?"

"I'm good. Thanks."

To her relief, Mary didn't mention her broken engagement but instead said, "I hear you're back living with Kyle and Justin."

"Yes, I am," Paige confirmed. "I hope to have my own apartment by the end of the year."

"I suppose you're going to have to find a new place once they sell theirs."

"They're selling the house?" Paige looked at Nancy for confirmation, but she simply shrugged and raised her eyebrows. "It's news to me."

"Oooh." Mary covered her mouth. "I hope I didn't speak out of turn. I just thought you knew. Ralph Jensen down the street gave them an appraisal. Maybe they changed their minds or want to wait until after they get back from Oregon."

"Oregon?" Again Paige looked at Nancy. This time it was apparent she wasn't in the dark about their plans.

"They've signed up for some seminars. Something to do with the business...you know, which plants to buy, diseases... that kind of thing." Nancy stirred the barbecued pork in the roaster as she talked.

"I can't believe they didn't mention it to me. How can they leave the business?"

"It's always slower in the winter, and now that Harry Bonner's going to be their partner, he can run things while they're gone," Mary said.

Kyle and Justin were taking on a partner? Paige didn't say anything. She couldn't. She was too hurt. Nancy looked uncomfortable, but Mary seemed unaware of what a shock it was for Paige. The two guys were supposed to be her closest friends. Mary asked Paige about her new job before getting the ice she came for and going back out to the party guests.

As soon as she was gone, Nancy said, "I'm sure nothing's definite on the house. I mean, they wouldn't do anything without talking to you about it first."

"I'm supposed to be a partner in their business, Nancy, yet they didn't even—" She stopped abruptly, worried she was going to break down in tears.

"I'm sure there's a reason why they haven't, Paige." Nancy tried to defend her son and his best friend, but there was no defense as far as Paige was concerned. She didn't understand why Justin hadn't said anything. Kyle was spending so much time with Tammy she rarely saw him, but Justin? Not wanting Nancy to see how upset she was, she changed the subject.

They worked side by side, talking mostly about Paige's position at her new school. Nancy understood the challenges and rewards involved in working with children.

Time passed quickly, with guests drifting in and out of the kitchen to say hello. When Justin came in, Paige was filling a serving dish with pickles and olives. He snatched one of the pickle spears.

"Are you hiding away in here? I haven't seen you all afternoon."

"I told you I wanted to help your mom," she said coolly, trying not to let Nancy see how angry she was.

"As long as that's all it is." He raised one brow.

"What else would it be?"

"I was worried you were avoiding me," he whispered so his mother wouldn't hear.

"No, I'm busy," she said shortly.

"Well, I'm glad you're not avoiding me, because I like seeing you. Did I tell you how glad I am that you're back in the house with me and Kyle?"

"I'm sure you are. There's food in the refrigerator when I'm home."

"You know that's not the only reason. I like having you around."

"Yeah, you like having another body in the house. You're a people person. You'd have trouble living alone."

"You make a good roommate," he complimented her.

She didn't want to have a confrontation with him in front of his mother, but she couldn't pretend that nothing was wrong. "Is that why you and Kyle are going to sell the house out from underneath me?"

He had the decency to look guilty. "We had it appraised. We haven't listed it with a real estate agent. We'd never sell it without telling you."

"Just like you'd never take on a business partner without telling me?" she shot back at him. "Or have you reneged on the promise you made that even though I only gave you my first paycheck, which was a fraction of what you needed to get started in your business, it was a contribution and I'm supposed to be a partner—a silent and small one, but still a partner."

He looked like a kid who'd had his hand caught in a cookie jar. "We were going to tell you." He shifted uncomfortably. "There have been some changes since you went away for the summer…"

She didn't let him finish. "This has nothing to do with me going away. You're keeping secrets from me." She didn't realize she'd raised her voice until Nancy turned her head.

Paige didn't want to sound upset, but she was. He was supposed to be her best friend yet he'd kept something this important from her?

"We had the real estate agent out in August...when we thought you were getting married. That's when we talked about bringing on a partner, too."

"And the trip to Oregon?"

"We would have told you about it but all you talked about this summer was your wedding plans and how you couldn't wait for the day when you no longer had to be the chief cook and bottle washer for me and Kyle."

"I never said that," she denied.

"Yes, you did."

Maybe she had. She'd floated through the summer in a fog of romantic fantasy. "It doesn't matter. I don't feel that way now." It had been a great comfort to come home to the familiarity of living with Kyle and Justin. Thanks to Angie she no longer was the chief cook and bottle washer.

Just then Nancy came over with a tray of appetizers, which she handed to Justin. "Be a dear and take these outside, will you?"

He had no choice but to do as she requested. He told Paige, "We'll talk later," before slipping out the back door.

"I'm sorry. I couldn't help but overhear you and Justin arguing. Is everything all right?" She had that maternal concern in her eye that made Paige want to pour her heart out to her, but she didn't. She couldn't.

"Yes, it's all right," she said, but the moisture in her eyes belied her words. She bit down on her lip, fighting the urge to cry. "They told me I could stay with them for as long as I wanted, when all along they were planning to sell the place."

Emotion closed her throat and she managed to mumble an "Excuse me" before rushing into the bathroom.

She splashed cold water on her face and blew her nose. What was wrong with her? Just because Justin and Kyle had decided to sell the house without telling her didn't mean she needed to bawl like a baby. And she was only a teeny-tiny shareholder in their landscape business. As much as she hated to admit it, what Justin said was true. She had been planning her wedding this summer, and had they mentioned they were selling the house and thinking of taking on a partner, she would have told them to go ahead. Still, she felt hurt that neither one had shared their plans with her.

When she returned to the kitchen she could see the concern on Nancy's face. "Are you sure you're all right?"

"I'm fine. I'm sorry I made a scene. I don't know what came over me. That was so not like me. I'm never emotional, but lately I feel as if I could cry if someone looks at me the wrong way. It must be tension related."

"You don't need to apologize. You've been through a major stress. Recovering from a broken engagement isn't easy. So don't be too hard on yourself. It's okay to cry a little."

"I know, but it's not Justin's or Kyle's fault that I'm no longer engaged. And getting all teary eyed doesn't resolve anything. Nor does it help that this morning—" She was about to tell Nancy that Michael had called, when Mary Adelmann reappeared carrying an empty dish. One again Paige noticed the fragrance the woman wore and wondered why she'd never found it offensive until today.

Normally Paige didn't have a problem with perfume scents, but as the afternoon progressed, several of the Collier guests wore fragrances that threatened to set off her gag reflex.

It crossed her mind that she could be coming down with a stomach illness. It usually happened every fall as soon as school reconvened. But by the time all the food was served, she didn't think any more about it because she was hungry and everything tasted exceptionally good. Not that she thought it wouldn't. Nancy was an excellent cook. It wasn't until later in the afternoon when she was helping serve coffee and cake that she again found herself nauseated by an odor.

This time it wasn't perfume, but the rich aroma of freshly ground coffee beans. Paige wrinkled her nose and took a step back. "Whoa."

Nancy could tell by the expression on her face that she didn't like the aroma. "I thought you were a coffee drinker."

"I am, but today for some reason the smell is disgusting. How weird is that?"

"It can be a rather pungent aroma."

"Is it a special blend or something?"

"No, just regular old coffee."

"Really? I wonder why it smells so awful to me. Maybe I'm getting the flu. The past few days I've noticed I have this weird sensitivity to smells. It's crazy. At least three or four times since I got here someone's perfume has made me want to gag. What's strange is that otherwise I feel good. Have you ever heard of anything like that?"

"Actually, I have," Nancy said. "Have you been having a lot of indigestion, too?"

"Yes. Is there a flu bug going around with those symptoms?"

"Not that I know of."

"Then what do you think is causing it?"

Nancy was silent for a moment, as if debating whether or not she should tell her. Then she said, "Paige, is it possible you're pregnant?"

Paige's mouth flew open. "No! Why would you even ask that?"

"I'm sorry. I didn't mean to offend you. But seeing you carrying around that big bottle of antacid tablets reminded me of when I was pregnant with Justin. It's the only time I ever had heartburn, and then when you told me about your aversion to smells…well, that's exactly the way I felt in the early months of my pregnancy. Sometimes the most benign odors would make me want to gag."

"It's got to be a coincidence," Paige said, trying not to think about the fact she couldn't even drink a glass of milk without getting heartburn lately. "There must be other reasons for someone to have similar reactions to smells."

"I'm sure there are. I didn't mean to get so personal, but you know I've always thought of you as a daughter, and if you were my daughter I would have asked you that question."

"I'm not pregnant," Paige assured her, trying to push aside the doubts her questions had raised. "I couldn't be. It's not possible."

"Then we won't talk about it anymore." Nancy wrapped her arm around her shoulder and gave her a gentle hug. "But I do want you to remember that if you ever need someone to talk to, I'm here for you."

"I do know that. You've always been there and I appreciate it." She hated that her voice cracked with emotion. "But I'm not pregnant."

Silently she repeated those words to herself throughout the afternoon, but the longer she stayed at the party the more anxious she became. As soon as the birthday cake had been served and she'd helped with the kitchen cleanup, she asked Justin to give her a ride home. Pleading the need to prepare her lesson plan for the upcoming week, she said her goodbyes to everyone and left the party early.

As soon as she was in her room she went online and read everything she could about early pregnancy signs. Then she went to the twenty-four-hour pharmacy and bought not one but two in-home pregnancy tests.

CHAPTER EIGHT

As SOON AS PAIGE finished teaching on Monday she drove to an urgent-care clinic where a nurse checked her vital signs, took a sample of her blood and asked her to urinate into a small cup. Now she sat in a small room on an examining table with a paper sheet draped over her naked body, waiting to talk to a total stranger about a very personal subject.

The nurse had said a Dr. Frampton would be in to see her shortly. When Paige was ushered into the examining room, she'd caught a glimpse of the two doctors on duty. One looked to be near retirement age, the other could have been one of the dreamy doctors on *Grey's Anatomy*. Now she wondered which one would be attending her. She raised her eyes to the ceiling and said softly, "Oh, please, let it be the older one."

When the door finally did open she saw that her prayer had been answered. The man that entered had a gray head. He stretched out his hand to Paige and said, "I'm Dr. Frampton. How are you today?"

"I'm okay," she answered cautiously.

"So you think you're pregnant," he said, looking at her chart.

Actually she didn't. Despite the fact that two in-home pregnancy tests had given positive results, she just couldn't believe that she was going to have a baby. Paige knew that even though false-positive results were rare with the tests, they did occur, and she assumed that she was in that small percentage.

"I'm not sure," she answered. She explained the symptoms she'd been having as well as the results of the in-home pregnancy tests. He didn't comment, but simply continued to write in her chart.

"Are you using birth control pills?"

"No."

"What method of birth control do you use?"

She wanted to say none, that there hadn't been a need for one, but she realized how foolish that would sound considering she came for a pregnancy test. "C-condoms," she stammered uneasily.

"Good for preventing sexually transmitted diseases, but not always the best method for preventing pregnancy," he said without looking up at her.

"I just don't see how I could be pregnant," she told him. "I had a period last week."

He continued to write notes in her chart. "Was it a normal one?"

"No, it was shorter than usual, but I had PMS and I had a headache," she stated. "And my periods have always been irregular. One month heavy, one month light."

"Do you tire easily?"

"Yes, but it's been a hectic few weeks at school," she told him. "I'm a teacher."

He asked more questions to which he made further notes in her chart. Then he examined her and said, "You can get dressed and I'll be back in shortly to talk to you."

Paige hopped down from the examining table and quickly pulled her clothes back on. Then she sat down on the chair next to the desk and waited. Finally there was a knock on the door and once again the doctor came into the room. He sat down on the stool in front of the desk and looked her squarely in the eye.

"Paige, you are pregnant."

Panic rose in her throat, blocking her airways and preventing her from saying anything. She simply sat in stunned silence as her mind filled with questions she couldn't answer. How was she ever going to manage to raise a child alone?

"It's still early," the doctor continued, "but from what you told me and from what I saw during the examination, I'd say you can expect to deliver a baby around the first of May."

She finally managed to find her voice, although it was wobbly when she asked, "But I had a period. How can I be pregnant?"

"It probably wasn't a menstrual cycle but implantation bleeding. That can occur ten to fourteen days after conception, and is probably what happened in your case. It's perfectly normal, but if you have any bleeding or cramping in the future, I want you to call the clinic right away." He opened a drawer and pulled out a packet of materials, which he handed to her. "That contains a lot of information you need to know about pregnancy and childbirth, and there's also a list of reference books you'll find useful." He wrote something on a prescription pad. "You should start taking vitamins right away. Here's the name of the one I recommend." He handed the slip of paper to her.

He continued to rattle off advice. Paige nodded in understanding, but she doubted whether she'd remember half of what he was saying about nutrition and exercise. How could she when all she could think of was that she was going to be having a baby. Justin's baby.

"So that pretty much covers it for now," he said, closing her chart. "Do you have any questions?"

She did, but not ones he could answer. Like what was she going to do with a baby? How would she tell her family and friends? How was she going to tell Justin? So she simply shook her head and said, "I can't think of any right now."

"Well, remember you can always call and talk to the nurses here at the clinic. There is also a helpline number on the back of that booklet that can assist you in finding the names of resources for pregnant women." She nodded and he continued. "So what you need to do is make an appointment with your family physician or gynecologist. We're only an urgent-care clinic, so you're going to need to schedule regular visits to make sure you have the proper prenatal care for you and your baby."

"I will," she said dutifully.

"Now, I want you to go home and eat well-balanced meals, get plenty of rest and try not to get stressed." He handed her a yellow slip of paper. "Give this to the front desk and you can be on your way. And remember, your baby experiences everything you do."

Her baby. It didn't seem possible. Alone once more in the examining room, she placed her hand on her stomach. Could there really be a tiny person growing inside her? Maybe she had imagined the doctor had said all those things.

But when she reached the front desk and heard the receptionist ask, "You do know that you're supposed to schedule a prenatal visit with your regular doctor in four weeks?" Paige wanted to say, "No, I'm not having a baby. I won't be needing another appointment."

But there was no avoiding the truth. She was pregnant.

It was something that was supposed to happen after she married Michael. They had planned a life together that had included children, but not until they'd accomplished a few goals. She'd planned to get her master's degree. He'd wanted to land a job with a major golf club. They had agreed that it was important that they be emotionally and financially ready to welcome a child into their lives. "Must want children" had been number three on her Top Ten list.

But Michael wasn't the father of her baby. Justin was. Justin who rarely planned anything. Justin who chose to think of the night they spent together as casual sex with no consequences. Would he make a good father? Would he even want to try? She didn't want to think about it. Right now the enormity of her situation threatened to overwhelm her.

She didn't have a clue how to be a parent. She didn't have a husband. She didn't even have a place to live. Even if Kyle and Justin didn't sell the house, it wasn't the kind of place she would choose to raise a child. She'd barely finished paying off her student loans. She hadn't even thought about saving money for a baby. For someone who'd always had a plan for everything, she couldn't have been less prepared for what was happening to her.

Panic hounded her as she made her way out of the clinic. It was unusually warm for September, and as she crossed the parking lot in search of her car she found herself breathing heavily. For the first time in a very long time she felt like the little girl who'd lost her way the day she found out her mother had died. She raised her eyes heavenward and said, "Oh, Mom. I wish you were here. I don't know where to turn."

But her mom wasn't there and the woman who'd tried to fill her shoes was also the grandmother of her baby. Although Nancy Collier might be the one person who could be the family support she needed, Paige couldn't turn to her. Not until she'd talked to Justin, and she wasn't ready to tell him about the baby. She wasn't ready to tell anyone. She needed time to think about what she should do.

The one thing she wasn't going to do was cry. She'd done enough of that the past few weeks and for no good reason.

She straightened, took a deep breath and blew it out. She needed a plan. Right now that plan wouldn't include anybody but her and her baby. If losing her mother at such an early age had taught her anything, it was that she could take care of herself. And she would do just that.

But what about Justin? a tiny voice in her head asked. He'd always been the one she called whenever she needed to talk to a friend. If it were Michael's baby, she wouldn't have hesitated confiding in him. But it wasn't Michael who was the father. It was Justin, and she didn't know what his reaction would be. And right now in the emotional state she was in, she couldn't risk having him treat their unborn child in the same manner in which he had treated their night together— as if it was something casual and unimportant.

That's why she wasn't going to tell him anything until she'd figured out what she was going to do. If she was lucky, when she arrived home she would be able to go straight to her room without seeing Justin or Kyle.

Unfortunately luck wasn't with her outside the doctor's office, either. When she turned onto Grand Avenue she saw the Colliers' Buick parked in front of the house. She frowned. Of all the days to have to see Justin's parents.

When she walked through the back door and into the kitchen, she saw Nancy and Elliot at the kitchen table drinking coffee with Kyle and Justin.

"This is a surprise," Paige said, setting her school tote down on the kitchen counter. Anxiety made her mouth dry so she grabbed a bottle of water from the refrigerator before joining them at the table.

"Mom and Dad brought back the table they borrowed for

the party. We were thinking it might be nice to have dinner at that Mexican place just down the road," Justin said. "Want to join us?"

The last thing Paige wanted to do right now was eat, and spending any time at all with the Colliers would be stressful, considering the circumstances.

"Oh, gosh, I'd like to but I have a ton of papers to grade." She looked at Nancy and said, "You know how it is when school's in session."

"Oh, I certainly do, but I also know you have to eat," Nancy said in a motherly tone.

Paige avoided looking at Justin. "I'll just grab a sandwich by myself. Don't worry about it. But Kyle and Justin can go."

"We're not going to go without you," Justin spoke up.

"Why don't we get takeout?" Nancy suggested. "That way Paige can be with us but it won't take up so much of her time."

"No, you're not going to do that just because of me," she protested. "Besides, what makes the food taste so great is the atmosphere. The Mexican place has the mariachi music and the piñatas hanging from the ceiling."

"I vote for takeout," Kyle said. The other three agreed, and before Paige knew it, Justin was taking everyone's order and left with his father to pick up the food.

Paige was grateful that Kyle had stayed behind with Nancy. At least she didn't have to worry about the conversation turning to her personal life. They talked mostly about the birthday party and the vacation plans Nancy and Elliot had for a winter getaway.

When Paige's cell phone rang, her heart missed a beat as she worried that it could be Michael. She excused herself from the kitchen to take the call in the living room. When she flipped open the phone and saw that it was one of her colleagues, relief spread through her. She didn't want to talk to Michael. The suspicion of pregnancy had shoved his phone message yesterday to the back of her brain and that was where she wanted it to stay. The debate in her mind no longer was whether or not she should call him back, but what she was going to do now that she was pregnant.

By the time she'd finished talking to her coworker, the guys had returned with dinner. Unfortunately, one whiff of the spicy Mexican food made Paige's stomach want to revolt when she stepped into the kitchen. She excused herself, made a hasty exit and went up to her room, where she fell onto the bed and willed her stomach to calm down. She hadn't been there long when a knock sounded at the door. It was Nancy.

"The guys are worried about you. Are you okay?"

Paige forced herself to sit up but the nausea returned and she had to lie back down. "I think I must have a touch of a flu bug. I'm not going to be able to eat dinner."

Nancy sat down next to her on the bed and placed her hand on her forehead. "You don't feel warm. Would you like me to bring you something? Maybe some soda to settle your stomach?"

She shook her head. "I think I just need to rest."

"Why don't I get you some water?" As she reached for the glass on the nightstand, her fingers bumped the velvet box containing Paige's engagement ring. As Nancy's eyes met hers, Paige saw the unasked question in them.

"He said I could keep it," she told her.

Nancy simply said, "I'll get the water." She disappeared and returned with a full glass.

Paige took a long drink, then set the glass back on the nightstand, pushing the ring box aside.

"Oh—I brought you this." Nancy produced the large tote Paige used for her school materials.

Noticing it was unzipped, Paige said, "I'll take it." She reached for the black bag just as Nancy set it on the bed and it went tumbling to the floor. Some of its contents spilled out onto the carpet. Paige scrambled off the bed to retrieve the pamphlets from the doctor's office, but not before Nancy had seen them.

There was a silence, then Paige said, "No, it's not the flu. I'm pregnant."

"And how do you feel about that?"

"Scared," she answered honestly, sinking back onto the bed. Nancy sat down beside her. "That's normal. I was scared, too."

"But you were married."

"I know, but I remember what it was like when the doctor told me the news. I was happy yet scared out of my mind." She looked at Paige. "Are you happy?"

"No," she answered honestly. "I haven't had time to be anything but scared. I just found out today."

"So you're still in shock."

She nodded. "I'm single. I don't even have a boyfriend, let alone a husband."

"That might change once the father hears about it."

She shook her head. "I doubt it."

"But you are going to tell him, aren't you?"

"Yes. I have to, but right now I just need time to accept that it's true."

"I understand."

Paige was grateful that she didn't inquire as to the father's identity. Kyle yelled up the stairs, reminding them the food was getting cold. "You should go downstairs and eat," she urged Nancy. "I'll be fine."

"What should I tell them?"

"That I think I have the flu. It's really important they don't know about this yet."

"You know I'd never say anything. You're the one having the baby. You should be the one to tell people."

"Thank you," Paige muttered softly.

"Should I come back up before I leave?"

"I'd like that," Paige said.

If she did return after dinner, Paige didn't know. She fell asleep and didn't awaken until the middle of the night when she got up and showered. She went back to bed, hoping that the symptoms of pregnancy went away soon, or she was not going to be able to keep her secret much longer.

"LOOK WHAT CAME in today's mail." Kyle held up two identical envelopes for Justin's inspection when he arrived home from work the following afternoon. "I'm hoping it's the news we've been waiting for." He handed one to Justin and kept the other, which he tore open. A broad smile spread across his face. "Looks like the nursery seminar in Oregon is a go."

Justin opened his envelope and found the same confirmation of acceptance into the continuing-education program.

"How's that for great news?" Kyle said with a beaming grin. "Do you know how much this is going to help us choose the right trees to plant?"

"Yeah, it'll be great. We need to talk to Paige, though. She wasn't happy that we didn't tell her about this when we applied in August," Justin said, remembering her reaction at his father's birthday party.

"I thought you were going to talk to her after the party."

"I was but she was already in bed by the time I got home. Then last night my parents were here and Paige went to bed early." He didn't tell Kyle that he had a pretty good hunch that she was avoiding him.

"You told her why we didn't tell her, didn't you?"

"Yeah, but that didn't make much difference. She's not happy with us."

"She just hasn't been herself lately. I thought she was over that zero Michael."

"I think she is," Justin said, although he knew it was probably wishful thinking on his part. "You know Paige. She's never been one to dwell on what's past."

"I tried to talk to her about him, but she just closes up. It could be that she's getting over him. Tammy did say that she saw her with some guy at the Olive Garden last week and she looked like she was having a good time."

Paige with another guy? Justin wondered why she hadn't said anything to him about seeing someone. In the past she'd always told him when she met a new guy, but ever since the Bulldog Reunion she'd said very little about her personal life. He wanted to think it was because she'd been so busy with school, but he worried there was another reason. They were in a place no couple wanted to be—more than friends but less than lovers.

"By the way, this was also in the mail." Kyle slid an envelope across the table. "It's the house phone bill. Do you think maybe we should cancel it? It's not like we need it. We each have our own cell phones."

"Makes sense to me," Justin said.

"I'm going to take a shower. Tammy and I are going to a concert tonight. Later." He started up the stairs. "Hey—Paige said the kitchen faucet's dripping. I think it's your turn for repairs."

Justin rubbed his hand across the back of his neck. "Yeah,

I'll do it," he said on a note of resignation. Ever since he and Kyle had bought the house they'd been taking turns with the maintenance projects. Even though he was tired from a long day's digging trees, he pulled his toolbox from the back of his pickup and crawled under the kitchen sink.

That's where he was when the house phone rang, a wrench in one hand, a flashlight in the other as he stared at a dismantled water pipe. There was no way he could get to the phone so he let the answering machine pick up.

Expecting it to be some telemarketer, he was surprised to hear, "Paige, it's Michael. I need to talk to you. It's important. I realize now what a mistake it was for me to put my career ahead of you. I know I hurt you and I'm sorry. Please call me. We need to talk."

The answering machine double beeped, indicating Michael's message had been recorded. Justin heard the tape rewinding and then silence. He dropped the wrench and shimmied out of the cupboard. Had he heard the message correctly? Had Michael Cross said it was a mistake to put his career ahead of her? He wiped his hands on a rag, then walked over and pressed the play button. After listening a second time, he wasn't any less angry than he'd been the first time. Who did the guy think he was that he could jilt Paige then call six weeks later and act as if he hadn't left her for another woman but because of a job?

Justin knew that if he didn't replay the messages now and take down the number, as soon as another call came in and no one answered, Michael's voice mail would be recorded over and lost for good.

And what if it was? Justin thought. Michael had caused enough trouble in Paige's life. She didn't need any more. He couldn't believe that she would want to even talk to the guy, so it made sense that she wouldn't want to know he'd called. Or would she? It was a question he debated in his mind until Kyle came back into the kitchen.

"Did you get the faucet fixed?" he asked when he saw the sink cupboard doors open and the tools on the floor.

"No, I was interrupted by a phone call," Justin answered.

"Not another telemarketer, I hope."

Justin didn't answer directly. "I think you're right. We should disconnect the land phone. What's the point in paying for nuisance calls?"

"I'll mention it to Paige. I think I hear her car now." He pushed the curtain aside to peek out the window. "Yup, she's home."

"Hey—you're just the person we want to see," Kyle greeted her with a smile when she walked through the door.

She was all business, barely giving either of them a glance. "If you need something, write me a note, will you? I have a ton of papers to correct." When she would have hurried up the stairs, Kyle stopped her.

"Whoa, whoa, whoa. Don't go running off. This is important."

She glanced at the clock then dropped her tote bag onto the table and sank onto a chair. "Okay. Start talking. The meter's ticking."

He briefly explained about the phone and she objected to canceling the landline. "That might be fine for you guys, but my school uses the house number to contact me, and besides, you guys are going to be gone. I'm the one who's going to be here using it."

Justin felt an enormous wave of guilt. He looked at the answering machine and saw the light was steady, not blinking. There would be no reason for Paige to hit the play button. Now would have been his opportunity to say that Michael had called, but he couldn't bring himself to do it. He remembered what breaking up with the guy had done to her emotionally and he didn't want to see her hurt anymore. So he stayed silent.

"Justin told you about our trip to Oregon, right?" Kyle asked.

Paige sent Justin that disappointed look she always gave him whenever he'd let her down. "No, he didn't. He got trapped and had to fess up. I wouldn't call it an explanation."

"You haven't exactly been around much lately," Justin pointed out.

"I've been working," she said defensively.

Kyle raised both of his hands in the air. "Hey—there's no need to get excited." He looked at Paige. "We're sorry we didn't say anything to you before now, but we knew you've been in a bad way over Michael."

"Just because my engagement is called off you think you don't have to tell me you're taking on a business partner, spending the winter in Oregon and maybe selling the house, to boot?" She was so worked up her cheeks were flushed. "In case you didn't notice, I'm not an emotional cripple because some loser walks out on me."

"We didn't think you were an emotional cripple," Justin said.

"Then you should have told me months ago what you were planning. I thought our friendship was based on honesty at all costs?"

Then Kyle did what he always did whenever Paige was angry at the two of them. He blamed Justin. "I wanted to tell you but Justin thought it would be better to wait."

Justin shoved his hand to his hips. "Now that's just flat out not true." He could see by the look on Paige's face that she didn't believe him.

"You're the one who wanted to keep it a secret?" she

accused him. "I guess that shouldn't surprise me. You're good at keeping secrets, aren't you?"

Kyle confronted him. "What's she talking about? Are you two keeping a secret I should know about?"

Justin didn't answer, which he realized only made him look guilty. The situation was deteriorating rapidly, and before it could get any worse, he said, "Look. We've all been friends long enough to know that there are going to be times when we disagree about stuff—"

"Disagree?" Paige shot back at him with fire in her eyes. "This is more than a disagreement."

"Would somebody please tell me what is going on? This is obviously about more than us going to Oregon for the winter." Kyle stood with hands on his hips, confronting the two of them.

Paige reached for her tote and hoisted it up to her shoulder. "You know what? I'm glad you two are leaving. I need a break from our friendship." Then she stormed out of the room.

"Paige, wait!" Justin went after her but she was too quick for him. She was up the stairs and had slammed the bedroom door shut before he could follow her inside. He knocked on the door but she refused to answer. "Paige, will you please talk to me?"

The only sound he heard was the Sheryl Crow album she'd put on her CD player. He went back downstairs to the kitchen, where Kyle sat at the table.

"Well, that went well," Justin said with a thick layer of sarcasm. "Why did you tell her it was my idea not to mention the Oregon trip?"

"Because I knew she'd forgive you or at least I thought she would. She always has in the past. I'm the one she likes to blame for everything. I can't believe she's upset over this. I mean, it's not like she'll mind staying here alone."

"She's upset because we didn't touch base with her when making our plans." Justin understood perfectly well why she had reacted the way she had. Regret filled every corner of his brain. He should have told her what was going on. Should have but didn't, because they'd been tap-dancing around each other, acting as if nothing was wrong between them, trying not to feel awkward. He sighed heavily.

"She had moved out and was planning a wedding! Sheesh. I will never understand women." Kyle shook his head. "And what was all that stuff about keeping secrets? You two were at each other's throats the whole time we were at the Cascading Waters. What aren't you telling me?"

Justin thought about lying, but Paige was right. What good was their friendship if there were secrets between them? Yet he was reluctant to tell Kyle without Paige's knowledge. "It's personal."

"That's all you're going to tell me—that it's personal?"

"Because it is. It's nothing for you to worry about. The problem is between me and Paige."

"So you do have a problem. I wasn't imagining things."

"Yes, but we're trying to get things back to the way they used to be."

"Is this about her breakup with Michael Cross?"

"Can we just drop it?"

"You tell me the two of you have a secret that is personal and you expect me to drop it?"

"Yes, because you're my friend and that's what friends do. They respect each other's wishes and trust them to make the right decision."

"But there aren't supposed to be secrets between the three of us," he argued. "What could possibly be so personal that you can't tell me? I'm your best friend."

"I know. And I will tell you, but first I need to talk to Paige. Will you let me do that?"

To his relief, Kyle said, "All right." But Justin had a pretty good idea that it wasn't right at all. "I'll see if Paige feels the same way." He left the room and went up the stairs. Justin could only hope that she would tell him the same thing he'd told Kyle—that it was a personal issue between the two of them.

A short while later Kyle came back down the stairs. "She wouldn't answer the door. I've got to go meet Tammy. I guess we'll have to finish all this later."

"Later," Justin said as his friend left the house. He made one more effort to get Paige to talk to him, but silence greeted him when he knocked on her door. Kyle was right about one thing. She could be stubborn.

He went back downstairs and did what he always did whenever they had words. He left her a note.

When you're tired of being on a break, let me know. I miss you. J.

CHAPTER NINE

BY THE END OF THE WEEK Paige had added another symptom to the growing list of signs that she was pregnant. She had started having cravings for foods she normally didn't eat. One of them was watermelon, which was why she stopped at a produce market on her way home from work.

She'd had an unusually tiring week in the classroom and was relieved to come home and find she had the house to herself. She cut off a chunk of the melon, grabbed a bag of onion-and-garlic potato chips and went upstairs. It was time to pull out the packet of information the doctor had given her and make a plan. She was over the initial shock of discovering she was going to have a baby. Now she needed to act.

As she alternated between bites of watermelon and potato chips, she read about taking care of herself and her baby. She took notes and wrote down questions, then went online to the referenced Web sites to learn as much as she could about the next seven or so months. By typing in her due date she was able to create a calendar with animated illustrations that showed the physical changes that would occur during the entire nine months. For Paige it was like a window into her pregnancy. Seeing the pictures of an unborn fetus developing from a small cell into a full-term baby made her realize what an amazing event was taking place inside her. Gradually, her fears began to fade away.

When she saw a link to a site for single expectant moms, she didn't hesitate to move her mouse and double-click on it. There she found a list of articles that included, "When marrying the father isn't a possibility, what to expect in child support from the father, and what you will need to live on your own." Paige didn't read any of them.

She didn't want to be a single mom. She wanted her baby to have a full-time father and a house with a fenced-in yard and aunts and uncles and grandparents. That's why the only piece of advice she took from the Web site was this: "If you're going to be a single mom, you're going to need help. Start talking with friends and family."

It sounded so simple. Two months ago she never would have imagined she'd have trouble talking to Justin or Kyle. Until this summer they had had the kind of friendship others envied—open and trusting. Now she and Justin were keeping a secret from Kyle, and she was keeping her pregnancy from both of them.

With good reason, she reminded herself. It was the kind of secret that could change their relationship forever. She was afraid of what the revelation that she and Justin had slept together would do to their friendship. And of course she had to tell Justin about her pregnancy first. She also knew that her pregnancy would eventually reveal itself and that the longer she waited to talk to them, the more difficult it would be to try to repair the damage that had already been done.

That's why the following morning she went downstairs with the intention of telling Justin she was going to have a baby. When she walked into the kitchen he was alone at the table reading the morning newspaper as he ate his usual breakfast—a bowl of cereal and a glass of orange juice.

"Where's Kyle?" she asked, pulling the remainder of the watermelon from the refrigerator.

"I don't think he came home last night," he answered with a lift of his brows.

"Oh." She cut a slice of melon. "Do you want some?" she asked, noticing his interest.

"No, but since when do you like watermelon?"

She thought about blurting out, "Since I became pregnant," but decided to break the news to him gently. "Since yesterday," she answered. She sat down across from him at the table. "I'm glad you're up this morning, because I want to talk to you."

He folded his newspaper and gave her his undivided attention. "Good, because I've been wanting to talk to you, too."

"I know. First I want to say I'm sorry about the other night. You know I'm not the kind to storm out like that, but lately I haven't been myself. But I've had time to think and I want to behave like an adult, not a petulant child."

"You have a legitimate complaint. Kyle and I should have told you our plans long before now. You are a silent partner in the business and we did invite you to live with us. I'm sorry we weren't more considerate of your feelings."

His apology was so unexpected it brought a tear to her eye. "Oh, it's so sweet of you to say that." She sniffled, which had him giving her another strange look. "I shouldn't have reacted the way I did. You don't need my permission to go to Oregon."

"No, but that's not the point. We should have talked to you about it."

"Are you going to sell the house?"

"We're not going to sell it out from underneath you," he said with a hint of indignation. "We'd never do that. Actually I was hoping that you might want to stay here this winter while we're gone. You know, house-sit. You wouldn't have to pay any rent in exchange for taking care of the place for us."

The offer was an attractive one, especially since Paige had been trying to figure out a new budget that included a baby. She knew, however, that at some point she was going to have to get her own place.

"I could do that, but I eventually want to get my own place."

He frowned. "Is this because of what happened between us?"

"Yes," she said candidly. "There's no point in pretending that things haven't changed, is there?"

He shook his head. "After you went upstairs the other night, Kyle asked me what the big secret was between us."

"And did you tell him?"

"Of course not. I wouldn't do that without you knowing about it. But I have to tell you, Paige. He suspects something's going on and I think it's only a matter of time until he figures out what it is."

"You're right. He's going to know. I've done a lot of thinking in the past few days, and if there's one thing that I don't want to live with, it's keeping secrets. Especially between you, me and Kyle. We've been close friends for too long."

"Yes, we have."

"That's why I need to tell you something. You've probably noticed a few changes in me lately...like I've been emotional." She stabbed at a chunk of her watermelon and said, "And I like this stuff."

"There's a connection between you crying a lot and liking watermelon?" He looked puzzled.

"As a matter of fact, there is." She ate the bite of fruit before saying, "Remember Monday night when your parents were here and I didn't eat dinner because I thought I was getting the flu?" When he nodded, she said, "It wasn't the flu."

"What was it?" he asked before taking a drink of his orange juice.

"I'm pregnant."

He began to choke and reached for a napkin. "That's not funny, Paige," he said when he'd cleared his throat.

"It wasn't meant to be funny."

His face paled. "You're serious."

She nodded and what little color was left in his face seeped away. "I took two in-home pregnancy tests."

"Those things aren't always accurate, are they?"

"I went to the doctor also," she added quietly.

"Damn." He slammed his clenched fist on the table. "I can't believe we did it without protection."

She kept her eyes on the watermelon, feeling an awkwardness that was totally illogical. She'd been as intimate as a woman could be with a man, yet she was embarrassed to be talking about contraception.

He squeezed his eyes shut and grimaced. "I can't believe this is happening. The one time I get a little careless—the only time I am careless—and this?" He threw his hands up in frustration. "How could I have been so stupid. I'm twenty-nine, not nineteen. I know better than to take chances when it comes to sex."

"It's just as much my fault. When you said you didn't have a condom I could have refused to do it." She wasn't sure that was quite true.

"You'd been drinking, Paige."

"Justin, I knew what I was doing and so did you. I thought we'd moved beyond blaming that night on alcohol."

Which was why she was having a hard time accepting that night had happened at all. At least if she'd been drunk she'd have had an excuse for her behavior. But the truth was, she had turned to Justin seeking comfort. And once she'd found it in his arms she'd discovered she liked it. A lot. *That's* why simply being around him now made her uncomfortably aware of his masculinity. For weeks she'd been avoiding him and hoping that with time things wouldn't be awkward between them, but now she realized that might never happen.

"Damn," he muttered, then without another word got up and left the room. She had a pretty good idea where he had gone. One of the bedrooms on the first floor of the house had been converted into an exercise and weight room. Hanging from the ceiling was a punching bag. For as long as she'd known Justin he'd taken his anger and frustration out on the bag. Judging by the faint sound of fist hitting leather, she figured that was where he was now.

He wasn't gone long. When he returned, Paige asked, "Feel better?"

"Not really." He sat down across from her again. "You're one hundred percent positive about this, right?"

"I saw a doctor on Monday," she said soberly.

He grimaced, running a hand across his neck and down his right shoulder as if massaging a sore muscle. "Damn," he said a second time.

"I know it's a shock," she told him. "I've had several days to absorb it and I still find myself wondering if it can possibly be true. We messed up big-time, Justin." Her voice cracked with emotion.

He reached across the table to cover her hands with his. "I'm sorry, Paige. I never meant for this to happen. I should never have let that night happen."

"I'm just as much at fault as you are," she said on a sigh, brushing a lock of her hair back from her face.

"That's not what you were saying the weekend of the Bulldog Reunion," he reminded her with a wry grin.

"No, I wanted to blame you. It made it feel less wrong somehow. But now it doesn't seem to matter why it happened."

"No, we need to focus on the problem, not the cause," he said pragmatically.

Hearing him refer to her baby as a problem reminded her of just how little emotional connection he had to her and her unborn child. She hadn't expected it would be any different, so why did his attitude make her want to cry?

"You don't need to focus on anything," she said with a sniffle. "I'll handle it."

"Don't be ridiculous. It's my problem, too."

"Don't say that," she said with a wobbly voice. "No baby should be called a problem. Babies are supposed to be gifts." As hard as she tried, she couldn't prevent the tears from pooling in her eyes.

"You're not going to start bawling on me, are you?"

"I can't help it. It's my hormones."

Justin came around to her side of the table and pulled her up into his arms, but she took one whiff of his cologne and pushed him away from her. She made a dash for the bathroom on the first floor, reaching it without a moment to spare. She splashed cold water on her face as she waited for the nausea to subside. When she saw Justin's jean-clad legs out of the corner of her eye, she said, "Don't come any closer."

"I want to help you," he said.

"Then go away," she said, leaning up against the cold porcelain sink. "I get sick when I smell certain things. Your cologne is one of them."

"Are you sure you're okay?" he asked from the doorway.

She nodded. "I'll be fine. I get these moments of sickness, but they pass. Please, go back to the kitchen." She was relieved when he did as she requested.

Paige dampened a washcloth and held it across her forehead. It didn't take long before the nausea abated and she was ready to face Justin. It was one of the things about her pregnancy that puzzled her—how she could feel so sick one minute, then as good as new the next. When she returned to the kitchen Justin had moved his chair as far away from hers as possible. He sat with a hint of a grin on his face.

"What's so funny?" she asked.

"I was just thinking about when we were kids and you'd get so mad at me that you'd say, 'You make me sick.' Never did I think the day would come when that would truly be the case."

"You won't make me sick if you throw out that bottle of cologne," she said, getting a drink of water before sitting down.

"Consider it done. I can't have the mother of my kid puking every time I come near her."

She stopped abruptly, her glass in midair. "Did you hear what you just said?"

As if he suddenly realized his own words, he said, "Yeah, the mother of my kid. We're going to be parents."

She nodded soberly. "Yes, we are. Do you think we'll be any good at it?"

"As good as anybody else."

She sank back down on the kitchen chair with a sigh. "Then you think I should have the baby?"

She held her breath as she waited for his answer. "Is there any other option for you?"

She shook her head.

"Then we'll become parents," he stated positively.

As hard as she tried, she couldn't stop the tears. Again he got up and left the room, but this time when he returned he carried a box of tissues. He set it down on the table in front of her. She blew her nose and swallowed back the rest of the tears.

"You know, I'm trying to keep things on an upbeat note

here," he told her. "It doesn't help if you're going to be crying every five minutes."

She dabbed at her eyes with a tissue. "Sorry. I told you. It's hormonal."

"I figured that. You've cried more in the last half hour than you've done in the past twenty years."

"I can't help it. The tears just come whether I want them to or not."

"I can imagine how much you hate that."

"You're right. I do." She took a sip of water. "We need to look on the bright side."

"Is there a bright side?" he asked.

"Of course there is. I don't know about you, but I'm going to make the best of this situation. I'm choosing to be positive."

A grin slowly spread across his face, crinkling the corners of his eyes. "Now that's the Paige I know and love."

He'd been telling her he loved her for years but it was always said with the affection of one friend to another. Today was no different. So why was she wishing it could be any other way? It must have been her hormones that had her wanting his words to carry the same sentiment that a guy in love expresses to his girlfriend.

"We're going to get through this," he told her from the opposite end of the table.

"Yes, we will because we're friends," she said with a confidence she wasn't feeling. "That's what's important."

"I would come over there and take your hands but I don't want you barfing on me."

"Real funny, J.C." The nickname brought another smile to his face. "So now you know."

His face sobered. "Yes, now I know. Do you have any plans for today?"

"Just to get caught up on my sleep. That's another one of the side effects—I'm tired all the time."

"So that's why you've been falling asleep on the sofa lately. Kyle thought it was all the long hours at school."

"That doesn't help. What are we going to do about Kyle?" She wondered how they were ever going to be able to tell him the truth.

"Having a baby isn't the kind of secret you can keep indefinitely, Paige," he said gently.

"I know, but it's going to be so hard to tell him. I don't know what I'm going to say to him."

"We'll do it together."

"When?"

He shrugged. "I don't know. We have a little time before you start to look as if you're having a baby, don't we?"

"Yes, but the longer we put off telling him, the angrier he's going to be."

"Do you want to tell him this weekend?"

"No." She was having enough trouble getting used to the idea of being pregnant. She wasn't ready to share her doubts and fears with anyone but Justin.

"Then we'll wait," he assured her. "You're looking a little pale. Are you sure you're okay?"

"No, I'm not okay," she snapped, then immediately regretted sounding like such a witch. "I'm sorry," she apologized, hanging her head in her hands. "But this is such a mess. I can't believe this has happened to us. There are so many things to consider."

"Then we'll consider every one of them. You can take your time. We're not, like, having this baby for a long time yet, are we?"

"No. It's due around the first of May," she answered.

"That's good. Kyle and I will be home by then."

He still planned to go to Oregon. So what had she expected? It didn't matter that she was pregnant and might need him. He'd made his plans with Kyle and he was going to go through with them. She should have expected as much. He and Kyle had gone off on plenty of adventures and not once had they allowed a woman to interfere with their plans.

While anger and disappointment simmered inside her, he added, "It's probably a good thing that we're going away because it'll give you a chance to prepare for the baby without us hanging around."

"Are you serious?"

"Why? What's wrong with that?"

She threw up her hands in frustration. "Oh, good grief. If I have to tell you then I'm lucky you're leaving, because you don't have a clue what happens to a woman when she's pregnant." She walked out of the kitchen and up the stairs to her bedroom, where she slammed the door.

She waited to hear the sound of his footsteps on the stairs, but they never came. What she heard was the purring of his pickup as he rolled out of the driveway. The noise faded away as he drove down the street. He was gone.

She placed her hand on her stomach and spoke softly, "So how do you like what you've seen of your parents so far? Not too cool, you say? Yeah, that's what I think, too. Hopefully by the time you arrive, the situation will have improved."

PAIGE DIDN'T SEE Justin the rest of the day. When her father called and suggested she have supper with him and Mary because he had something he wanted to discuss with her, she accepted the invitation and told him she had something she wanted to tell him, too. She'd taken care of the first name on her list of people to be told about her pregnancy. Her father was next. Maybe Justin wasn't going to be around to provide support to her during her pregnancy, but at least her father would be there for her.

They'd never been very close, not even before her mother died. People assumed that with the death of her mother, the bond between father and daughter would be strengthened.

But that hadn't happened. Paige and her father knew why. No matter how many conversations they had, how often they agreed to forgive and forget, the past haunted them. Paige's mother haunted them.

Still, she wanted her child to have a grandfather. And she wanted to keep their father/daughter bond—no matter how fragile it was—intact. That's why she was going to tell him about the baby at dinner. It didn't matter that Mary Adelmann would be there.

She decided to wait until dinner was over just in case there was a chance that her father did find the news upsetting. She expected that when she did tell him he would offer to do whatever he could to help her out. She hadn't lived with her father since her college days, but she wasn't ruling out the possibility that she might have to move back in with him for a short time before the baby was born.

Just as Justin and Kyle's house was big, her father's was small. As Paige sat in the tiny dining area she noticed how cluttered it was. He'd added some new pieces of furniture since she'd been there, including a cherry-wood hutch that took up nearly one-half of the dining-room wall. When Mary pulled three china dessert plates from inside the glass cabinet, Paige asked, "Did you get a new hutch, Dad?"

"No, it's Mary's. Would you pass the sugar, please?" He

pointed toward the small china bowl near Paige's water goblet. "She thought we might as well be eating off her good dishes."

"No point in saving them," Mary added with a chuckle.

"And since we needed a place to keep the china," her father continued, "we decided we might as well bring over the hutch, too."

We. It should have been a tip-off to Paige. Along with the new drapes on the living-room windows. And the way Mary's hand touched her father's shoulder whenever she passed him. But Paige was too absorbed in her own situation to recognize what was right before her eyes.

"So we both have news," he said cheerfully as they finished the remaining bites of the strawberry shortcake Mary had made. "Who's going to go first? You or me?"

Paige dabbed at her lips with a napkin. "You go," she said, feeling suddenly nervous.

"All right," her father said with a glance toward Mary. "The reason I wanted you here tonight is because I have something to tell you. I've decided to retire at the end of the year."

"That's great news, Dad," Paige said with a lift of her water goblet. "Congratulations. You've certainly earned it."

"Yes, he has," Mary seconded. "He's spent more nights in hotels than anyone I know."

"It's the nature of the job—can't make the lumber sales if you're not willing to travel," her father said with a wink.

Paige knew all too well how many hours her father had spent away from home. It was the reason she'd spent so many hours at the Colliers', and why her parents had argued that night her mother died. It seemed as if he was always gone.

"So what are you going to do with all your free time?" Paige wanted to know. "Since you've been on the road so much throughout your career, you probably want to stay home."

"No, not me," he said with a grin. "I can't wait to get in the car and drive without having anything on my mind except having a good time."

"Really?" Paige was surprised by his answer. "You're not going to become a snowbird, are you?"

"Not unless my new bride wants me to," her father answered.

Paige momentarily froze, wondering if she had heard him correctly.

But then he said, "I've asked Mary to be my wife and she's accepted."

Paige hoped her face didn't show how stunned she was by the news. Although Mary had been like a part of the family for over eight years, Paige never thought there was anything but friendship between their neighbor and her father.

Somehow she managed to smile and say, "That's wonderful, Dad. I'm really happy for you...for both of you." She pushed back her chair and walked around the table to give Mary a hug. "My father's a lucky man."

"Thank you, Paige. I'm so glad you approve. I know it's been a long time since you lost your mother and you probably never expected your father to marry again."

Paige shook her head. "I didn't."

"She didn't think anyone would want an old coot like me," her father said good-naturedly.

"That's not it at all," Paige insisted, noticing for the first time how young her father looked. Maybe it was the knowledge that he was retiring that had erased the lines on his face. Or maybe it was his love for Mary. Whatever it was, he looked happy.

"Paige probably remembers how devoted you were to her mother and didn't see how you'd ever want to take a chance at finding happiness with anyone else," Mary suggested.

Paige didn't want to tell Mary how wrong she was about

her parents' marriage. To the outside world they might have appeared to be a happy couple, but Paige knew differently. But it wasn't her place to inform her father's fiancée about the state of his previous marriage. "I guess I could say the same thing about you and your husband, Mary."

Mary smiled wistfully. "My Frank was a keeper—just like your mother. It's because we both had such good marriages that we're willing to take another chance." She glanced affectionately at Paige's father.

Paige was relieved when talk turned to possible venues for the wedding, which had already been set for the end of October. She thought she did a good job of pretending not to be shocked by the news, but it had caught her off guard. Ever since she'd learned she was going to have a baby she'd felt as if she was setting out on an uncertain journey. Now one of the parts she'd thought would be a constant was no longer going to be there.

Later, as her father walked her to her car, he said, "We spent so much time talking about wedding plans I just realized that you didn't get a chance to tell us your news. What is it?"

Suddenly Paige felt as if the timing was wrong for her to tell her dad that he was going to be a grandfather. He was making plans to start a new life with Mary. She didn't want to make him feel that he needed to help her out and she certainly wasn't going to ask him if she could move in with him and Mary until she found a place for her and the baby.

"Oh, it was nothing," she said with a flap of her hand.

"Do you need money?"

"No," she answered quickly.

"I know you sank a lot of money into a wedding that didn't happen," he said. "If you need a little extra cash until you get settled in that new job, I can help you out."

She shook her head, her throat blocked with emotion.

"Are you sure you're okay with me getting married again?"

"Why wouldn't I be?"

He shrugged. "That's what I'm asking you. Mary might not have noticed, but I saw how uncomfortable you were when we were talking about marriage in there." He jerked his head toward the house.

"That was surprise on my face. I thought you and Mary were just friends."

"We were for a very long time and then things changed, but you don't need to hear the boring details of the romance of someone my age," he said with a dismissive wave of his hand. "I'm not sure how we got to where we are, but it's good, Paige. It's not what I had with your mother, but it's good."

"I hope it's not what you had with Mom. Mary deserves better." Paige couldn't keep the bitterness from her voice.

"Ah. So that's what this is all about. It's been almost twenty years, Paige. How long are you going to punish me for your mother's death?"

"I'm not punishing you," she denied, growing more uneasy with their conversation by the minute.

"I'm worried about you, Paige."

"You don't need to be. I can take care of myself."

"I know that, but you should be married."

"Yes, well, it helps to have the right man to marry," she pointed out with a touch of cynicism.

"There's a right one out there for you, but I'm worried you won't find him because you're too afraid."

"Afraid?" She laughed without humor. "Dad, I'm not afraid of men. I've dated lots of guys...I was even engaged to one and would have been married if he hadn't dumped me."

"None of them was the right one, Paige," he said as if he

were imparting wisdom. "Not even Michael. You chose them because they were safe."

"That's ridiculous."

"Is it?" He leaned back and stared at her for several moments before continuing. "To love somebody you need to take a risk."

"Why are you telling me this?"

"Because I'm worried that you're letting what happened to your mother keep you from taking that risk. That's why you've chosen men who were safe. Because you've been afraid to risk losing your heart to someone who might break it."

She swallowed with difficulty. "You mean the way you broke Mom's?"

"I never wanted to hurt your mother, Paige. I loved her."

She didn't want to be having this conversation. Not tonight. "Good night, Dad," she said, and climbed into her car.

As PAIGE PREPARED for bed later that night she looked at her pregnancy plan. She crossed off the possibility of moving back home with her father. Finding a place of her own or staying with Justin and Kyle were the other two options.

She glanced at the clock. It was ten o'clock and she hadn't seen Justin all day. As happened so often late in the evening, she felt both nauseated and hungry. She still didn't understand how a person could be both at one time, but she went downstairs in search of relief.

She found it in the freezer. She opened a pint of double-fudge ice cream. She didn't need a bowl but ate it straight from the carton. She was sitting there alone in the kitchen in her pajamas when Justin returned.

The first thing he said to her when he walked in was "I'm not going to Oregon."

"Why not?"

"You know the answer to that question."

"Hey—I'm not going to lay any guilt trip on you. You want to go to Oregon, you can go. I can take care of myself." She tried to make her voice sound disinterested, but she knew she had failed.

"I told you. I don't want to go."

"That's not what you said earlier," she reminded him.

"Yeah, well, earlier you dumped a pretty big news flash on me. Maybe my reaction wasn't what it should have been, but it took me a while to process all of this." He looked tired and his jeans had dried mud on the legs.

"Where have you been all day?"

"At the nursery."

She watched as he unlaced his work boots and tossed them into the garage. "You were working?"

"I do some of my best thinking when I'm with the trees," he told her. "And I've been doing a lot of thinking. Actually it feels like that's all I did today. Can I have some of that?" He pointed to the ice cream.

"Grab a spoon," she said.

He did and sat down at the table. She pushed the ice-cream carton closer to him so they could share.

"How was your day?" he asked.

"Okay. I found out my dad's getting married."

"To Mary?"

"Mmm, hmm."

"Wow. That's cool. She's a nice lady."

"I'll tell them you're happy for them," she said with a dose of sarcasm.

"Aren't you?"

"It's not that I'm unhappy, it's just…" She paused, wondering how to explain all the emotions her father's news had stirred inside her.

"You don't think your dad deserves a second chance at happiness because he was unfaithful to your mom?"

"I don't want to talk about that," she said, digging deeper into the ice cream. "If you must know, I was hoping that maybe I could move back home with my dad—at least until the baby came. Now I know I can't."

His spoon stopped in midair. "I thought it was settled that you're staying here."

"Do you really think Kyle is going to want me around once he finds out what happened?"

"The house is half mine, Paige."

"And I can stay in your half? Is that what you're saying?"

"No, that's not it. I know Kyle's going to be upset at first, but I'll explain to him what happened. He's not an unreasonable guy."

She stared at him. Could he really be so naive as to think that their friendship with Kyle would survive her having Justin's baby? "I'm sorry. I never wanted to come between the two of you. It's one of the reasons I pretended I didn't know he had a crush on me all these years."

"Maybe this won't mean the end of our friendship," he said optimistically. "If he knows that we're willing to do the right thing, he might not take the news so hard."

She frowned. "What do you mean, do the right thing?"

"Get married."

It was not the answer she was expecting. "You want us to get married?" she squeaked.

"We're having a baby together."

"That doesn't mean we have to get married!"

"No, but it makes life a lot easier for a kid if his mom and dad are married."

"Only if the two people are happy living together."

"Paige, we've lived together over six years. What's the difference whether we share a house as friends or as husband and wife?"

"What's the difference? Hello. We're not in love. In order to have a happy marriage you have to be in love."

"Statistics show that's not true. Just look at divorce rates in countries with arranged marriages. They're much lower than those of cultures where men and women marry for love."

She stared at him in bewilderment. "And you would know that because…?"

"I took a family-studies class in college. Contrary to what you thought, I was paying attention and I did learn something."

"But I don't want an arranged marriage. When I get married it has to be for love."

"You mean like the kind of love you had for Michael Cross?"

"That's a rather low blow," she told him.

"I'm sorry," he apologized. "Have you heard anything from him?"

"No!" she was quick to lie. "Why would I?"

He shrugged. "Just wondering if the zero tried to contact you, that's all."

"This isn't about Michael and I don't think we should waste time talking about him."

"You're right. We need to find a solution to our situation. Notice, I did not call it a problem," he added with a half smile.

"Thank you." She leaned back in her chair and sighed. "I just can't believe that you think marriage is a solution. It's a huge commitment."

"Having a baby or getting married?"

"Both." She couldn't believe he was talking about it so calmly. They were sitting at the kitchen table eating ice cream straight out of the container and talking about marriage as if they were talking about sharing household duties.

"Why can't we just live together?" she asked.

"Because whether or not you want to admit it, marriage legitimizes a child's existence." He took another spoonful of ice cream.

"It shouldn't. There are children everywhere being raised by single parents who are just as healthy and happy as those in two-parent families."

"Of course there are. But answer me this." He waved his spoon for emphasis. "If you had a choice, which would you rather have for your child—an intact family or one where you shuffle the child back and forth between parents?"

She didn't answer the question because he already knew the answer. "I can't believe you're saying these things. You've never had much regard for tradition and family values," she pointed out.

"That's not true," he denied.

"You can't even stick with one girlfriend for more than a couple of months."

"I haven't wanted to. It's not because I can't." He paused when she looked skeptical. "What? You think I'm some commitmentphobe or something?"

"I know you are."

"Haven't I been a loyal friend to you?"

"Yes, you have, but that's not the same thing. We're talking about marriage."

"Well, our marriage would be an act of friendship. I would never do anything to be disloyal." He playfully tugged at the hand in which she held her spoon. "Hey, slow down. You're eating twice as fast as I am."

She licked a bit of chocolate from her lip. "I'm eating for two people." She quickly dug her spoon back into the container. "So you're proposing a marriage that would be more like a partnership between friends?"

"Uh-uh. I know if it were any other kind you'd have to pass because I don't have the necessary Top Ten traits."

"I told you I burned my list," she said with a mock frown.

"So it wouldn't matter if I didn't have stick-to-itiveness?" he teased, and she slugged him playfully.

"Don't make fun of a serious subject. I'm not going to marry you because it's not a good idea."

"So what is a good idea? How are you going to be a full-time mom and a full-time teacher without any help?

"I have a plan."

He chuckled. "Of course you do."

She'd thought of little else since she'd learned she was pregnant. "Since the baby isn't due until May, I'll be able to finish out this year's contract. Then next year I'm going to apply for a position at a school with on-site day care. That way I'll be able to bring the baby to work with me. One of the teachers I work with belongs to this single-moms group that provides babysitting services as well as emotional support. I can probably join once the baby comes."

"So you won't need a man around. Is that what you're saying?"

"What I'm saying is that I'm going to take care of my child." And when she did get married it would be for love, not friendship.

"What about me? What if I want to take care of my child? How do I fit into this plan?"

"You're the father. Of course I want you to be a part of its life."

"Just not in the traditional way." He shook his head. "I don't get you. For as long as I can remember, you've been the traditional one. You wanted a husband first, baby second. I offer to give that to you and you tell me you don't want it."

"Because if I marry it will be for love, not friendship." She didn't add that she doubted that would ever happen because she didn't think she would ever find a man she could trust.

He made an incorrect assumption. "Well, I'm sorry. I can't wave a magic wand and make Michael the father of your child. Not that he would do the right thing and marry you even if he were."

"I already told you. Michael has no place in this conversation."

They'd run out of ice cream, so he set his spoon down on the table. "What happens next?"

"We're going to have to tell our families. Your mother already knows I'm pregnant." She told Justin about the night they ordered the Mexican food. "She just doesn't know it's her grandchild."

"She probably thinks it's your ex-fiancé's baby."

"If she does, she was too polite to mention it to me," Paige told him.

He sighed. "So when do we tell Kyle? It needs to be soon because I have to tell him I'm not going to Oregon."

"Maybe you should go with him," she suggested.

He rolled his eyes. "First you're upset because I say I want to go. Then when I make the decision not to go you tell me I should go. Do you or do you not know what you want?"

She didn't. She was confused. About so many things. "I'm sorry. My hormones are out of whack. You're going to have to get used to it."

He rolled his eyes and groaned. "This is so not like you."

"I know. I don't like it any better than you do. I like having control of my emotions." She yawned. "I need to get to bed. This baby has zapped my energy."

"Will you at least think about the two of us providing the kind of family a child needs?"

"Yes."

"Good. That's a start."

As she climbed the stairs to her room, she thought about how surreal her life had become. Just two short months ago she'd been planning a wedding with the man she thought she'd love forever. Now she was thinking about getting married to a man she'd loved forever, but as a friend.

But she wasn't seriously thinking about marrying Justin, or was she?

CHAPTER TEN

JUSTIN DIDN'T SLEEP much that night. How could he? Two words had turned his life upside down. "I'm pregnant."

There had been no reason for him to ask Paige if he was the father. He knew he was. She'd never had sex with Michael Cross. Just thinking about her ex-fiancé made him angry.

But she was pregnant and there was no point in thinking of what might have been. He needed to come to terms with the reality that he was going to be a father. Until today he'd never given much thought to marriage and having a family. He'd never even come close to wanting to move in with any of his girlfriends. He was too young to settle down. None of his friends were married, nor were any of them thinking about it. And he wouldn't be thinking of it now if Paige wasn't pregnant.

But she was having a baby. His baby. He still couldn't get his mind wrapped around that one. One night of recklessness was about to change his life forever.

And he had been careless. He still couldn't believe that he'd given in to temptation and risked not using protection. Until that night he'd been the best-prepared Boy Scout on the planet, never going anywhere without a sufficient supply of condoms.

If there was one thing he was sure of, it was that marriage to Paige would not be without its rewards. Just thinking about the way their bodies had fit together made him ache with desire.

He knew she had assumed he meant for their marriage to be platonic. What he hadn't told her was that he hoped that in time she would come to love him the way he loved her and it would be a real marriage. Maybe they weren't madly in love now, but that didn't mean they couldn't enjoy being married. He needed to stop thinking about the sexual aspect of their relationship. There was a very good possibility she wouldn't marry him. Once Paige made up her mind she seldom changed it, and she had decided that when she did marry it was going to be to the love of her life, not her best friend.

What he needed to focus on was the baby. He was going to have responsibilities. Big responsibilities.

Until today he'd never had to worry about supporting anyone but himself, but with two words that had all changed. He now was responsible for two other people, because whether or not Paige liked it, he was going to take care of her and the baby.

After an hour of tossing and turning and thinking about their situation, he decided to get up and go downstairs into the family room. He turned on the big-screen TV and surfed through the infomercials and old movies, looking for something that would distract him from the issue foremost on his mind. Suddenly he heard the back door open and in came Kyle.

"I didn't expect to find you up," Kyle said, draping his jacket over the back of one of the chairs.

"I couldn't sleep. Where have you been?"

"At Tammy's. I was going to spend the night but we had this big blow-out fight." He sank onto the sofa at the opposite end from Justin. "I've been feeling guilty about leaving her this winter, but the way she was behaving today makes me think she's not going to miss me when I go to Oregon."

Justin knew he had to tell Kyle he wasn't going to make

the trip. "I need to talk to you about that." He turned off the TV and leaned back against the arm of the sofa so he was facing Kyle. "I'm not going to Oregon."

"You have to go. It's all set. We've registered for the seminar, all the arrangements have been made. This is for the good of the business." He leaned forward, his hands folded, his elbows on his knees.

"I know, but I can't go. Something's come up."

"What could have possibly come up that is more important than this?"

He knew there was no easy way to tell him. "I'm going to be a dad."

"Whoa. You're joking, right?"

"No, it's no joke."

"I can't believe it! You got a girl pregnant? You are the last person I would expect to tell me that kind of news." He looked as if he didn't know whether to laugh or feel sorry for his friend.

"Yeah, well, believe it was a big shock for me, too. At least now you know why I can't go to Oregon."

"When's the baby due?"

"Not till the first of May."

"Well, that's not a problem," he rationalized. "We're only going to be gone for three months. You'll be home in plenty of time."

"Yes, but I wouldn't feel right being away from her while she's going through the pregnancy."

"It isn't Tara, is it? I didn't think you were seeing her."

"No. I never hooked up with Tara."

"Then who is it?"

"I'm not sure she'd appreciate me spreading her news... know what I mean?" He stood up and stretched. "It's late. We can talk about this tomorrow."

He started for the stairs, but Kyle stopped him. "Wait a minute," he demanded. "You aren't going to drop a bomb like that on me at two o'clock in the morning and then trot off to bed. We've been best buddies since kindergarten. You ought to know that you can tell me anything and I won't go blabbing it around."

Justin hesitated, feeling torn between two friends. He felt a loyalty to Paige, but he also knew that he and Kyle had shared stuff only guys shared. He decided to take a chance and tell Kyle the truth. "It's Paige."

Kyle swore at him and the last thing he saw before he blacked out was a fist coming at his face.

When he awoke, Paige was bending over him, soaking up the blood with a wet cloth.

"I can't believe you did this to him," she said to Kyle.

"I can't believe he took advantage of you the way he did," Kyle said with disgust. "God, you've been like a sister to him."

"Just stop with the indignation and go get me some vinegar," Paige ordered, "or he's going to get blood all over the carpet."

Justin sat up and blood poured out onto the wet cloth Paige held against his face. "Thanks," he murmured.

"Why didn't you wait until I was here to tell him?" she asked.

"If I had known he was going to clobber me a good one, I would have."

Kyle returned with the bottle of vinegar.

"I need some cotton balls, too," she told him. "Look in the vanity in my room."

He disappeared up the stairs without an argument.

"What are you doing up?" Justin asked her.

"I heard Kyle shouting at you."

"He's pissed."

"I can see that."

Kyle came thumping back down the stairs. He tossed a bag of cotton balls at Paige.

"I can't believe you kept this from me. How long have you two been carrying on behind my back?" Kyle demanded, pacing back and forth in the living room.

"We haven't been carrying on," Justin denied, his voice muted by the cotton Paige had stuck under his nose. "Not that it's any of your business if we had been."

Paige shushed him then said to Kyle, "If you must know, it happened the night before the Bulldog Reunion."

"Which would explain why you two were behaving so weirdly." He turned then to Justin. "You're supposed to be my best friend. I trusted you. I trusted both of you. What a fool I was."

"He's still your best friend and you can still trust him," Paige said, surprising Justin. "And what happened here is the reason we didn't tell you. You're wrong if you think we don't care about you. Because we do."

"Oh, don't make me laugh," he drawled sarcastically and spun around and left.

"Well, at least the cat's out of the bag," Justin said as he gingerly patted his nose.

"I wish you had waited until I was with you to tell him."

"I'm sure I could find another place to bleed if you want to take out your anger on me," he said irritably.

She sighed. "I'm not angry. I'm all out of emotion at the moment."

He reached for her hand. "I'm sorry. It didn't go as I thought it would."

"Are you going to be all right?" she asked, eyeing the

swelling on his face. "I'll get you an ice pack. I'm afraid you might have a shiner in the morning."

She disappeared briefly. returning with a cold pack that she told him to hold close to his puffy cheek.

"We're going to get through this—all three of us," he assured her.

"Do you mean three as in us and the baby or three as in you, me and Kyle?" she asked.

"I had meant Kyle, but I guess I should say all four of us."

"Yeah, I guess so." And without another word she placed the cap back on the vinegar bottle and went upstairs.

SEVERAL DAYS PASSED before Paige saw Kyle, and then it was only briefly. He was coming out of the house as she was going in. She asked if he had time to have a cup of coffee with her and he answered that he was already late for an appointment. Justin told her later that evening that he had bumped into Tammy at the gas station and she'd told him that Kyle had been spending a lot of time at her place.

It was a reminder to Paige that she needed to make a decision about a place to live. On Friday night she left messages for both Justin and Kyle to call her so they could meet and come to a decision about the house. By lunchtime Saturday, neither of her roommates had called or put in an appearance. After a quick sandwich, Paige decided to treat herself to something she'd read about on one of the many pregnancy sites she'd visited—a facial mask for her dry skin.

Working cautiously in case the smell played havoc with her olfactory sense, she mashed carrots and avocados, then added honey and egg. When she was confident the smell wouldn't make her sick, she slipped a headband over her hair to keep it away from her face and applied the mixture. Then she set the timer and sat down on her bed with the newspaper to scan the want ads for apartments to rent.

That's what she was doing when Justin passed by her open door. "What do you have on your face? You look like you should have a spear and headdress."

"It's a mask."

He chuckled. "No kidding."

"A facial mask to soften my skin."

He stepped into her room to get a closer look and saw that she'd been circling ads in red ink on the newspaper spread out in front of her. "Looking for something?" he asked.

"Yes. An apartment."

His eyes narrowed. "What does that mean?"

"It means that I can't stay here indefinitely. Sooner or later I'm going to need my own place. It's rather obvious that it's sooner."

"Why? Has Kyle said he doesn't want you living here?"

"No. I've hardly seen him since he blew up at us. What about you…have you spoken to him at all?"

"Only at work, and then it's strictly about business."

"When I have tried calling him I get his voice mail," Paige told him. "I'm sure he's not picking up when he sees it's me. I guess we shouldn't be surprised. We both knew that he would be hurt by what we did."

He sat down on the edge of the bed. "I'm going to have a talk with him. We need to get this resolved."

"I hope he'll listen to you. This is not how I wanted to see our friendship end."

"What makes you think it has to end?"

She chuckled sardonically. It was so like a guy to think that any relationship could be repaired. "I can't believe this has happened. Ever since we were kids I've tried so hard to be impartial, to never step in when the two of you had a disagreement. Now I'm the one who has come between you."

"You can't blame yourself for this, Paige. I've always known how Kyle felt about you, yet I broke the number-one unspoken rule among guys. It didn't matter whether or not his feelings for you were one-sided. I should have respected that he had them."

"I think I should be the one to talk to him," Paige said. "So I can explain why we spent the night together."

"Do you really think he wants to hear that?"

"Probably not, but if we're going to work this out between the three of us, we need to be honest with him. He doesn't realize the emotional wreck I was the night before the Bulldog Reunion."

He leaned closer to her. "So what are you saying? We only had sex because you were depressed over losing Michael?" He pinned her with his intense blue eyes while he waited for her answer.

Her heartbeat quickened and her mouth went dry. "What other reason could there be?"

He eyed her with a wary expression. "I don't know, Paige. Maybe you should tell me."

She shifted on the bed, putting some distance between them. "Why are you being like this?"

"Like what?"

"Contrary. You're the one who said it was casual sex."

"It certainly wasn't the consummation of our undying love for one another that you thought it should be."

"Do you have to remind me of that?" she retorted. "Why are you arguing with me anyway?"

"We're not arguing," he corrected her. "We're discussing."

"It feels like arguing to me, and all I'm trying to do is find a solution to our problem with Kyle."

"And I've already told you I'll talk to him," he said on a note of frustration.

She was saved from responding by the ringing of her timer. She hopped off the bed, waving a hand in the direction of her face. "I need to wash this stuff off."

When he got up and headed for the door, she asked, "Where are you going?"

"Downstairs. I think I heard Kyle come home."

"Wait for me and I'll go with you," she told him before disappearing into the bathroom, where she scrubbed the hardened mask away. By the time she'd washed away the dried mixture and returned to her room, he was gone.

As she hurried downstairs she heard voices coming from the kitchen. She pushed open the door and saw Kyle with his hands on his hips, a scowl on his face. Next to him was Justin, standing in an equally confrontational pose. It was obvious that they'd been arguing.

"What's going on?" Paige asked.

"I came to pick up some of my things," Kyle said. "I'm moving in with Tammy."

"But you live here," Paige told him.

"Not anymore," he said bitterly. "You two will just have to play house here without me."

"We are not playing house," Paige denied at the same time that Justin said, "It's not like that, Kyle."

"If anyone should leave it should be me," Paige said. "It's your house." She included both of them in a sweeping gesture of her arm.

"No one has to leave," Justin stated in no uncertain terms.

"I'm not staying here." Kyle's voice was steely. "If you're worried about the bills, don't be. I'll pay my share."

"I can't believe our friendship has come down to this—a

shouting match in the kitchen." Paige directed her comments to both of them. "We're friends—or doesn't that mean anything to you anymore?"

Kyle pointed to Justin. "Obviously it doesn't to him."

"Of course it does to me," Justin said. "That's why I'm trying to find a solution to this mess we're in."

"You mean the mess you're in," Kyle corrected him.

"Will you two stop?" Paige begged a second time. "Why are you acting like this?" she said to Kyle.

"Acting like what?" Kyle asked.

"Like Justin betrayed you."

"You don't understand," Kyle said. "You're a girl."

Which only made her more frustrated. "Wait a minute. I understand perfectly well that you're upset by all of this. Well, guess what? So are we." She included Justin in her gesture. "I'm having a baby. It's not the way I planned it, but it's going to happen no matter how much you two argue about it." She pointed her finger at both of them. "You are my best friends and I want both of you in my baby's life. Maybe everything about this situation has gone wrong from the start, but if there was one right thing I thought I had going for me it was that the two of you, being my friends, would help me get through this."

"We will." It was Justin who spoke.

Kyle remained silent until she asked, "Are you really willing to walk away from our friendship over this?"

He raked a hand over his dark head. "I don't know."

"Please don't do it," she pleaded with him. "If you want to move in with Tammy, fine, but please don't cut us out of your life."

He appeared to be thinking it over and was silent for several moments. Finally he said, "I've got to go. Tammy's waiting for me to take her to her nephew's birthday party."

Paige would have pressed the issue, but Justin was giving her a look that said, "Let him go." There was one thing, however, that she did need to ask him. "You haven't told Tammy I'm pregnant, have you?"

"No, although I should. She still thinks Justin and Tara are going to hit it off."

Paige worried that Justin was going to get right back into it with him, but at that moment Kyle's cell phone rang and he stepped away to answer it. He was only gone a minute when he returned and said, "I've got to go."

"Are we okay?" Paige asked as he started to leave.

"I don't know" was all he said before walking out the door.

When Kyle was gone, she said to Justin, "I don't like what's happening to the three of us."

"It'll all work out. It's not like Kyle and I haven't had a rift in our friendship before now." Then he did something she never would have expected him to do. He kissed her on the cheek. It was a simple brushing of his lips across her skin, but it sent a tickle of excitement through her.

She looked at him and asked, "Why did you do that?"

"I wanted to see if the mask worked. It did. Your skin is really smooth. It tastes good, too." Then he grabbed his keys and said, "I've gotta go, too. I'm going to watch the game with the guys from work." And with a quick bye tossed over his shoulder, he was gone.

JUSTIN MISSED KYLE, especially on weekends when they would spend hours in front of the TV watching college football. Although Paige liked football, if she had something better to do, she wasn't around on Saturdays. That's why he was surprised when she burst into the family room with an order.

"Grab your coat and let's go."

"Go where?"

"To the convention center. Remember you said we were going to do everything together when it comes to the baby? Well, today there's a baby expo and we're going to look at furniture."

Justin groaned. "On football Saturday?"

"TiVo it," she said, grabbing the remote. "What games do you want to see?"

He took the remote from her. "I don't want to watch them after they're over. I'll already know the scores."

"Not if you don't turn on the radio or TV."

"Can't we go to this baby thing tomorrow?" he pleaded.

"No. Tomorrow I have a date."

"You're joking, right?"

"No. Why would I joke about that?"

"Because you're pregnant."

"Yes, and your point would be?"

"Does this date know you're pregnant?"

"No, he doesn't. One of my fellow teachers was sweet enough to ask me to go hear a concert at the high school and I accepted."

Jealousy knifed through him, surprising him with its intensity. "I would have taken you to the concert if you had asked me."

"And miss the pro football games?"

"I'd rather miss pro football than college football."

"I can't very well ask this guy to take me to the baby expo when he doesn't even know I'm pregnant, can I? Besides, you told me you wanted to be involved with the baby."

So she was resorting to that tactic—hitting him with his own words. "I do want to be involved, but the number-one and number-two teams in the nation are playing each other today."

"And that's more important than finding the right crib for your child?"

The right crib? Weren't they all safety approved? "Isn't it a little early to look for cribs? The baby's not going to be here until next year."

"That's the point. I need to figure out how much everything's going to cost me. That's the purpose of the baby expo. To give parents an idea of what to expect."

"I understand, but do you need to plan this far ahead?"

"Yes. Just come with me this one time and I promise I won't ask for another Saturday. Deal?"

Did he have a choice? Not really. "All right," he drawled miserably. "How long is this going to take?" He began to punch in the numbers on the remote.

"We should be home in time for dinner. Unless we want to eat out."

"No! We'll get takeout if we have to."

She smiled. "All right. My treat. Now stop looking as if I'm dragging you to get a flu shot."

"It's worse than that," he told her.

Later as they strolled through the exhibition hall he knew exactly why Paige had insisted on attending the expo. It had everything she needed to know about setting up for a baby. The good news was that Paige, with her usual efficiency, visited only the booths that interested her. They finished well before dinnertime, and he asked her if she wanted to stop for a cone as they passed an ice-cream parlor on their way to the parking ramp.

"What do you think? Is your stomach up for a scoop of chocolate-chocolate chip?"

"Yes. Mornings and evenings seem to be the worst times for my stomach, afternoons I'm usually fine," she told him.

"You want your usual?" he asked before going up to the order counter.

"No. I want cherry."

He frowned. "You don't like cherry."

"I never used to like it but I do now." She shrugged. "Just like the watermelon. Maybe it's your fault. You always order cherry."

"What does that mean? That the kid has my preferences?"

"You know, it would be nice if you'd stop referring to it as the kid," she commented.

"What would you like me to call it? We don't know if it's a boy or girl."

"Not yet we don't."

"When will we find out?"

"I'm scheduled for an ultrasound at the end of November. We can find out the sex at that time if we want."

"What do you mean if we want to? Of course we want to."

"I'm not so sure I do."

"Why not?"

"I don't know. It just might be *fun* to have it be a surprise."

He raised his eyebrows. "This from someone who hates surprises? Who plans every detail of her life?"

"Don't you think it would be more fun not to know?"

He didn't want to tell her that the word fun had yet to make an appearance in his lexicon for describing her pregnancy. "If you're not having the ultrasound for another month there's no reason we need to decide today, is there?"

"I guess not," she conceded, following Justin to a small parlor table.

They hadn't been there but a few minutes when a voice called out, "Well, look who's here."

Justin glanced up to see a very pregnant woman approaching. She stopped at their table and said, "Paige, how are you?"

"I'm fine. Carrie, you've met Justin, haven't you? Justin,

you remember my cousin Carrie and her husband Daryl?"
Justin turned to see a slightly balding, bearded man behind her.

Justin noticed how quickly Paige hid the shopping bag of
pamphlets and information she'd gathered at the expo under
her coat. She hadn't missed that her cousin's husband also had
an expo bag.

"I can't believe I ran into you," Carrie gushed. "We
heard about your dad getting engaged. Tell him congratulations from us."

"I will," Paige assured her. "It looks as if you don't have
much longer to go before you'll be hearing congratulations,
too."

"Yes, in January. That's why we're downtown. There's a
baby expo at the convention center."

"There is? Oh, how fun," Paige said.

Her cousin rambled on about babies and families and after
what seemed like an eternity of small talk, finally dragged her
husband over to the ice-cream counter.

"I think we should leave," Paige said.

Justin didn't argue with her and shielded her as much as
he could from her cousin as she slipped her coat on and made
her way to the door.

As soon as they were outside the shop, she said,
"Ohmigosh! Do you realize how lucky we are that we didn't
run into them at the baby show? She would have blabbed to
my aunt who would for sure have told my dad."

"I know you're trying to keep this a secret for as long as
you can, but don't you think it's time we tell our families
what's going on?" Justin asked.

"We will. I just want to wait a little longer," Paige answered.

"For what?"

"Until I'm sure nothing's going to happen."

"What could possibly happen?"

"A miscarriage."

He stopped abruptly. "Have you been having problems you haven't told me about?"

"No, but if a miscarriage is going to occur it would be in the early months. I want to make sure this is a viable pregnancy before we tell our parents."

"And when will that be?"

"Once I'm past my twelfth week the risk decreases to three percent."

"So that would be what? The middle of next month?"

She nodded. "I thought we could tell our folks at Thanksgiving."

It was a long time to wait, but Justin respected that it was her decision. As they drove home, the question of marriage weighed heavily on his mind. Finally he asked her, "Have you thought anymore about us getting married?"

"Of course I have." She sounded as if it were an insult that he would even ask such a thing. "How could I not think about it?"

"Do you want to tell me what those thoughts are?"

She hesitated briefly before saying, "I know to you it seems like a logical thing to do, but I don't think it's a good idea."

"Why not?"

"Because there could come a day when you regret your chivalry."

"Isn't that a chance all couples take—even those who are in love? They risk regretting their decision someday?"

"Well, I think it's less likely to happen if you're in love with someone than if you're simply getting married to provide a home for a child."

He wanted to tell her that it wasn't simply a chivalrous

decision on his part, that he'd been in love with her most of his life, but things were awkward enough between the two of them. And there was that little nagging fear in the back of his mind that warned him if she knew he was in love with her, she for sure wouldn't marry him.

So instead of saying what was really in his heart, he said, "I disagree. I've been thinking about this a lot, too, and it seems to me that, more often than not, people are disillusioned by love. If you had married Michael, he would have run off on you and you would have ended up divorced."

"What an awful thing to say!"

"You think a wedding ring would have kept him from being unfaithful? An engagement ring didn't."

"I don't want to talk about Michael. This has nothing to do with him." She stared out the side window of the pickup.

"No, it doesn't." He could see just the mention of her ex-fiancé's name caused her to get agitated. Was she still in love with the guy? He didn't want to think about it so he tried another tactic. "Since Kyle has been staying at Tammy's it's been just the two of us in the house and we've managed to get along okay, don't you think?"

"Justin, there's a big difference between living together and being married."

"Why does there have to be?"

"Just the fact that you're asking me that question tells me we're not on the same page. Can we please just not talk about this right now?" The exasperation in her tone made him feel as if the subject wasn't important enough to discuss.

"Fine," he said stiffly. "I won't say any more about it for now, but you know our parents are going to ask about marriage when we tell them you're pregnant."

"I know," she said a bit impatiently.

They didn't say another word on the subject but drove the rest of the way home in silence. When he pulled into the driveway he saw the reason. She'd fallen asleep. As he watched her, he thought of how odd it was that she was the one who was avoiding making a decision about marriage. The Paige he knew saw a problem, weighed the possible solutions and took action. In all the years he'd known her, he couldn't remember her ever being indecisive for more than a day or two. Now weeks had passed and she still couldn't decide whether or not they should get married. It had to be her hormones. Or maybe she still wasn't over Michael Cross. He hoped it was the hormones.

PAIGE WOULD HAVE TAKEN just about anybody's suggestion as to how to mend the tear in her friendship with Kyle and Justin, which was why she listened when Tammy called to discuss the subject. Her advice was to get the guys together to do what they loved most—watch Vikings football. Having a houseful of people on a Sunday afternoon to watch professional sports had never been on Paige's list of favorite things to do. She preferred the company of a few rather than many, but if it meant a chance to get Kyle and Justin to patch their friendship, she was willing to give it a try.

Shortly before noon on Sunday the doorbell rang and Paige went to answer it. Standing on the step was a woman dressed all in green and wearing a plastic slice of cheese on her head. In her hands she carried a covered dish.

"Hi. I'm looking for Justin."

"You must be here for the game."

She smiled then. "Yes. I guess my hat gave me away. And my bean dip." She lifted the covered bowl. "I'm Sarah."

"Come on in. I'm Paige. You're the first to arrive." She led her into the room that housed the wide-screen TV.

"I'm early for everything," she said apologetically.

"Me, too. Are you from Wisconsin?" Paige asked, pointing to the cheese hat.

"No, I'm from Iowa, but I've always rooted for the Packers."

They made small talk and finally Paige asked her, "And how do you know Justin?"

"I work for him."

"Oh, you're that Sarah." One of the new hires. If Paige remembered correctly, Sarah was recently divorced and looking to make new friends. Paige gave her an extra smile, curious to see how Justin would greet her.

He shook her hand. "Sarah, hi. I see you've met Paige."

Again the doorbell rang and Paige went to get it. On the step was Tammy but no Kyle. She looked past her shoulder to see if he was still parking the car, but there was no sign of him.

"He's already here," Tammy said as she stepped inside. "He decided to shower here since Tara and I were monopolizing the bathroom this morning." She rolled her eyes. "I'll go upstairs and find him."

It wasn't necessary. A few seconds later Kyle came thumping down the stairs. Paige watched anxiously as he and Justin greeted each other. To outsiders they gave no indication that anything was wrong, much to Paige's relief. Fortunately more friends arrived, and talk turned to the upcoming game between the Vikings and Packers.

While everyone retreated to the living room to watch the game, Paige sought the quiet refuge of the kitchen to make appetizers. She would have been content to stay there indefinitely, but Justin came looking for her.

"Why are you hiding out here?" he wanted to know.

"I'm not hiding. You know I'm not crazy about a crowd."

"There are only nine people in that room."

"Well, that's about six too many for me."

"If you'd come in there and sit down I'd talk to you instead of them."

"You don't need to talk to me."

"What if I want to?" He moved closer to her and she felt the hairs on her neck rise in excitement. Uneasy with the signals her body was sending her, she moved away from him. "Are you feeling…you know, sick, like…because of the…" His eyes flew to her stomach and she glanced over her shoulder nervously.

"Shh. There are people in the next room." He took a step closer and she moved to the other side of the kitchen on the pretext of needing to wash her hands. "Your date is in the next room," she added.

"Sarah's my employee."

"Does she know that's all she is?" she asked with her back to him.

He came and stood right next to her. "Yes, she does, as a matter of fact, and so does her boyfriend. You know I'm not dating anyone. I haven't in months."

"That has to be a first." She sounded surprised.

"No, actually it isn't. But that's beside the point. If I were going to date anyone it would be you."

If he had said those words two months ago she would have laughed them away with a sarcastic comment. Back then those words wouldn't have made her jittery the way they were doing now. She couldn't think of a single clever thing to say.

"It doesn't seem right for us to be dating," she finally said, stepping away from the sink.

"Why not?" he asked, following her.

"Because it's never been like that between us." She moved across the room to the table, where several bags of snacks sat half-empty, and busied herself with making sure they were neatly tucked together.

"It was like that the night before the Bulldog Reunion," he said, watching her hands make work out of nothing.

She blushed. "Would you stop talking like this? Anyone could walk in."

"And would that be so awful?"

She faced him. "Yes, it would."

"Then come outside with me." He extended a hand to her.

Reluctantly she placed hers in it and allowed him to lead her to the backyard.

When they were far enough away from the house so that no one would hear their conversation, he said, "Maybe it's time we leave the past behind us and start over. We're not the kids that played flashlight tag and rode our bikes to the caves along the river, Paige. We're adults."

"And what about Kyle?"

"He already knows the worst, Paige. If I were in his shoes I'd be upset, too, but at least I would respect his attempt to do the honorable thing and make a go of the relationship."

"The honorable thing?" She shook her head. "You ought to know me better than that. I don't want some guy taking me out because it's the honorable thing."

"What is it you want from me, Paige?"

"I don't know, but I know I don't want you to feel sorry for me. Marriage is about mutual love and respect. It's about honesty, dependability, sensitivity—"

He interrupted her before she could finish. "I thought you said you burned your Top Ten list."

"Well, I probably shouldn't have," she retorted.

He took her by the arms and made her face him. "Take a good look at me, Paige. I may be short some of those ideal traits you have on your list for the perfect guy, but I've been a loyal and faithful friend to you, which is more than you can say for your ex-fiancé."

"Why are you bringing him into this?" she cried out angrily.

Suddenly the back door opened and Kyle came out. "Are you all right, Paige?"

"Of course she's all right." Justin bristled. "Stop looking at me as if I'm going to hurt her. I would never hurt Paige."

"What do you mean? You already have." Kyle shot back at him. "Why don't you just leave her alone?"

Paige stepped in between the two of them. "We're done talking. Would you please go back inside before you have everyone else out here?" she begged Kyle. "I'm okay."

Kyle looked as if he wanted to argue that point but turned around and went back in the house. Paige threw her hands up in frustration.

"Now look what's happened. Today was supposed to be about bringing you two back together. You're friends."

"So are we, Paige," he said soberly. "What has happened to us?"

"I don't know," she said on a long sigh, rubbing her fingers across her forehead. "We shouldn't be talking out here when there are people inside."

"No, we shouldn't. Let's take a walk."

She allowed him to steer her toward the sidewalk. When she shivered, he took off his Vikings football jersey and wrapped it around her. She murmured a thank you, appreciating the warmth.

"I don't want to argue with you, Paige, especially not over someone like Michael Cross."

"Then it's best if we don't mention his name again. Ever."

"I agree. There's no place for him in any of our conversations."

"No, there isn't."

"And my wanting to date you has nothing to do with him," he continued. "We need to convince our parents that we're serious about each other."

"Our parents?" Any hope that he might say the reason he wanted to date her was the same reason any other guy dated a girl evaporated.

"Yes. What are they going to think if all of a sudden we tell them you're pregnant and I'm the father? Don't you think we should try to make it look like we're a couple rather than a one-night stand?"

In other words pretend it was a real date. She tried to hide her disappointment. Resigned to the fact that he was only dating her for appearances, she said, "Yeah. I guess we should try. When do you want to go on this date?"

"How about next weekend?" he suggested. "We could go to a movie."

She shrugged. "That sounds like fun. I'll look at my calendar, but I'm pretty sure I can do it on Saturday."

"Okay. Then it's a date."

CHAPTER ELEVEN

PAIGE DIDN'T UNDERSTAND why she should be nervous about her date with Justin. She'd been to the movies with him more times than she could count, yet she felt like a teenager waiting for the most popular boy in school to pick her up. Only he didn't have to come to the door since they lived in the same house. They agreed to meet in the kitchen at a quarter to seven.

When she went downstairs he was waiting for her. Usually she was the prompt one and he was the one running a few minutes behind, but she'd spent more time than usual trying to decide what to wear and was pulling on her corduroy blazer as she walked into the kitchen. Instead of her usual ponytail her hair hung loosely across her shoulders.

He noticed right away. "Your hair's different."

"I thought I'd try it down for a change," she said, feeling very self-conscious about the way he was looking at her. He'd never paid any attention to her hair before. So what was up with tonight?

"It looks nice," he said, then immediately turned his attention to the newspaper on the table. "I suppose you want to see the romantic comedy."

"What are the other choices?" she asked.

"Sci-fi, action adventure, horror, horror and animated. Oh, and one more horror."

"You can tell it's getting close to Halloween," she commented. "What do you want to see?"

"I'm willing to try the romantic comedy."

"You are?"

"Sure. If we're going to act like it's a date we should probably see a date flick."

It turned out to be a good choice. Not overly sentimental, the film had a good combination of comedy and romance and had both of them laughing. It also gave them something to talk about as they shared a pizza afterward.

Except for the fact that they had officially called it a date, this could have been just another of the many times they'd gone to the movies together and out for pizza. At the restaurant, she expected him to order their usual favorite—Italian sausage with green olive and onion on one half and pepperoni, green peppers and mushrooms on the other.

"Give us a couple of minutes," he told the teenage girl who came to wait on their booth.

"Why didn't you order our usual?" Paige asked.

"Are you okay with that? I mean, I know how some foods make you queasy."

"I think I can handle it. Just don't add any extra Parmesan cheese or I might have a problem," she warned him.

They had just finished placing their order, when Paige saw her dad and Mary enter the pizza parlor. They noticed Paige and Justin right away and came toward them.

"This is a surprise," Paige said. "Dad, isn't it past your bedtime?"

He grinned. "Just about."

"Your father had a craving for pizza so we thought we'd pick one up and take it home."

"Have you ordered?" her dad asked.

"Yes," she answered.

"Why don't you tell them to make it to go and you can come back to the house with us," her father suggested.

Mary quickly said, "Art, they don't want to spend their Saturday night with a couple of old people."

"We're not old," Art corrected her, "and it's not like they're on a date."

Paige met Justin's questioning glance. It was the perfect opportunity and he took advantage of it.

"Well, actually we are on a date."

Paige's father looked around. "Where are the other two?"

Then Mary elbowed him. "They mean *they're* on a date."

Her father frowned. "You two are on a date?"

"Yeah, Dad, we're on a date." Paige wondered if she could feel any more uncomfortable than she did at that moment.

"I hope you don't mind," Justin said.

"Naw. You've proven yourself hundreds of times over." Her father clapped Justin's shoulder.

Paige avoided her father's eyes, wondering if he thought she had taken his advice and was dating one of the men in her life who definitely wasn't safe.

They were granted a bit of a respite from further questioning when the waitress reappeared. Paige was relieved when her father said they were going to take their pizza to go. Talk turned to football as it usually did whenever Justin and her father were together, and Mary asked Paige about school.

As soon as their pizza arrived, Mary and her father left, and the first thing Justin said was, "Well, the news is out."

"Your mom will hear about it tomorrow morning."

"Does that bother you?"

"Mary will make it sound as if we're a couple. I can tell by the way she kept looking at us." As much as she liked her future stepmother, Paige knew that she would also take great pleasure in sharing the discovery she'd made this evening.

"I thought you wanted them to know."

Paige wasn't sure what she wanted. "What if this is a one-off?"

"What kind of a question is that?"

"An honest one. I don't know what we're doing here, Justin." To her horror she got choked up and almost started to cry.

He reached across the table and took her hand. "Hey, don't go all girlie on me. I don't know how to deal with a weepy Paige."

She reached for a tissue in her purse, dabbed at her eyes, sniffled a couple of times then put it away, annoyed by the hormonal mood swings that came with her pregnancy. She took a deep breath before saying, "Sorry. I'm okay now."

She liked the way his fingers felt holding her hand. They gently caressed her skin and suddenly she had another hormonal surge. But this one was desire. She gently pulled her hand back.

"I'm in unfamiliar territory, too," he admitted. "I've never dated a girl I really cared about."

His words sent a ripple of pleasure through her. "Is that supposed to be a compliment?"

"It's just the truth. If there's one thing we've always been with each other it's honest. It's why we've been able to stay friends for so long."

She knew what he said was true. At times they had been brutally honest with each other, but she never doubted that he was there for her if she needed him and that she would get only straight answers.

"You've been there for me whenever I've needed you." She pleated her napkin to avoid looking at him.

"And I always will be. That's what friends are for."

She wanted to ask him if that's why he'd invited her on the

date. Because he knew she needed someone to share the pregnancy with? But she didn't, because she didn't want to hear the answers.

By the time they'd finished their pizza she felt comfortable enough to ask him, "Are we going to have a second date?"

"I want to." The words sent another shiver of pleasure through her until he said, "I mean, if eventually people are going to know that the baby is mine, shouldn't we at least make it look as if we had more than a one-night stand?"

He didn't say that he wanted them to try to make it work. Or that he wanted to give the romance angle a shot. Or that maybe if they dated they might fall in love. He wanted to date her for appearances' sake. And that was a big disappointment.

"I'm not sure it really matters what people think," Paige said. "I mean, they're going to think whatever they want anyway."

"And our parents?"

She paused, then sighed. "I guess it would be easier for them if we made it look like we were in love. Okay, we'll have another date."

He chuckled. "I suppose you're going to whip out your date planner and schedule it."

She reached into her purse. "As a matter of fact, I am. There's a teachers' Halloween party next weekend. I wasn't going to go, but maybe I should bring you and let people see I have a boyfriend."

"Have you told anybody at work yet?"

"You mean about the…" She trailed off, uneasy with using the word *baby*.

She shook her head. "I haven't. And frankly I'm worried. It's a private school, Justin. I don't think they're going to like the fact that a single teacher is having a baby."

"You don't have to be single. I told you I'd marry you."

He made it sound like an obligation. She flipped her date book shut. "Can we just focus on the next date for now? We're going to need to wear costumes. Do you have any ideas?"

His eyes lit up. "Hey—remember when we were in high school and Kyle and I went as the Blues Brothers to that party? I bet we still have those old suits in a box in the basement somewhere."

She could see the evilness in his grin at the thought of Paige as a Blues Brother. "I don't know why I put up with you."

"Because I'm the best friend you've ever had."

"Why don't we skip the Halloween party and make my father's wedding our next date?" she suggested.

"Weren't you planning on going with me anyway?"

"Well, of course I was, but not as a date." She glared at him. "I thought the three of us would go together…but who knows whether Kyle will be talking to us by then."

"He hasn't asked me to buy out his share of the business, so that's a good sign," Justin pointed out. "You know Kyle. He doesn't let go of his anger easily."

Paige knew exactly what he meant. She also had a stubborn streak but she couldn't hold a candle to Kyle when it came to grudges. He clung to perceived injuries the way caramel stuck to her teeth.

She figured eventually he would get over it and act as if nothing was wrong, because that's the way he operated. Get angry, don't talk for a while, then behave as if nothing ever happened.

That's why she wasn't surprised to arrive home from school the following Monday and find him at the house.

He stood with the refrigerator door open. "Are you out of soda?"

"I think there are a couple of cans on the bottom shelf in

the back." She walked over to him and left him no choice but to hug her. "It's good to see you. I've missed you."

"I hope you mean that." He pulled out a can of root beer and popped the top. "I moved back."

That did catch her by surprise. "I thought you were living with Tammy."

He took a sip of the soda before saying, "She asked me to leave. She said she wasn't ready to make that kind of commitment yet."

Silently Paige applauded the decision. The world needed more women like Tammy, women who weren't afraid to say no to a man, but she also knew how much Kyle had wanted to make their relationship work.

"Living together *is* a commitment," Paige agreed. "Maybe she just needs more time before she feels comfortable with her decision."

He shrugged. "Maybe, but I doubt that's why she wanted me gone."

"Why do you say that?"

"I think she wants to date some guy Tara introduced her to."

"Well, if she does, then she wasn't ready for the kind of relationship you wanted." Paige filled a kettle with water to make herself a cup of tea.

"If you're trying to cheer me up, you're not succeeding."

She set the kettle on the stove. "I'm sorry. You really cared about her, didn't you?"

"Yeah, I did. Rather ironic, isn't it? That I finally found someone I want to be with and she uses the line on me that I've been using on women for the past twelve years." He took another sip. "Payback can be a bitch."

"She didn't say that she didn't want to see you again, did she?"

"No. Is that supposed to be the silver lining?"

"No, living with me is the silver lining," she said with a grin. "Lucky for you we didn't rent out your room."

"I'm not sure it'll work out, the three of us under one roof," he warned her.

"You may be surprised to know I have the same doubts as you. I mean, I don't think it's a good idea to be three roommates and a baby, do you?" She pulled a mug from the cupboard and slipped a tea bag into it.

"So when do you plan to move out?"

"I don't know," she answered honestly.

"Have you told your dad that you're pregnant?" he asked her, leaning back against the counter.

"No. I'm going to have to do it soon, though, before I can't button my pants anymore. You haven't said anything to anyone, have you?"

"No. I told you I wouldn't do that and I haven't."

"Thank you." She wanted to approach the subject of their disagreement, but knew she needed to tread carefully. "Kyle, I'm sorry if I hurt you. You have to know that I never meant for this to happen between me and Justin."

He held up a hand. "You don't need to tell me that, Paige. I don't blame you. Justin should have known better. You were vulnerable that night, hurting badly, and he disrespected you."

"No, he really didn't. He—"

Again he stopped her with his hand. "You know what, Paige? It's better if you don't get in the middle of what goes on between me and Justin."

"But I am in the middle and there's no place for me to go. I don't understand why my having a baby should pull us apart."

"That's because you're not a guy and you don't get what's happened here."

"We didn't do this to hurt you," she continued, trying to reason with him.

"I know you didn't," he said, clearly indicating that he'd forgive her. "But Justin and I have always had a code we live by. He violated that code." He thumped the can down on the countertop. "End of discussion. I'm going to go up and shower. It's music-trivia night at the Shout House."

The Shout House was a bar in downtown Minneapolis that held a weekly competition to see who could get the most correct answers to questions about music. Kyle, Justin and Paige had teamed up on many occasions to see if they could take home the first-place prize. More important than winning the hundred bucks was the pride in knowing the correct song titles and artists from the different music genres.

"Is Justin going with you?"

"No. I'm going with some guys from work."

"But he loves music-trivia night. And he's really good." She gave him a look of appeal.

"Don't go there, Paige," he warned. "You can't fix this."

She wanted to try to convince him she could but she knew it was useless. "All right. Forget I mentioned it."

"Look, I've got to take a shower. I'll catch you later." And with that he disappeared up the stairs. Not exactly the way she wanted their conversation to end, but at least he hadn't sounded angry.

He was upstairs when Justin arrived home. The first thing he said to Paige when he saw her was, "Kyle's here?"

She explained that he'd decided to move back in, expecting Justin to comment, but he went over to the DVD player to retrieve a couple of rented movies. "I've got to go. I only stopped home to pick up these. I'm going down to the Shout House to meet a couple of guys on our fantasy-football league for dinner. Want to come along?"

Paige thought about warning him that Kyle was going to the same bar but decided to say nothing. She simply declined his offer. "I have too much to do."

"If you don't want to come for dinner you could come for the music trivia. We could use another team member—especially one who knows country-western."

Until tonight she hadn't tried to get Justin and Kyle to reconcile, but now with Kyle moving back home she wondered if it wasn't time to see if she could calm the troubled waters between them. So she changed her mind and said, "Okay. I'll meet you for music trivia. That way I can get my work done first."

They agreed on a time and a place to meet. As soon as he was gone she took her school tote into the living room and sat down on the sofa. She leaned her head back briefly and closed her eyes, remembering how simple life had been when the three of them were younger. She didn't realize she had dozed off until the sound of the doorbell awoke her with a start.

When she opened the front door she was stunned to see Michael on the front porch. He flashed her that devil-may-care smile of his that used to make her heart miss a beat. To her dismay, she had the usual reaction and she had to cling to the door for support when her legs weakened.

"What are you doing here?" she asked, her heart thumping madly in her chest.

"I needed to see you. Can I come in?"

"No." The reply was automatic.

"Please. It's really important. And it's cold out here." It was October and the frost had already been on the pumpkins. Paige could feel the bite in the nighttime air. Something about the way his head tilted to the side as he looked at her brought back a pleasant memory from another time. Here was the man she almost married. She hesitated briefly, then stepped aside and gestured for him to come inside.

As soon as she'd closed the door, he said, "Leaving you was the biggest mistake of my life, Paige."

Paige could hardly believe what she was hearing. How many nights had she lain awake in bed and fantasized that this very moment would occur? That Michael would come to her and tell her he'd made a mistake. Now it was happening and all she could think was that he looked out of place. His skin had a golden tan from spending so much time in the Nevada sun and he wore a short-sleeve golf shirt and beige khakis instead of a sweatshirt and jeans.

Just then Kyle came jogging down the stairs. "Why are you here, Cross? Did you forget where you put your wife?"

"Kyle!" Paige said.

"I'm not married," he told Kyle, and Paige's eyes widened.

"Oh really? I hope that means that the woman you ran off with wised up and saw that you are nothing but a worthless piece of crap. I ought to beat the hell out of you for what you did to Paige." He pulled back his arm and looked as if he wanted to hit Michael, but upon hearing Paige's plea thought better of it.

"Kyle, stop. I'm the one who let him in."

"You're not going to listen to what he has to say, are you?" Kyle asked with a look of disbelief.

"I can take care of myself," she told him. "You know that. Would you please just go?"

He looked as if he was going to protest, but finally said, "You know how to reach me if you need me."

As soon as they were alone, Michael said, "You look good, Paige."

She didn't want compliments from him and she didn't want to feel any pleasure from anything he had to say.

"Why did you come here, Michael?" she asked.

"To talk to you. You wouldn't return my phone calls."

"You mean phone call. You called me once on my cell."

"I called twice. The second time I left a message on your answering machine here at the house."

She frowned. "When?"

"At least three or four weeks ago."

"You didn't leave any message. Otherwise I would know about it."

"The way your two roommates feel about me?" he scoffed. "Don't bet on it."

Would Kyle have deliberately kept messages from her? She knew that he had many faults, but censoring her calls wasn't one of them.

"Are you saying the only reason you didn't return my calls was because you didn't get them?" His face brightened at the possibility.

"No. I got the first one. But even if I'd heard the second message, I wouldn't have called you back. You left me to be with Chelsea. Do you realize how much that hurt me?"

"I didn't leave you for Chelsea. I went away because I needed time to think." He placed his hand on her arm. "If I had wanted Chelsea, I wouldn't have had to go to Vegas to get her."

She shrugged off his hand and took a step backward. "So Chelsea wasn't with you?"

"She came to Vegas, yes, but not because I wanted her to. She was looking for a job—just like I was. I left you that note telling you I loved you."

"A man who loves a woman doesn't leave her a note calling off the wedding."

"I'm sorry I did that, but I didn't think it would be fair for you to have to follow me to Las Vegas....especially if I couldn't get a job."

Was he telling the truth? she wondered. Then he smiled that special smile, the one that made her want to believe every word that came out of his mouth, only today she saw it as a flirtatious grin, and she wasn't in the mood for flirting with anyone.

"I came here today hoping you would tell me that you would give me a second chance," he said in a voice that was as smooth as silk.

A second chance? He wanted her back? A few months ago she would have been over the moon with joy to hear those words. But today she could only stare at him in stunned disbelief.

He gave her another smile. "I've never seen you speechless. That has to be a good sign."

It was not a good sign and she didn't waste any time telling him so. "It's been almost three months, Michael."

"I know. I've been living in Vegas getting established. I hired on with one of the golf courses out there and never went back to Cascading Waters. This is a much better opportunity for me. The people I work for are great. They were nice enough to give me some vacation time so I could come get you."

"Come get me?"

"Yes. I want you to come back with me. You're the only woman I've ever really loved, Paige."

"It's too late, Michael. You're too late."

It was as if she hadn't said one discouraging word. "Remember how we talked about moving to a warmer climate? The weather in Vegas is fantastic. And the people are nice. Do you still have my ring?"

"Yes." It was a reluctant admission.

"That's a good sign, don't you think?" Then he made a

move to kiss her. Only his lips never made it to hers, because the scent of his cologne sent her racing into the bathroom.

JUSTIN LOOKED at his watch. Paige was now half an hour late. It was so unlike her to be late. But then she hadn't been herself since she'd become pregnant. After several unsuccessful attempts to reach her, he began to worry in earnest.

He decided to walk over and talk to Kyle. Ever since he'd seen his partner enter the bar he'd been debating whether or not to say hello to him. Now the mental debate was over.

"Have you talked to Paige today?" he said by way of a greeting.

"Yeah, I saw her tonight. Why?"

"She was supposed to meet me half an hour ago and she's still not here. Paige is never late."

"It might be because Michael Cross was at the house when I left."

Justin had a sinking feeling in his stomach. "She let him in?"

"Oh yeah. I asked her if she wanted me to escort him out but she said no. I can't believe she even opened the door. But you know Paige. She hangs on to a relationship long after it ends."

Justin's anxiety turned into anger. He couldn't believe she would be taken in again by the likes of Michael Cross. Especially not after everything he'd put her through the past three months. Kyle had to be wrong.

"She knows what a jerk he is," he told Kyle. "She wouldn't be fooled by him a second time."

"Well, at one time I would have agreed with you, but she no longer uses the best judgment when it comes to men."

Justin knew the criticism was directed at him. He wanted to tell Kyle that he would never hurt Paige the way Michael Cross had hurt her, but he didn't want to get into a war of words with him. He was too worried that something had happened to Paige.

So he simply walked away.

He wasted no time in leaving the bar and driving home. When he arrived at the house he saw an unfamiliar car in the driveway. *Michael Cross*, a little voice in his head taunted him.

When he walked inside, his suspicion was confirmed. Seated on the sofa as if he were at home, arm slung across the back, was the golf pro.

"Where's Paige?" Justin demanded, giving the room a quick perusal.

"She went to freshen up," he said with a cocky grin.

"What are you doing here?"

"I'm visiting Paige—as if it's any of your business."

"It is my business if it means I have to worry about you hurting Paige."

"I'm not going to hurt her. I love her."

Justin made a sound of disbelief. "Is that why you ran off to Las Vegas with another woman?"

"I did no such thing—not that it's any of your business."

"I don't know why Paige even let you in the door."

"Oh, but she did. And that bugs the hell out of you, doesn't it? The fact that she'd rather have me than you?" He got up and stood close to Justin, taunting him.

Justin could have easily punched the guy but Paige came into the room. "What are you doing here?" she asked Justin, as if he was the one who didn't belong there, not Michael Cross.

"You were supposed to meet me an hour ago," he reminded her.

"I'm sorry. I forgot." She looked pale and uncertain.

Justin didn't miss the gloating expression on Michael's

face. It was a look that said, "See, she was so happy to see me she forgot about you."

Then the little weasel had the nerve to say, "Paige and I are having a private conversation. Do you mind?"

"Yes, I do mind. This is my house and I want you out of here. Now." He pointed his finger toward the door.

"Justin! You can't order my guests out of this house!" Paige protested.

"Yes, I can."

"No, you can't."

With a false bravado Michael said, "You heard her. I'm staying."

"Is that what you want?" Justin looked at Paige.

"I'm perfectly capable of telling him to leave if I want him to leave," she answered.

If she wanted him to leave. Justin knew that one word said it all. She still had feelings for Michael Cross.

"Then I guess I'm the one who should leave." It was her last chance to show him he was wrong, that she didn't want her ex-fiancé, but she let him walk out the door without saying a single word to him.

"I DON'T KNOW HOW you've stayed friends with that brute for so long," Michael said as soon as Justin had gone.

"Can we not talk about Justin?" she asked on a weary note, still feeling sick to her stomach.

"You're right. We shouldn't be talking about him. We should be talking about us and our future."

She ambled over to the sofa and dropped down, leaning her head back.

"What's wrong with you? Are you sick?"

"Yes," she answered. "Now will you please leave?"

"You want me to come back later when you're feeling better?"

She noticed that he kept inching his way closer to the door as if he was worried he'd catch her disease. "No. There's no point in your coming back."

"I know I hurt you and I'm sorry, but I'll make it up to you, I promise. Just tell me what I need to do."

"I want you to go back to Vegas and find someone else," she told him.

"Please tell me you don't mean that."

"I do." She straightened and tried to stand, but the smell of his cologne hung in the air, causing her stomach to rumble, so she sank back down into the cushions. "I really think you'd better go, Michael."

To her relief he did as she requested. As soon as she heard the door shut behind him, she got up off the sofa and climbed the stairs to her room. She fell across the bed, thinking how weird it had been to see Michael again. She'd expected that she'd feel something for him, but she'd felt almost numb.

As she lay on the bed her nausea gradually subsided. She lifted her head to see what time it was and noticed the velvet ring box on the nightstand. She took it in her hands and stared at it, rolling it between her fingers until finally she opened it. Sparkling as brilliantly as it had the first day she had put it on was the diamond solitaire. She looked at it for a long time before slipping it on her finger. To her surprise it didn't fit. The water retention of early pregnancy had made it too small. She pulled the ring from her finger and put it back in the box. Then she got up and went over to the closet, where she shoved the box into the bin marked To Be Donated To Charity.

There was no longer a reason to keep it.

CHAPTER TWELVE

PAIGE DIDN'T SEE Justin until the next morning. Already suffering morning sickness, she felt out of sorts when she walked into the kitchen. One glance from him told her that he was angry and she knew the reason. Michael. She figured she might as well clear the air now.

"You don't have to look at me that way," she said.

"And what way is that?"

"Like I'm a fool for even talking to Michael last night."

"I didn't say that."

"No, but you're thinking it."

He didn't deny it but kept eating his cereal.

"I know you think I took his side last night but I didn't. I just didn't like your being so heavy-handed with that macho stuff about this being your house and ordering my guest out of it."

"Why did you let him in after what he did to you?"

"Aha! See! I knew you were thinking that." She couldn't help a feeling of satisfaction. "I wanted to talk to him."

He picked up his bowl and walked over to the sink to rinse it out. "I think I've heard enough."

She followed him to the sink. "Did you know that he called here and left a message on our house phone but no one gave it to me?"

Justin's silence told Paige he did know.

She gasped. "It was you! I thought it must have been Kyle. How could you do that to me?"

"Do what? Protect you from a spineless piece of crap like Michael Cross? It was easy. He'd already hurt you enough. I wasn't going to let him do it again." He stuck his bowl and spoon in the dishwasher.

"I don't need you to protect me!" she declared emotionally.

"No? Look what happened last night when I wasn't here," he pointed out, slamming the door of the dishwasher shut.

"Nothing happened," she insisted. "Except I found out my best friend deliberately kept a phone message from me."

He sighed. "Look, I'm sorry I did that, but at the time I thought I was doing you a favor... I can see you don't want or need my protection so I'll stop." He held his hands up in surrender. "Happy? Now I have to go to work."

"Wait!"

He paused on his way to the door and she asked, "What about my dad's wedding? Are you going to take me?"

"I thought maybe you wanted your ideal man to take you." His attempt at sarcasm failed.

"No, I want you to take me." She didn't want to sound so angry, but it irritated her that he thought she needed him to protect her like some kind of big brother.

"It doesn't sound like you do and it sure didn't look like it last night."

"Last night was not what you think," she said on a sigh of frustration. "I don't want us to argue over Michael. Tomorrow is my father's wedding. I want it to be a happy occasion. Could we just start over and forget this morning happened?"

She thought he might say no, but then he said, "Okay. What time are we supposed to be at the church?"

"Four o'clock."

"I'll be ready. Oh, and one more thing." He leaned toward her as if he was going to kiss her, but a knock on the back door had him jerking away. The door opened and Paige's father poked his head inside.

"Am I interrupting anything?" he asked.

"No, I'm just heading out," Justin said, grabbing his jacket from the hook next to the door.

Paige was left feeling cheated. She looked at her dad and asked, "Why are you here?" She immediately apologized. "I'm sorry, Dad. I didn't mean that the way it sounded."

"Are you sure?"

"Yes. Please. Sit down. Do you want some coffee?"

"No, I'm not staying long," he said, taking a seat at the table. "I'm on my way to get the car tuned up so Mary and I can get out of town. And I know you have to get to school, but I have something I wanted to talk to you about so I thought I'd stop in."

"I'm glad you did, Dad. Really." She took a seat across from him and folded her hands on the table, waiting for him to tell her the real reason he was there. It wasn't like her father to simply drop by. He had something in mind.

"I wanted to talk to you about the wedding," he began.

"Dad, if this is about you worrying that I'm unhappy that you and Mary are getting married, you don't need to bother. I already told you I'm okay with it. Mary's nice and it's obvious the two of you are happy."

"Yes, we are happy. She's a good listener." He smiled. "I know she has the reputation for listening a little too much at times, but she's the reason I'm here talking to you. She told me the only way we can start our marriage on the right foot is for me to tell you a few things about your mother."

Uneasiness clawed at Paige's insides. "I don't think I want

to hear this." When she attempted to get to her feet, her father's hand on her arm stopped her.

He leaned forward so he could stare into her eyes. "I know you think your mother and I didn't have a good marriage, but we did. Sure we argued, but all couples argue at times. Maybe I spent too much time traveling for my work, but I never cheated on your mother. Not once."

There was such sincerity in his expression, Paige didn't doubt for a minute that he was telling the truth. "But I heard Mom say something about a woman…"

He shook his head. "A business contact, not a mistress," he said quietly.

"How come you never told me this?" she asked.

"Because it's always felt like your mother's ghost has been between us," he answered sadly. "We did argue before she got in the car that day. You think I don't regret the last words I said to her were in anger? Believe me, if I could redo those last few hours I had with her I would, but there's no guarantee that she wouldn't have still gotten into the car and driven away."

"Oh, Dad. I'm so sorry for blaming you. It wasn't your fault." She rose to her feet and held out her arms. How long they stood hugging each other she didn't know, but they were interrupted by Kyle, who walked into the kitchen with a "Hey!"

Her father pushed her away. "Look at the time. I've got to go." He headed for the door. "I'll see you two tomorrow?"

"We'll be there," Kyle answered for both of them.

It was a good thing because Paige was too choked with emotion to say anything.

PAIGE HAD TOLD Justin that her future stepmom had picked out the simple blue dress she was to wear at her father's wedding.

The dress may have been simple, but on Paige it looked splendid. It had an iridescent sheen to it that made it look as if it was continually changing color and was the perfect contrast to Paige's pale skin. It had two skinny straps that held up the scoop-necked bodice and Justin thought it was the perfect style for her. Her hair hung loose around her shoulders, reminding him of how she had looked that day she sent him the picture of herself in her wedding dress.

"You look great," he said to her. "That dress makes you look—" He almost said sexy, but stopped himself. She would not appreciate him calling her sexy.

"It makes me look what? Can you tell I'm pregnant?" Her voice held a note of panic. "I'm growing in places that I don't want to be growing," she said, tugging at the bodice of her dress.

Justin had noticed, but no way would he admit it. She'd always hated any talk of women's breasts and he knew better than to comment on the changes in her figure.

"No, I can't tell you're pregnant," he said. "What I was going to say is that the dress makes you look more like a woman and less like a third-grade teacher. Heads are going to turn in your direction."

"I hope not. This is supposed to be Mary's special day, not mine. Thank goodness this dress came with a wrap." It was then that he noticed she carried a long scarf made out of the same fabric as the dress. "Kyle's not here?" she asked, adjusting her left earring.

"No. He called and said we should meet him there."

Thunder rumbled in the distance, causing Paige to grimace. "Shoot. I should have had my raincoat dry-cleaned for today."

Justin opened the closet door with a gallant gesture and

pulled out her trench coat wrapped in plastic. Her eyes widened as she realized what he'd done.

"You took it to the cleaners for me?"

"I had to take mine so I figured I'd take yours, too. I also had the oil changed in your car."

She gave him a bewildered look. "Why?"

"Just because I wanted to."

She shot him a suspicious look. "What's the real reason? Do you want to borrow my car?"

"No, I want to apologize for the way I reacted to your ex-fiancé showing up here," he said honestly.

She gave him a coy smile. "Apology accepted."

She tore away the plastic and stared at the trench coat in amazement. "This is so sweet. Thank you."

"You're welcome." He held the coat open for her so she could slide her arms inside.

"I owe you one, J.C.," she said. "Let me know when you want to collect."

He almost said, "I'll take it now in a kiss," but stopped himself. She wouldn't appreciate his attempt at flirting with her, especially not when she was so nervous about her father getting married.

To his relief the wedding was brief. Justin hardly noticed the bride and groom. He only had eyes for the groom's daughter, who sat in the front pew of the church trying not to sniffle. He would have liked to have been sitting beside her, but he told himself he should consider himself lucky that he was her escort and not Michael Cross.

He and Kyle sat a few rows back in an area filled with neighbors and friends. When Paige held Mary's bouquet as she said her vows, Kyle whispered in his ear, "At least they have girls doing girls' work and boys doing boys'."

Following the ceremony the guests were invited to a reception held at a hotel in downtown St. Paul. Again Paige was forced to sit with family, leaving Justin to share a table with Kyle and their friends. As soon as dinner was over, Paige joined them, the shawl wrapped tightly across her shoulders.

"How's everyone doing at this table?" she asked. Kyle acted as if there hadn't been any friction between the three of them. Justin didn't know if it was for appearances' sake or if he truly wanted to move forward.

The only unsettling moment in the evening came when Mary said to Justin, "I'm so glad you and Kyle were the ones to bring Paige tonight. I was worried that she'd show up with that Michael Cross."

"I don't think she'll be seeing much of him anymore," Justin told her.

"I hope you're right, but I'm worried he's like a bad penny. He'll just keep turning up. I heard he even went to see her at her school yesterday."

So Michael Cross had been at her school? Paige hadn't mentioned it, but then why would she? She got very defensive whenever Michael's name was mentioned.

By the time the reception was over, Paige looked tired. Although Kyle suggested the three of them go out for a nightcap, she told him she was tired and asked Justin to take her home.

He'd wanted to ask her about Michael coming to see her at school, but she'd fallen asleep almost before they were a few blocks from the hotel. He was determined to confront her before she went upstairs to bed.

"Why didn't you tell me Michael came to see you at school?" he asked as soon as they were inside the house.

"Who told you?"

"Mary."

"I should have known. She has a way of finding out everything." Her voice sounded weary and he thought about letting the issue slide, but he couldn't.

"So why didn't you tell me?" he pressed her for an answer.

"I didn't think about it." She kept her eyes downcast, which made him wonder if she was being honest.

He decided he wasn't going to beat around the bush. He was going to find out what was going on. "I thought he had a job in Las Vegas."

"He does."

"It's a good place for him. There are lots of losers in that city. So what was he doing at your school?"

"All right, I'll tell you." She sounded impatient and he could see she really didn't want to tell him about it, but he wasn't about to let her off the hook. "He showed up at school with one of those singing-telegram people who serenaded me with a song and asked for my forgiveness."

"And did you forgive him?"

"Yes."

He grimaced. It was not what he wanted to hear. Pride kept him from asking why but she supplied the answer to his unasked question.

"I had to forgive him, Justin. I teach my kids the importance of forgiveness. I couldn't stand up there in front of them and not be a good example." She yawned. "I have to get out of these shoes. My feet are killing me. I think they're swollen."

She headed for the stairs but he stopped her. "Want me to massage them for you?"

"And wouldn't you be surprised if I said yes."

He didn't want her to go to bed. He wanted her to stay and talk with him. "I'd do anything for you, Paige."

"Would you put that in writing?" she asked with a chuckle.

"How about if I seal it with a kiss?" He reached out and pulled her to him, then kissed her long and hard. When it was finally over and they were both breathing heavily, he said, "There. How was that?"

"I liked it. A lot." She sounded breathless.

He kissed her again, and this time she wrapped her arms around his neck and met his mouth with equal passion. He was surprised by the intensity of the kiss and the fact that she didn't want it to end, keeping him close when he would have pulled away from her. When they finally reluctantly pushed away from each other, he said, "Would you like more?"

For an answer she took him by the hand and led him up the stairs to her bedroom.

WHEN JUSTIN AWOKE he was alone in his bed. Had it all been a dream? He and Paige together again? He glanced down at the floor and saw the blue dress. "No, it wasn't a dream."

He smiled and sighed. She must have sneaked back to her own room, not wanting Kyle to see that they'd spent the night together. That was okay with him. Even though they were starting to repair their friendship, it was best not to push it.

He showered and dressed, then went to look for Paige. When he didn't find her in her room, he went downstairs. Kyle sat in the living room watching a football game.

"Where's Paige?" Justin asked him.

"Couldn't tell you. She got a phone call from some guy and out the door she went."

Justin's stomach dropped. "Not Michael Cross?"

"It could have been. She was in the bathroom and her phone rang so I answered it. It was some guy. I didn't recognize the voice." He looked at Justin and said, "If it's bugging you, why don't you call her?"

"It's not bugging me," he lied, but he did flip open his cell only to snap it shut again. What would he say to her? Where are you? What are you doing with him? How could you make love to me the way you did and rush to be with another guy?

There had to be an explanation for her behavior. They'd been friends too long for him not to trust her. And he did trust her.

But the longer he sat staring at the football game, the more he began to lose the little bit of faith he had in his own instincts. He didn't realize that he'd been pacing back and forth between the sofa and the window until Kyle pointed it out.

"Hey—either call her or take that pacing upstairs," he said irritably. "I'm trying to watch the game here."

"Aren't you worried about her?" Justin asked him.

"No, but obviously you are, which has me wondering why." He looked at Justin curiously.

"Why? Because she could get her heart broken again and I don't think she's told him about the baby, and when she does, how do you suppose a guy like that is going to react?"

"If he still loves her he might tell her he doesn't care that she's pregnant with another guy's kid. Or is that what's really bothering you?"

Justin knew there was no point in lying. "He's not good enough for her," he said quietly.

"And I suppose you think you are?"

"As a matter of fact, I do. And you should think I am, too. I've always been good to her and you know it." It was a challenge and he held his breath, waiting to see how Kyle would respond.

He took a long sip of his beer before answering. "I do know it."

Justin heaved a sigh of relief. "Then you must know that I would never hurt her."

"Not intentionally anyway."

That was enough of an admission for now. "I don't know if I already told you this, but I'm glad you're back. The house wasn't the same without you."

Kyle grinned wryly. "Her hormones were getting to you, were they?"

Justin grinned back. "She's unpredictable, that's for sure."

"Yeah, well, I'm not sure how long I'll be around. I don't want to horn in on the two of you."

"You're not horning in on anything," Justin assured him.

Just then the doorbell rang and Kyle went to answer it. Two of their friends had stopped by to watch the game. Justin greeted each of them and briefly made small talk before excusing himself on the pretext of having to make a couple of phone calls. If he was going to pace the floor worrying about Paige, he would do it upstairs in his own room without an audience.

He picked up the dress from the floor and found an earring beneath it. He went to her room with the intention of putting it on her desk.

As he did, he bumped her computer mouse and her PC screen lit up. For as long as he could remember she'd always had a photo of the shoreline of Lake Superior at sunrise as a screen saver. Today, however, it wasn't a Great Lake that flashed on the monitor, but a calendar. It had a pink background and next to it was an animated photo of a developing fetus. Beneath the picture of the unborn child was the caption "This is what your baby looks like today."

Justin stared at the photo of a twelve-week-old fetus, amazed at how much detail was actually visible. He could see legs and feet, the beginning of fingers on its tiny hands. So engrossed was he in studying it that it took him several minutes to realize that scrolling at the bottom of the screen saver were facts about fetal development.

Your infant is about three inches long and weighs just under an ounce.

He spread his finger and thumb to what he estimated would be three inches, trying to imagine that a tiny person would fit inside the span. That was what he was doing when Paige entered the room.

"Hey—what's going on?" she asked.

"How long have you had this baby calendar on here?" he asked, pointing to the screen saver.

"Since I went to the doctor and found out I was pregnant." She kicked off her shoes and sat down on the bed behind him.

"And you didn't show it to me?"

"I didn't know you'd be interested."

"Interested? Are you kidding? This is incredible."

She got up on her knees and leaned against his back, looking over his shoulder. "If you click on the calendar you can go either backward or forward in time. That way you can see what changes will happen next week or next month or whatever date you choose."

He did as she suggested, first going back in time to the moment of conception and then going forward so they could see the changes that would occur in the months ahead.

"It looks like it's in a bubble," Justin noted when they were back on today's date. "I hate to say it but it has your big head."

"It does not. You should be happy the head is so big. That's where all the important stuff is getting done. I start every day by looking at the calendar to see how the baby is developing and what new piece of information will be there."

Justin looked back over the past week and saw, *The chance for miscarriage gets much lower after this week.* "Was that why you were in such a good mood yesterday?"

She nodded. "I want this baby, Justin. At first I wasn't sure, but now I am."

"I want it too, which is why you can't go back to Michael. I won't let you do it, Paige. I don't care what the man says or does, you can't trust him."

"I know that. Why would you think I would?"

"Where were you just now?"

"One of the teachers at work had an appendicitis attack and her husband called first thing this morning. A few of us went over to her house to clean so when she gets out she doesn't have a big mess waiting for her. I left you a note downstairs."

"I didn't see it," he admitted.

"So where did you think I was?" When he didn't answer, she said, "Not with Michael?" He knew guilt flashed all over his face. "You thought I would spend the night with you and then get out of bed and go be with him?" She looked appalled at the suggestion.

"You told me you'd forgiven him."

"Yes, and you know why. That doesn't mean I want him back." She made a face as if she were sucking on something sour.

"You told me your life was over when he left you." He didn't want to remember those words, but they were hard to forget.

"Because at the time I believed that was true, but I realize that I was never really in love with Michael. I was in love with being in love. I had this plan of what my life should be. He was just a temporary mark on a time line that was easily erased."

He put a finger under her chin. "And what about me?"

She shook her head. "You have a permanent spot there. I can't believe you would even think I would go see Michael after what happened last night."

"I didn't want to think it, but when I went downstairs and Kyle said you'd had a phone call from a guy, he was the only person I could think of who would get you out of the house on a Sunday morning."

"You and Kyle didn't get into it again, did you?"

"No. It was more like the opposite of what you'd expect."

"You patched things up?"

"Not exactly, but it was a step in the right direction. I think it helps that he knows I'm in love with you and I'm not just looking at this baby as some new adventure."

"You're in love with me?" she repeated, her mouth dropping open.

"Yeah, I told you that last night."

"Well, yes, but I thought you just said that because the sex was so good," she admitted honestly.

"I said them because it's true and I thought you meant them when you said them, too."

"I—" she began only to stop, as if she regretted telling him she loved him. "I thought we were having buddy sex," she finally said. "We're best friends."

He felt as if someone had punched him in the stomach. All the pleasure he'd felt when she'd told him she didn't ever want to see Michael Cross again faded away. "Paige, I don't want buddy sex from you. I want the real thing."

"I want that, too." She didn't look at him when she spoke.

"Are you sure?"

"No." There it was. The honest admission. He expected nothing less even though it hurt like hell.

"Why not?"

"Because I know I can handle being friends. I'm not sure we'll make it if we're more than friends."

"But we're having a baby together. We need to do it all, Paige. Marriage, a house, kids. I want everything."

"You say that now because it's something you've never

even thought about before. A challenge, and we both know you love a challenge until you conquer it."

"Is that what this is about? *My* shortcomings?"

"I didn't say they were shortcomings."

"You didn't have to. We've been friends so long there are some things that don't have to be said."

"You want something until you get it, Justin."

"And you think that's what will happen to you and the baby? That once I have you I'll get tired of you and toss you aside?"

"I don't know, but I'm not sure it's a risk I can take."

"Paige, life is a risk, yet you don't stop leaving the house."

"You sound like my dad."

He groaned. "I'm doomed."

"No, when he was here the other day we had a really good talk."

"About your mom?"

She nodded. "You know I've always blamed him for what happened. I wanted to believe that it was his fault she drove away angry."

"You probably haven't been any angrier with him than he's been with himself," Justin noted.

"You're right. He carried that burden for a long time, but he's happy now. And he wants me to be happy. As in happy and married." She sighed. "He thinks I'm not because I've been choosing the wrong guys—guys who were safe."

"Guys who never argued with you."

"Yes. Ones I thought wouldn't leave me. Ones I hoped I could trust."

She yawned and curled up on the bed. "I don't want to be afraid of love. Really I don't."

"You don't need to be afraid of me," he whispered close to her ear.

"I'm not. You're my best friend," she said sleepily.

He could see by the weariness on her face that she was worn-out. So he got a lap robe from the chair and draped it over her, then kissed her on the cheek.

"You rest. We'll talk later." And before he'd even pulled the door shut she was asleep.

WHEN PAIGE AWOKE it was dusk and the room was in shadow. She reached for the lamp on her nightstand. It was then she saw the CD case. On top of it was a note that simply said *Play Me.*

She went over to her desk and slipped the disk into her computer. A slide show of photos featuring Justin, Kyle and her soon replaced the pregnancy calendar. Pictures from their past flashed on the screen to the sound of Faith Hill singing "Breathe," one of Paige's favorite songs. A few of the photos dated back to childhood, but most were from their high-school and college days. There were pictures of the three of them floating in inner tubes down the Apple River, in-line skating in Canal Park in Duluth, and hiking in the Superior National Forest. It was a lifetime of memories and Justin was in all of them, but it was the last picture in the slide show that had her clicking on the pause icon. Justin was in a tuxedo and she was in a light blue prom dress. She reached for her cell and texted him a message.

Ineedu.

Within minutes he was in her room. She was still at her PC, staring at the photo of the two of them from prom night.

"You took me to the prom when Matthew Warner backed out on me at the last minute," she said.

"You'd already bought your dress."

"And you smacked Jamie Edson when he called me a skank when we went to Valley Fair for the school-patrol picnic," she reminded him.

He rubbed a hand across his jaw. "I should have done it long before that. He was always teasing you."

"And you picked me first when we were choosing sides for volleyball."

"You've got a great kill shot for a shorty," he said with a half grin.

She pointed to the computer screen. "You did this to show me I was wrong, didn't you."

He reached for her hands. "I know I don't have all those traits on your Top Ten list. I'm a lousy cook. I have a tendency to start and not finish things, but, Paige, you, Kyle and I have been friends since we were in elementary school. Doesn't that prove that I have staying power when it comes to people I care about?"

She got up then and went into his arms. She wanted to tell him yes, it did, but tears were streaming down her face, emotion blocking her throat. He hugged her tightly. "I won't ever betray your trust, Paige. I love you."

She finally managed to squeak out, "I love you, too."

He pushed her back then and stared into her tear-streaked face. "I know you love me, but are you *in* love with me?"

For an answer she placed her mouth on his and kissed him in a way that left no doubt as to her true feelings for him.

"Does this mean your original baby plan can be revised?" he wanted to know.

"To include you?"

"To include marriage."

She didn't hesitate to say yes, but she quickly added, "Do you really think it will work?"

"We'll make it work."

"But we're total opposites in so many ways. I like everything scheduled and you like to do everything on the spur of the moment."

"Which is probably a good thing. I can loosen you up when you get too rigid and you can give structure to my life when I tend to lose sight of the goal. I think we'll be good together."

"But what if you get tired of me? None of your girlfriends have lasted more than three months."

"Did you ever think that the reason for that may have been that I've been in love with the one who was living right next door?"

She giggled as he swooped her up in his arms and carried her to the bed. When he set her down gently and leaned over her, she said, "Do you think we were ever just friends?"

"We may have been, but one thing is for certain. We never will be again." And he proceeded to prove it to her.

EPILOGUE

THE SOUND OF THE PHONE ringing woke Kyle from a deep slumber. His right hand reached for the cordless on the table next to his bed. "Kyle," he said in a sleepy voice against his pillow.

"It's me."

He pushed himself up onto one elbow. "Paige?"

"And me," a male voice said.

"Justin?" Kyle glanced at the clock. "Do you guys know what time it is?"

"It's barely past midnight. Were you sleeping?"

"Yes, I was sleeping," he grumbled. "What's so important that it couldn't wait until morning."

"We have someone here who wants to meet you."

A baby's cry sounded in Kyle's ear. He heard Justin say, "Zachary Kyle Collier, meet your godfather, Kyle Langdon."

Another wail screeched across the phone line and Kyle grinned. "Hey, little guy! What are you doing here already?"

After a moment Justin spoke into the phone. "How's that for a set of lungs?"

"He sounds great, but I thought he wasn't supposed to be born for another couple of weeks?"

"He wasn't but I guess he couldn't wait to meet us," Paige said.

"He must have heard how much fun his mom and dad have with his Uncle Kyle and wanted to get in on the action," Justin added.

"Who does he look like?" Kyle wanted to know.

"Paige. Justin," they answered simultaneously.

"Guess I'll just have to see for myself."

* * * * *

Nate Dempsey has returned to Whitehorse to uncover the truth about his past...

Nate sensed someone watching the house and looked out in surprise to see a woman astride a paint horse just on the other side of the fence. He quickly stepped back from the filthy second-floor window, although he doubted she could have seen him. Only a little of the June sun pierced the dirty glass to glow on the dust-coated floor at his feet as he waited a few heartbeats before he looked out again.

The place was so isolated he hadn't expected to see another soul. Like the front yard, the dirt road was waist-high with weeds. When he'd broken the lock on the back door, he'd had to kick aside a pile of rotten leaves that had blown in from last fall.

As he sneaked a look, he saw that she was still there, staring at the house in a way that unnerved him. He shielded his eyes from the glare of the sun off the dirty window and studied her, taking in her head of long blond hair that feathered out in the breeze from under her Western straw hat.

She wore a tan canvas jacket, jeans and boots. But it was the way she sat astride the brown-and-white horse that nudged the memory.

He felt a chill as he realized he'd seen her before. In that very spot. She'd been just a kid then. A kid on a pretty paint horse. Not this one—the markings were different. Anyway, it couldn't have been the same horse, considering the last time he had seen her was more than twenty years ago. That horse would be dead by now.

His mind argued it probably wasn't even the same girl. But he knew better. It was the way she sat the horse, so at home in a saddle and secure in her world on the other side of that fence.

To the boy he'd been, she and her horse had represented freedom, a freedom he'd known he would never have—even after he escaped this house.

Nate saw her shift in the saddle, and for a moment he feared she planned to dismount and come toward the house. With Ellis Harper in his grave, there would be little to keep her away.

To his relief, she reined her horse around and rode back the way she'd come.

As he watched her ride away, he thought about the way she'd stared at the house—today and years ago. While the smartest thing she could do was to stay clear of this house, he had a feeling she'd be back.

Finding out her name should prove easy, since he figured she must live close by. As for her interest in Harper House... He would just have to make sure it didn't become a problem.

* * * * *

Be sure to look for
MATCHMAKING WITH A MISSION
and other suspenseful Harlequin Intrigue stories,
available in April
wherever books are sold.

HARLEQUIN® Romance®

presents

The Wedding Planners

Planning perfect weddings...
finding happy endings!

Amidst the rustle of satins and silks, the scent of red roses
and white lilies and the excited chatter of brides-to-be, six
friends from Boston are The Wedding Belles—they make
other people's wedding dreams come true....

But are they always the wedding planner...never the bride?

Who will be the next to say "I do"?

In April: Shirley Jump, *Sweetheart Lost and Found*
In May: Myrna Mackenzie, *The Heir's Convenient Wife*
In June: Melissa McClone, *S.O.S. Marry Me*
In July: Linda Goodnight, *Winning the Single Mom's Heart*
In August: Susan Meier, *Millionaire Dad, Nanny Needed!*
In September: Melissa James, *The Bridegroom's Secret*

*And don't miss the exciting wedding-planner tips and
author reminiscences that accompany each book!*

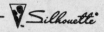

SPECIAL EDITION™

Introducing a brand-new miniseries

Men of Mercy Medical

Gabe Thorne moved to Las Vegas to open a
new branch of his booming construction
business—and escape from a recent tragedy.
But when his teenage sister showed up pregnant
on his doorstep, he really had his hands full.
Luckily, in turning to Dr. Rebecca Hamilton for
the medical care his sister needed, he found
a cure for himself....

Starting with

THE MILLIONAIRE
AND THE M.D.

by *TERESA SOUTHWICK,*

available in April wherever books are sold.

Celebrate the joys of motherhood!
In this collection of touching stories,
three women embrace their maternal
instincts in ways they hadn't expected.
And even more surprising is how true
love finds them.

Mothers of the Year

With stories by
Lori Handeland
Rebecca Winters
Anna DeStefano

*Look for Mothers of the Year,
available in April
wherever books are sold.*

REQUEST YOUR FREE BOOKS!

2 FREE NOVELS PLUS 2 FREE GIFTS!

HARLEQUIN®

Super Romance®

Exciting, emotional, unexpected!

HSR08

HARLEQUIN *Presents*

He's successful, powerful—and extremely sexy....
He also happens to be her boss! Used to getting his
own way, he'll demand what he wants from her—
in the boardroom and the bedroom....

Watch the sparks fly as these couples
work together—and play together!

IN BED WITH
THE BOSS

Available April 8
wherever books are sold.

COMING NEXT MONTH

HSRCNM0308